Deal With The Devil
(Circles in Hell, Book Three)

by

Mark Cain

ISBN-13: 978-1518622199
ISBN-10: 1518622194

'Deal with the Devil' is published by Perdition Press, which can be contacted at:

hellssuper@hotmail.com

Cover design by Dan Wolfe (www.doodledojo.co.uk)

To Linda

Chapter 1

A dull, red glow, like that of a wildfire in the distance, or the burning ocher of a lava flow, suffused the sky, driving back the shadows of night. They weren't gone. They were never gone, but lingered always along the edge of sight, nightmares that would not end but lost some of their potency in the light of day.

Well, they would have anyway, if this weren't Hell, where nightmares are pretty much the steady diet of the eternally damned. Besides, the lurid radiance I'm talking about was emanating from the Throat of Hell, that great yawning chasm that stretches from the Mouth of Hell at Gates Level all the way down to Satan's office suite in the Ninth Circle. Still, the scary shadows weren't as obvious, because the Infernal Realm was now cooking on high instead of a slow boil. A new day, or what passes for day around here, had begun.

I took in Hell's version of dawn from the steps leading to my office. To be accurate, it was not really an office, but more of a beat-up trailer that wouldn't have been allowed its rectangle of concrete in any self-respecting trailer park back on Earth. Still, it was command central for the Underworld's Superintendent of Plant Maintenance (me) and my trusty sidekick, Orson, as we endured our never-ending punishment of being lousy handymen.

Hey, it's a lot worse than it sounds. Have you ever been bad at something? I mean really, really bad, stinko, like someone with two left feet and an inner ear infection trying to execute a pirouette during the climax of *Swan Lake*? Not pretty. So doing something you really suck at, not to mention hate, for all eternity is an excruciating, if highly specialized, form of Hell for me and Orson.

Speaking of Orson, he had beaten me into the office that day, something almost unheard of, since he was famous during his lifetime for being late and I was obsessive about being early. I knew he had preceded me because the door was already slightly open, so for once I didn't have to fight the stupid doorknob to get into my own office.

That the great Orson Welles got to work before me was noteworthy. I'm an early riser, as evidenced by my getting to watch Hell's version of sunrise every morning. Orson, on the other hand, didn't give a damn about punctuality, but there he was, early for work, sitting on his work stool, waiting for me, his Blimpie's mug in hand.

"Morning, Steve."

"What are you doing here so early?" I asked, closing the door behind me.

"Couldn't sleep," he said.

For some reason, this struck me as funny, and I chuckled. "Good grief, Orson. This is Hell. Nobody can sleep."

He shrugged. "Yeah, but last night was worse than usual." Probably true, judging from his eyes, which were especially bloodshot this morning, with dark bags under them, as if he'd stayed up the night, drinking and smoking while he pondered the mysteries of the universe. "I keep thinking about my Hell movie."

"That again," I said, rolling my eyes. "You know there's no way, correct that, there's no way in Hell that Satan's going to let you make a promotional video about Hell."

My assistant's face reddened. "He might. It would help get him some more demons. You know he always needs more demons."

Orson had a point there. While a few demons, like incubi and succubi, were native-born, most were converted humans. They actually volunteered to be repulsive devil-wannabes. "Okay, that's probably true. But it's not going to happen."

"And why not?" he snapped.

Okay, we'd started the morning off on the wrong foot. Now it was time to calm things down. "Look, Orson. I know you'd make a great movie, but you'd, well, you'd enjoy making it, right?"

"Well, of course I'd enjoy making it, and ... oh ... well. Right. We're in Hell." Orson's face assumed a mournful expression, like I'd just killed his dog or something.

I smiled sympathetically. "Yeah, and we don't get to enjoy anything down here."

The smell of burnt java filled the room, so I stepped away from my disgruntled assistant and his hanged-dog expression. From my desk, a rusted and dented All-Steel model that could have been constructed from a World War II depth charge, I grabbed my "I'm not With Stupid. I AM Stupid," mug and headed to our antediluvian Mr. Coffee. I took my first sip of the day, straining loose grounds with my teeth. "Shit," I mumbled, singeing my tongue.

"Nothing like a good cup a' joe, eh?" Orson said, a little twinkle coming back in his eye. Only one of them, though. The other was hanging onto its depression.

"Yes, but unfortunately, this isn't one," I grumbled, using thumb and forefinger to pick a ground off my still-burning tongue. "I haven't had a decent cup of coffee since the grande Sumatra I got at Starbucks the day I died."

Orson set his cup on the edge of my desk and stretched expansively. Of course, since my friend's ectoplasmic frame was a reasonable facsimile of his mortal one toward the end of his life, said frame was pushing four hundred pounds. Almost by definition, Orson was expansive, and so, gargantuan as he was,

9

he had a hard time doing anything in less than expansive fashion. "Starbucks was around when I died in 1985, but I never got around to trying it."

"Just as well," I said, wincing as I took another sip. "I still remember, which makes our morning coffee ritual just a little enhancement to my eternal torment."

"Lucky you," Orson said, grabbing his own mug and taking a swallow of the hot, black liquid. "Still, even Folgers was better than this. Speaking of coffee, are you and Flo still on for this morning? ... I guess so, judging by the way you're blushing."

"She has a way of doing that to me," I replied with a rueful grin.

"Nervous?"

"A bit." Florence Nightingale (yes, that Florence Nightingale - is there another one?) and I had only recently gotten past an early rough patch in our relationship. Rough patch: that's a euphemism for Satan and his underlings humiliating us by filming me and Flo in the sack and then turning the footage into the most popular porn movie the Underworld had ever seen. And by Underworld, I mean all of it. Apparently, everyone in Hell had seen "Flo Does The Super." Many devils and demons even owned it on Blu-ray, complete with 3-D and Smellovision®. Pretty humiliating, though that's par for the course down here.

Anyway, Flo had been particularly upset by the movie. After some months, though, she had adjusted to the situation. Only a few days ago, after the successful conclusion of the HVAC Affair - hmmm, doesn't have the same panache as "The Thomas Crown Affair," but there you go - she had confessed the surety of her love. (That's exactly how she'd said it: "surety." I'd never even used that word in a sentence, but then I hadn't been born in the Nineteenth Century, as she had, back when the language had a lot more elegance to it than what I'd lived and died with in the second half of the Twentieth Century.) We had agreed to take it slow. Well, she had wanted to take it slow, and I'd reluctantly acquiesced. Me, I would have been perfectly happy to get back in the sack with her immediately, but then I'm a guy. We are simple creatures, driven mainly by lust and bacon.

Having coffee at the hospital today was our way of restarting the relationship. I was a bit nervous, but mostly excited. Now if only nothing important came up that the Plant Department had to handle. As Hell's only maintenance team, Orson and I were expected to fix everything that broke down here. That was a boatload. After all, no one really expects Hell to function flawlessly. If it did, it would be Hea … the other place.

Well, we didn't fix everything, as evidenced by the four-foot high piles of unresolved work orders filling one corner of our office. There was no way we could take care of everything that broke. If it were even possible to do so, this wouldn't be a particularly good form of eternal punishment, now would it? Still, we did our best to fix the important stuff.

I looked around our trailer. The office could use a little repair itself. All of the wallpaper, a drab gray pattern that added nothing to the décor except that it was something else to maintain, was sagging like a dowager's chin. One piece, damp from a leak in the roof that we'd never been able to find, had finally pulled away completely from the wall. The top half of it was now touching the floor. Without thought, I lifted the stapler off my desk and, with a rapid series of clicks, tacked the sheet back to the wall. No more than a second after I finished, while admiring my own handiwork, the staples began to pop out of the drywall. One of them hit me in the right eye.

"Shit," I cursed, without much enthusiasm - after all, I'd only had half a cup of coffee and didn't really feel awake yet - and reached to one of the two spools of duct tape hanging from each side of my tool belt. With a quick pull, I dispensed about eighteen inches of the stuff, what I judged the width of the wallpaper to be, made a clean tear, and taped the top of the paper to where it met the ceiling.

"I'm surprised you didn't reach for the duct tape first," Orson commented.

"Me too," I said, once again admiring my handiwork, and once again being struck in the same eye by a tardy but nonetheless rebellious staple. The wallpaper stayed put, though. Duct tape, the one tool of the handyman trade with which I had any competence, had never failed me. It was also gray, so it didn't look particularly bad against the wallpaper, though the paper in the middle of the wall still sagged like that chin I mentioned earlier.

Splat! A long, skinny package, about the size of a salami, emerged from the pneumatic tube above my wire inbox. That's how we got most of our work orders, but this obviously wasn't one of them. Curious, I picked up the package. It was addressed to both of us.

"What the hell?" Orson said, when I showed him the return address. It said Sintas Uniform and Apparel. "You don't think it's two of those HOTI gimme caps they were trying to get us to wear last year, do you?"

HOTI was the acronym for Beelzebub's operation down here: Hell's Office of the Interior. Plant Maintenance was a department within the HOTI division. The hats hadn't worked out very well. They made us look too dignified, so we'd had to return them.

"One way to find out," I said, opening the parcel. Inside were two long, narrow maroon-rimmed ovals, with yellow centers that matched the color of our coveralls. There was also a set of simple instructions: "Peel off the paper and affix fabric to the location indicated by the diagram."

Orson slapped his hand to his forehead. "Great, just great."

I shrugged. "We knew this would happen sooner or later, so let's just get it over with. Turn around. I'll do you, then you can do me."

"Fine." My friend put his back to me, displaying the maroon HOTI insignia on the back of his coveralls. I peeled off the wax paper from the back of the fabric and affixed the oval to the narrow space between the O and the T, doing my best to stick it on straight. Then I turned and let Orson do the same for me.

Our divisional acronym now read, "HOOTI," except that one of the "O"s was extra skinny to fit in the limited space available to it. This was a pretty cheap solution, but actually better than getting a whole new, properly-spaced logo that we would have had to sew on ourselves. After we took the old ones off, of course. Since I'm a terrible seamstress, a skinny peel-and-stick letter was okay by me.

Still, this was a regrettable if completely predictable eventuality. The old acronym had never accounted for the "of" in "Hell's Office of the Interior." This new one did.

Orson was staring over his shoulder, examining the logo in the cracked and yellowed shard of mirror we had in our office. "HOOTI. Just marvelous."

"Actually, it says 'ITOOH.' Mirror, you know."

"Very funny," he grumbled. "Dora will have a field day with this."

I nodded. "It was the first thing I thought of too." Dora, who ran the Parts Department, was fond of calling us Hotties. "Now she'll call us Hooties, I guess."

He frowned. "Knowing Dora, she'll probably call us a big pair of Hooters."

13

"Ooh!" I said, grimacing. I went over to the Mr. Coffee and topped off my mug then sat back at my desk. "Hadn't thought of that."

Splat!

"Now what?" Orson groused.

"Work order?" I said, not looking up from my coffee.

"No. Wrong color."

I glanced at my inbox. Our work orders were printed on paper stock that was the color of bile, but this packet had blue and white sheets stapled together. With suspicion, I picked it up and got popped in the left eye this time by the staple holding the packet together. All the papers tumbled to the floor.

On my hand and knees, I gathered the pages from off the linoleum and put them in order then took a gander at what I had and scowled. "Crap!"

"What is it?" Orson asked, putting down his coffee cup.

"I HEARD that!" boomed a voice from the office PA system.

Fuck! Beezy was paying attention. I got off the floor and pressed down the talk button of the intercom that sat on a corner of my desk. "Come on! A performance evaluation?"

"Union rules," said Beelzebub, the great Lord of the Flies and, not insignificantly, my boss down here.

I had been on the last bargaining team for the union, so I knew the current contract by heart. There had been no such provision in it. "I don't remember the SEIU agreeing to personnel evaluations."

That's Satan's Employees' Infernal Union. Don't confuse it with the Earth-bound union having the same acronym. Just a coincidence, like the APA standing for both the American Psychological Association and the American Poolplayers Association.

Beezy laughed in that endearing way of his. It sounded like a rock polisher working on a large chunk of concrete. "You don't remember it because Management slipped it into the contract when you weren't looking."

Swell. That means they rewrote the contract without telling us. Nice.

"Besides," Beelzebub continued, "it only applies to humans in positions that report directly to one of the princes of Hell."

"Oh," I said, somewhat mollified. "There can't be too many of us in that situation."

"You're right about that. Demons supervise most of you."

I thought about all the princes of Hell, and realized with some surprise that almost none of them had direct contact with humans. "That," I said hesitantly, "that would narrow it down to just me and Bruce then, right?"

Bruce the Bedeviled was Satan's personal assistant.

"Not Bruce," Beezy said. "At least, not anymore. Remember he was promoted to demon recently."

"Oh right, right." I stared in bemusement at the speaker mounted on the wall. "Then, that means this portion of the contract only applies ... to me?"

That piece of concrete got a little bit shinier. "Right you are! But if you're going to report to me, you must be held accountable for your actions, Minion, even in Hell. Besides, it's best practice. All the management consultants, and believe me, we have a lot of that type down here, agree."

In life, I had been a professor of economics. Faculty members, probably more than anyone, hate having their performance evaluated, but in most cases, they only have to put up with it for their first seven years on the job. After getting tenure, I thought I was done with that forever ... well, except for those stupid evaluations done on Scantron forms I had to let students fill out - number two pencil - for the occasional course. Seems I was wrong. My lips curled down into a fair imitation of a toddler's pout. "It just doesn't seem fair that I'm the only one in all of Hell that has to have a performance evaluation."

Polish, polish. "Tough shit. Besides, Hell isn't about fair play, and you know it. Now quit your whining and come down to my office this morning. Make sure you complete that self-evaluation before you get here."

"Yessir," I mumbled, as an ear-piercing screech came from the speaker. The PA system had lasted just long enough for Beelzebub to ruin my morning before failing.

It failed about twice a week.

Great. Though it could be worse, I suppose. At least he didn't say immediately. This means I have time to have coffee with Flo then fill out the stupid personnel form as I ride down on the Escalator to the Eighth Circle.

"What's the point of an evaluation?" Orson said, sharing my outrage as he stared at the forms crushed in my hand. "We're in Hell. Everything we do sucks, not to mention being completely pointless. And even if you did a great job, Beezy would never admit it."

I stroked my chin. "Don't know about that." My boss and I had been getting along pretty well, especially since I'd had success with some big projects recently. Also, despite his bluster and innate cruelty, Beelzebub was the most fair-minded of all Hell's princes. *Good thing I don't report to Asmodeus. He'd rake my butt over the coals.*

Asmodeus, the Lord of Lust, had a double axe to grind with/on me. Only the other day, Flo had very publicly snubbed him at a reception at which she'd been the honored guest. That had been partly my fault.

Not to mention that his own assistant has the hots for me. As I thought about the redheaded succubus, I began to blush. She was one sexy demon, the only woman in Hell other than Flo who I'd ever been attracted to.

But this was the worst time to think about Lilith, right before my date with Flo. Putting my coffee cup down on the desk, I stuffed the self-assessment form into my pocket, stepped before our mirror and tried to make my hair appear a little less unkempt.

"Orson, while I'm gone, would you take a pen and draw some narrow O's on our letterhead?"

My friend flexed his right hand and frowned. "That sounds like a guaranteed hand cramp. Couldn't we just order fresh stock?"

"Sorry. We're over budget in the Supplies line."

"Oh, okay," he said with a sigh.

"Thanks." Pivoting on my heel, I headed toward the exit.

"Good luck, Steve! With both Flo and Beelzebub!" Orson yelled, as the door closed behind me.

Chapter 2

Ah, the ripe smell of Hell in the morning. The cess pools along the sidewalks were bubbling, sending their fetid odor into the air. The exhaust from the cars and trucks that traveled along the Road to Hell, off of which our office was located, added to the olfactory effect. Then there was the contribution made by next door's oil refinery, as well as the omnipresent scent of sulfur, which permeated the air on every level of Hell. Have to have a lot of brimstone, ya know, to really make Hell, well, Hell.

Despite this noxious assault on my nose, I chuckled. The sulfur reminded me of burnt matches, like what grandma used to light to cover the perfectly natural but impolite odors that might arise during a prolonged stint in one of her bathrooms. I'm not sure the smell of burning sulfur was an improvement over anything the human body was capable of producing, but whatever. Besides, in Hell's case, sulfur did not hide other noxious scents but worked with them synergistically.

Hell is more than just its stench and the glow of fire, which at dawn came from the Throat of Hell but usually emanated from the fire pits that were scattered liberally on all nine levels. What wasn't lit by red flame. was a drab-beyond-drab gray. That was actually worse than the hellish fire. The gray was rigor mortis, ennui, boredom, depression.

Hopelessness.

There were treats for the ears too. Jackhammers were going non-stop; sirens helped too, as did the screams of anguished souls just cranking up in earnest for a new day. And then there was the traffic noise on the Road to Hell. The cacophony made that at Broadway and 42nd Street seem, in comparison, like the gentle sounds of an Amish buggy on a country road: a slight creak of metal springs, the gentle clop-clop-clop of the horse's hooves. Hell knew how to do traffic, and my ears actually hurt as I walked on the cracked sidewalk next to the Road.

I used to joke that the Road to Hell was paved with good intentions. That's not really true of course. Very little good can be found down here. The main avenue on Level Five, where it was paved at all, was all about bad intentions, as evidenced by the gridlock caused by ill-timed traffic lights; demon bus drivers who intentionally blocked multiple lanes of traffic; blind human cabbies regularly slamming into curbs, cars and their fellow damned souls who could not scurry across the street quickly enough to avoid being run over.

Despite this overwhelming sensory onslaught, and despite what promised to be a humiliating performance evaluation at the hands of Beelzebub, I found myself whistling while strolling - when I wasn't tripping over a patch of broken pavement. My destination was just ahead: the stainless steel twin towers of Hell's Hospital, or the Giant Toaster, as I usually called it. Soon I would see my true love, Florence Nightingale.

That the founder of modern nursing reciprocated my feelings was still a marvel to me. Nothing good is *ever* supposed to happen in Hell, and Flo's love was the goodest, pardon, best thing to happen to me in life or death.

Satan had tried to break us up, but there was something about Flo that thwarted even him. I think it's because she, who was destined for Heaven, came to Hell of her own free will, to do good down here, in a place where good was supposedly impossible. She seemed to have an aura about her - a Florence Nightingale Zone - that warped the reality of Hell. Somehow, when I was with her, the aura extended to me. We found that we were in love, and because of the FloZone, Satan couldn't do a damn thing about it.

There was a grumbling in my mind when I had that thought - the Devil had been listening - and an entire section of pavement rose from the sidewalk and landed on me. With a groan, I crawled out from under the concrete, shoving any smugness or satisfaction out of my brain.

Satan was a mind reader. You forgot that at your peril.

In a few minutes, I walked past the entry ramp that corkscrewed its way down to the hospital parking garage. I'm not sure anyone ever used the garage. To begin with, very few humans had cars down here. If they had them, the purpose was to cause aggravation.

For some people, Hell is a car that won't start. For others, it's being caught in a traffic jam. For still others, it's not being able to find a parking space. All of those people own cars down here and are subjected to their personal version of damnation. Maybe they're the ones who use the hospital parking garage.

Certainly, all the T's had been crossed and the I's dotted in the design of the garage. For example: the handicapped spots were as far away from the hospital entrance as possible. All the close spaces were reserved for the doctors, nurses, administrators and so forth that ran the Toaster. Unsurprisingly, these were all demons. A few humans did work in the hospital, but they had menial jobs, and they certainly didn't have cars or parking spots. Still, those few humans who were allowed to navigate the Toaster's garage got to experience a concrete maze designed to maximize fender benders and minimize the find-ability of your car, not to mention dealing with exit bars that wouldn't rise after you paid.

This attention to detail is what makes Satan so good at his job.

I bypassed the parking garage and headed toward the hospital's main entrance. As usual, the automatic doors weren't

20

working - we had a work order somewhere for that, but since they never stayed fixed for more than five minutes, we routinely ignored such minor assignments - so I pried them apart and stepped into the waiting room.

It was massive, as big as the waiting area in Grand Central Station. Hundreds of damned souls - some sitting, others standing, and still others in wheelchairs or on gurneys - were in queue to register, be called into the ER, settle a bill or meet with an insurance counselor. Some had been waiting so long they were covered in dust; as I entered, demons were going through the waiting room with feather dusters, tidying up the waiting damned.

Near the front of the room was a big man in a nurse's dress. He was squatting like a baseball catcher, and in his left hand was a bedpan. That was Jim, an inmate in Hell like me. I think in life he'd been a truck driver or something. Anyway, he was a nice guy, and other than the fact that he smoked like a chimney, pretty pleasant company.

I walked over to say hello. Unusually, he didn't have a cigarette in his mouth; instead it was tucked behind his ear. The cigarette, I mean, not the mouth, which would have been really creepy, though not unheard of in Hell's Hospital, where the surgeons were famous for doing weird things like that. In fact, a mouth behind an ear would have been mild compared to the experiments in surgical cubism that I'd seen conducted on some patients.

But I digress. As I approached Jim, I noticed a sheen of sweat on his face. I also noticed the demons nearby. One was standing before him, a baseball bat in hand, concentrating fiercely on another demon who stood about twenty yards away. Behind Jim was a third demon in umpire garb. He also had a pitchfork in hand.

"Hi, Jim," I said uncertainly. "What's up?"

Jim, momentarily distracted, looked up at me. "Uh, hi, Steve. Look, this isn't really a good time ... "

The demon pitcher, seeing his opportunity, spun on his heel, crouched and let fly.

Oh. Ugh.

"Ball!" screamed the ump.

"Sorry, sorry," I mumbled, backing away, as Jim used his sleeve to wipe the crap off his face.

Newly motivated, he caught the next pitch squarely in the bedpan. "Strike!" yelled the umpire, clearly disappointed.

Jeez. Demons have warped senses of humor. And speaking of demons, it's usually about this time when I run into ...

Uphir, the demon physician and head of Hell's Hospital, entered the waiting room in scrubs. He was pulling latex surgical gloves from his hand. I noted without surprise that the little, puce colored jerk dropped them precisely on the heads of two people parked nearby in wheelchairs.

"Steve Minion, as I live and breathe!" Uphir said in mock surprise. "Well, I don't do either of those things, but fancy meeting you here. Aren't you going to ask what I've been doing?"

I sighed. *I'm going to regret this, but sometimes it's best just to play along.* "Okay, Uphir. I'll bite. What have you been doing?"

Uphir rubbed his chin. "Difficult case. Very difficult case. Patient needed a new brain."

"*Another* brain transplant?" A few months ago, he'd swapped Mao Tse Tung's brain with that of a chicken. "Who was it this time, Albert Einstein?"

The little demon chuckled. "Good idea, but no. This fellow was one of the great unwashed, just a regular Joe. Still, even the anonymous damned deserve the best medical care, don't you think?"

"Yeah, but then why did he get you?"

"Watch it, human!" Uphir snapped with typical demonic arrogance. "My skill with a surgical can opener is unsurpassed. In any event, there were no brains available, so I had to improvise."

I sighed quietly. "So, what did you do?"

Uphir smiled in satisfaction. He loved having me for a straight man. "I used a large head of cauliflower. It looks a little like a brain anyway, so ... "

One. Two. Three. "And how did the operation go?"

The little creep shook his head. "Mixed results, I'm afraid. The operation was a complete success, but unfortunately, the patient will be a vegetable from now on."

Somewhere in the distance a rimshot sounded. As Uphir laughed hysterically, I scurried away and headed for the coffee shop. Fortunately, Flo had beaten me there. One look at her, sitting demurely at a table in the corner, drove from my mind all thoughts of Uphir and his inventive torments for the damned humans under his care.

"Hey, beautiful," I said, slipping into the seat next to her and kissing her cheek. "Come here often?"

She blushed. As a woman who grew up in the Victorian era, she wasn't accustomed to public displays of affection (PDAs ... the other kind). Yet she dimpled with pleasure. "Hello, Steve. Would you like some coffee?"

"Sure," I said. "Let me get it."

I went to the counter and got two coffees. The demon at the register charged me only $700. Must have been half-price day.

I set Flo's coffee before her and sat back down. She looked gorgeous, as usual, even in a simple white nurse's dress.

Florence had a killer figure, fat in all the right places as some people say, and she filled out the garment in spectacular fashion. It always amazed me that she seemed unaware of how attractive she was. Even more astonishing: this beautiful woman was in love with a nondescript middle-aged man in yellow coveralls. Lucky me.

As she sipped on her coffee, Flo stroked my hand. "You're a few minutes late. I thought you had stood me up," she said, grinning impishly.

"You? Never. No, I just got delayed in the waiting room."

My love frowned. "Uphir?"

"Of course."

"What is he up to now?"

I shook my head. "Let's not talk about him. We're on a date, remember?" I snagged her hand and held it in mine.

Florence blushed slightly. "I remember," she said softly.

We talked for a while, nothing important, just chitchat, but it felt great, and for a moment, I forgot that we were in Hell. We were just a guy and a gal in love.

Yes, I know I'm old-fashioned and corny. I probably should have been alive during Orson's heyday, when people said things like that, when they used words like "swell" and "gee" and didn't mean them ironically. Instead, I lived my life during a period when we humans, especially those from the States, could never be completely genuine. We had to be too smart by half and never say anything with total sincerity.

I guess I'm a strange mixture of two eras. I have all the cynicism of the age in which I lived, but my tastes align with that period between the First World War and the Korean one. I love Art Deco and old movies ... and words like swell and gee. And I was most definitely a guy in love with a wonderful gal.

"So, what do you have on your agenda today?" I asked.

Flo looked around. None of the coffee shop regulars, neither the humans, who hated coffee and were being given it intravenously by attendants in Candy Striper outfits, nor the demon physicians in the corner, who couldn't get enough caffeine and drank it by the gallon, were paying us any attention. "Well," she said quietly. "I've heard through the hospital grapevine that the administration plans a raid on the Dermatology Unit. I intend to be there to stop it."

"What are they planning to do, pop a few zits?" I said lightly but then sobered up when I saw her expression.

"Yes, and probably treat some skin cancer. They're going in with Brillo pads."

I winced. "Sorry. Of course that would be horrible."

"Yes," she said primly. "But don't worry, the demons shall be disappointed."

"Of that I have no doubt," I said with a smile, kissing her cheek again.

"I'm also thinking about attending a lecture by William Playfair."

"Hmm?" I hmmed, taking another sip of coffee. The shop's cup 'o joe was even worse than what Orson and I made at the office, but with Flo for company, my beverage tasted better to me than a mocha Frappuccino. "Who's he?"

"He's the statistician who invented the pie chart."

"Oh."

I dearly love Flo, but she has this thing about pie charts, an interest of hers that goes back to her mortal existence. Back on Earth, when I was an economist, I had to stare at the bloody things all the time, and I was sick of them. In fact, one of the best parts about being in Hell was not having to deal with dumb statistics. But I'd never tell Flo that.

25

We spent about thirty minutes visiting before I decided it was time to head down to Beelzebub's office and get my stupid evaluation over with. "Darling, I have to go down to Level Eight now and see my boss."

"That's okay. The raid on the Dermatology Unit will start in a little while, so I need to head up there anyway. I'll walk you out."

"Great," I said, pulling back her chair.

"Thank you, my love," she said standing. "You are a gentleman. One of a dying breed."

"Well," I opined, "I don't think there are too many down here in Hell, but I do my best."

We walked hand in hand toward the waiting room, but as we passed a large closet off one of the nursing stations, she pulled me inside and closed the door.

The kiss almost made me swoon. (Another one of those old-timey words I like.) "That was, that was wonderful," I said, breathlessly, as we held each other tightly.

"Yeah!" said a little voice at our feet. A pint-sized creature was sitting on a cinderblock, sipping on a Slurpee, staring up at us. "Did you use lots of tongue on him, Flo?"

Florence grabbed a broom and swatted the imp to the floor. She opened the door and swept him through. "Get out of here, you horrid little creature!" Then she slammed the door shut.

I winced. "I'm sorry, Flo. You're such a private person, and to have to deal with the constant ogling ... "

She leaned the broom in the corner, brushed her hands together briskly then straightened her dress. With an effort, she calmed herself. "It's all right, Steve. I'm getting used to this sort of harassment. We are in Hell after all, and Satan and his minions simply will not stay out of our affairs. Having to conduct our relationship under occasional watchful eyes is just something with which we will have to contend."

"Does that mean I get another kiss?"

Ten minutes later, both of us slightly flushed, we left the closet. We said our goodbyes for the nonce, then I headed toward the exit, whistling again.

Chapter 3

Hell's Escalator is a very long affair, starting near Saint Peter up there with all those clouds, where you'll find both the Pearly Gates and those for Hell. The heavenly ones are pretty impressive, glowing, massive columns supporting gates wrought in silver or white gold or platinum - not sure which, since I've never been able to get very close to them - that open automatically when one of the saved approaches.

The Gates to the Inferno are not nearly so grand. They might have been once, but if so, that was way before my time. These days, the ominous entrance to the Underworld is the top platform of a monstrous escalator surrounded on three sides by garish marquee-style light boards. The top one, though, still displays Dante' famous "Abandon All Hope" line, and with that quotation, tradition is maintained.

From Gates Level, the Escalator descends into Hell, circle by circle, including the Fifth, and ending on the Eighth. Level Nine, Satan's office and also the location for the supreme sinners of all time, is only accessible by Hell's Elevator. Or by magic. Or by falling through the Throat of Hell, which is a series of openings in the centers of Hell's circles.

One can reach Beezy's office on Level Eight in all sorts of ways. Falling through the throat is certainly possible, but tricky. You have to sort of kick out your heels at just the right moment to throw off your trajectory as you descend below the Seventh Circle. Get it right and you'll go splat somewhere near the edge of the Throat on Eight. Get it wrong and you'll still end up on Nine, though with some pretty nasty burns from brushing up against the molten hot sides of the hole that burrows through Eight. And you'll be in Satan's office without an appointment, which is never a good idea. Not to mention that the fall is scary as Hell. Few people travel this way by choice.

The Elevator is always a possibility, but the demon who animates it enjoys making prospective passengers wait, as they endlessly press the call button before the doors on each level, thinking this will somehow accelerate the arrival of the lift. As far as I can tell, this button doesn't work. It's like one of those idiot lights on your car, saying "check engine" or "maintenance required," but it doesn't really do anything useful. Well, it probably alerts the Elevator demon that he has a potential passenger, but that only means he's been forewarned, so he can be sure to avoid that particular level. Even the demon Elevator eventually has to pick up a would-be passenger, and once it does, the thing moves very quickly, but a body could spend an entire day waiting for that pick up.

Then there's the stairs. The Stairway to Paradise, or to Hell, depending on which direction you're traveling, will get you to Eight, but it's really hard on the calves. Besides, I had some writing to do, and that's hard to manage as you're trudging down three or so miles of stairs.

For these reasons, I opted to take the Escalator. It was slower than the first two methods, less work than the third, and generally pretty dependable. Besides, I was in no hurry to have my evaluation, and I needed time to fill out the forms anyway.

One thing about Hell's Escalator: it has a habit of moving around the surface of each level of Hell. A few days previously, its landing point on Five had been relocated to a place several miles away from my office, too far away to walk in a reasonable amount of time. I warmed up the old thumb, preparing to signal for a cab, when I noticed that the Escalator had moved back to its previous location between the Hospital and the trailer. I didn't know if this was an omen for good or ill or simply one of the random bits of chaos (as opposed to a non-random bit of chaos) that was part of the unreality of Hell. In any event, this saved me time and cab fare. I hopped on a metal tread and in moments descended beneath the surface of Five.

I immediately teared up, not because riding the Escalator is an emotional experience, though it can be when the mechanical beast decides to buck you off. Descending beneath the surface of one of the Circles of Hell exposes you to intense heat. Not only was I crying, I was coughing from the searing touch of superheated air on my lungs. The next few moments were mostly spent wheezing, with my eyes squeezed tightly shut, until I emerged into the sky above Level Six. The air was frigid, a stark contrast to my time spent inside the Fifth Circle, but I could see again. The surface of Six looked a mile below me, though distances in Hell, being more metaphysical than physical, cannot be relied upon. It still seemed very far away. Despite that, I could see a huge, gaping cavern some distance away. A long black line, which I knew to be a train track, zigzagged from the entrance of the hole to some indeterminate location out of sight. The cavern was Hell's main sulfur mine, where two of my least favorite damned humans, Thomas Alva Edison and Henry Ford, were spending eternity digging for sulfur.

A scientist would tell you that's not how you get sulfur, but that's how we get it down here. Hell operates by its own rules.

The rest of the Sixth Circle was much like other parts of Hell: fire pits, seas of thorns, communities with special punishments for the different types of sinners, like hoarders or lusters or gluttons, murderers, thieves, goof-offs (Sloth is one of the Seven Deadly Sins, an often overlooked fact that would no doubt trouble couch potatoes everywhere if they ever made the effort to look it up.), people in bad moods (Sullenness doesn't win any "good guy" points either.), etc. You get the drift. In the distance was a German Stalag, an American Detention Camp, and a couple of concentration camps ... fun places, all of them.

I'd been to the Sixth Circle many times, though, so all of these sites didn't hold much interest for me. I was far more vested in getting my stupid self-evaluation complete before arriving on Eight. The trip between each circle went much faster than you'd think, and I only had three of these during which to complete the form. Pulling the paperwork and a number two pencil from the inside breast pocket of my coveralls, I got to work. The wind above Six was pretty strong, and it threatened to pull the form from my hand, but anticipating that, I kept a good grip on the stack of papers. I began to work, using the Escalator's hand rail as a writing surface.

HELL'S OFFICE
OF THE INTERIOR
"HOOTI: We die to serve ..."

SELF-APPRAISAL

Employee's Name: Steve Minion
Title: Hell's Superintendent of Plant Maintenance
Department: Plant Maintenance, like I said
Supervisor: Beelzebub, Lord of the Flies
Date: Whenever [It's hard to be specific here, since I don't even know what year it is.]

<u>**Instructions: As part of the performance review process, complete this self-appraisal and then discuss it with with your manager.**</u>

1. Describe your position. For each of your major responsibilities, what were the expectations and outcomes?

I'm Hell's Superintendent for Plant Maintenance, Hell's Super for short. Also known as Hell's Handyman, Mr. Fixit of the Underworld, and so forth. I report to Beelzebub, the magnificent Lord of the Flies,

Doesn't hurt to brown-nose a little here

and supervise a department of two (counting myself).

My major responsibilities are:

1. Supervise Orson Welles. I expected him to help me. I guess that went ok.

2. Fix things. Well, that was a mixed success. I'm not a very good handyman, so my expectations weren't particularly high. Besides, since this is my eternal damnation, I don't think your expectations of my success were very high either. Anyway, what I worked on got fixed [sort of], but I couldn't keep up

with my workload. There may have been a few projects I haven't gotten to yet.

Like those twelve pillars of work orders in the far corner of the trailer.

2. Describe any projects you have been responsible for which are not in your position description. What results have you achieved?

<u>Play detective:</u> I didn't know what the hell I was doing, so my expectations were quite low. Still I managed to figure out who was trying to break Hell's Escalator. At another time, I deduced who had sabotaged the HVAC system. I give myself an A for my detective work. Wait, make it a B. I don't want to be accused of grade inflation.

<u>Be a patriot:</u> Well, I didn't think I could do it, but I put down a revolution in Hell during the Escalator Escapade.

I liked the sound of that better than the "HVAC Affair," but that's probably because I'm fond of alliteration.

<u>Fight mythical creatures:</u> Steve 1, Ymir 0

3. Describe any changes you suggested/ implemented this year that resulted in improvements to your area. (Examples of

improvement: quality of work life, cost savings, efficiency).

To be candid, my suggestions generally get ignored by management. Not by you, of course, Lord Beelzebub. You took my recommendation to let Orson supervise rebuilding the Stairway to Paradise and then later to be interim Hell's Super, both times freeing me up to play detective. That was pretty efficient, and I appreciate that you let Orson out of his eternal punishment long enough to actually fix some things without me.

4.   What action(s) have you taken this year to increase your understanding of the organization and your place within that organization?

Hmm. I worked up an organization chart of the universe and saw my place in it. It's still hard for me to believe that I'm only three organizational rungs below ~~Go~~ ... the top Boss, which I think puts me on the same level as a solar system, but then, there you go.

5.   Give   examples   of   inter-departmental collaborative efforts you participated in this year. What contributions did you make? Were you a team player?

Team player. Give me a break. This is Hell.

Well, heck, Orson and I work great together. If we look at the entire Office of the Interior, though, I collaborated with some workers from the Department of Mines on at least two occasions. They weren't very helpful. My main contributions, I think, were putting up with them at all and firing them when I saw how useless they were.

6. Describe goals/developmental steps you set out to accomplish since your last evaluation. Of those, which did you accomplish?

Argh. I hate questions like this. Besides, I've never had an evaluation in Hell before.

My main goal was not to drown in work orders. Orson and I continue to keep our head above water, but just barely. Didn't do much toward professional development. Practiced my duct tape skills, and I continue to improve, however, since Hell really isn't much about self-improvement, I guess I'd say we're all about as low as we can go and meant to stay there. I'm not sure you really want us to develop anyway. Grade: C-

7. What do you think has been your most important contribution to the department? What are you most proud of?

Proud of? Hmm. I guess I would say my positive working relationship with Orson.

35

I hadn't expected to get hit with a coconut cream pie, half a mile above Level Eight, but I suppose saying something nice about Orson qualified as a pie-worthy punishment. I cleaned the cream off my face with the last page of the form, the one that said "This Page Intentionally Blank."

8. What would you have liked to have done this year, but were unable to? Why?

Spend more time with Flo, but I can't say that. Hmmm ...

Learn more about the workings of other departments within the Office of the Interior. I mean, I did a little of this, spending some time in Mines and Gluttons' Gap, but my workload doesn't exactly make doing a job swap with someone in another department a viable option.

9. What goals have you set for yourself during the next year? What types of projects would you like to be involved in?

To get through each day of Eternity without succumbing to soul-destroying hopelessness. I expect that, along with my normal workload, will preclude me from taking up too many new projects.

10. What developmental activities would you like to participate in? For example: seminars, training classes, and so forth?

Nothing involving pie charts, please.

11. What kind of support/guidance would you like to receive from your manager?

Nothing more than what you already do, Lord Beelzebub. You're the best supervisor <u>ever</u>!

Okay, so I'm sucking up here, but how can I imply he's anything but the world's greatest supervisor?

12. Where do you see yourself in five years?

Huh? Hell is eternal, and job growth or self-improvement here seem oxymoronic.

Heh. I love that word, oxymoronic. What I wrote was

In Hell, doing pretty much what I'm doing right now.

I finished this last response just as the Escalator reached the surface of Level Eight.

Whew! With only seconds to spare!

Hopping off the Escalator, I landed on the sandy surface of Eight, right next to an Arabian bazaar. Beezy's office was diagonally across the bazaar from me, so I threaded my way through the large and smelly crowd to reach him. I stepped in some camel shit near the camel lot (I know it sounds a bit bizarre), then, as I was cleaning my boot on a Persian rug, someone tried to pick my pocket. I hit him with my hammer, which pretty much discouraged him. I reached Beelzebub's office with all my possessions, including the all-important assessment form, and pushed my way through the revolving door.

The office, little more than a large screened-in porch, was flooded with a dull, yellow light. In the center of the room was what appeared to be an altar with a massive statue, like that of an ancient idol, placed on top. Altar and statue were wreathed in dense smoke, like that emitted by wet wood burning.

That was what appeared to be before me. On getting closer, I realized that the altar was really a desk, and the ancient idol was nothing more than the top half of Beezy, who was sitting behind his workstation. Since he normally stood over seven feet, and was of a rotund figure (yes, I mean fat), even half of him looked like a pretty large statue. And on closer examination, the dense smoke was a whirling vortex of flying insects, orbiting the center of their universe, Beelzebub, the Lord of the Flies. A few of them flew over to check me out, but finding no one as interesting as their lord and master, they returned to the swarm engulfing him.

Bugs loved Beezy. Unfortunately for them, he did not return their affection. "Damned nuisances," he muttered then reached up and gave a couple of tugs on the string of the ceiling fan that was suspended above his desk. It kicked into reverse and began to spin at a very high speed. The fog of flies was sucked away from my boss, through the blades of the fan and out a hole in the ceiling that had conveniently just opened.

"Pretty neat trick," I said. "I see you finished the modifications to your ceiling fan."

Beelzebub stuck a finger in his mouth and pulled out a fly. He squished it between two fingers then flicked it to the floor. "Yeah. They'll find their way back in here soon enough, but for now I have a few minutes of peace." He looked at me critically, as if I were another irritating insect he had to deal with. "Sit down, Minion." In front of my boss's desk was a metal folding chair, and I settled into it.

Hell's Secretary of the Interior stretched out a clawed hand. His reach was long; it was a simple matter for him to snatch the evaluation from my grasp. Like a card dealer with a new deck, Beezy gave the pages of my evaluation a quick flip then tossed them in his trash can. A puff of flame consumed them.

"Hey!" I protested. "I spent a lot of time filling that out."

My boss snorted. (Beezy snorted a lot.) "No you didn't. You spent all of fifteen minutes filling it out on the escalator ride down here."

How did he know that? Satan made a regular display of his near omniscience, constantly reading my mind, knowing things from afar that it shouldn't have been possible for him to know. Beelzebub, however, had always been more circumspect about the extent of his abilities. He had never given definitive proof of mind reading or seeing across vast distances or instantly teleporting to some far-away section of Hell. I suspected, though, as a prince of the Underworld his powers were much the same as Satan's, so I wouldn't be surprised if he'd been watching me rush through the self-appraisal as I rode down on the Escalator.

"Besides," he continued. "I read your responses. We'll start with them, and then I'll give you your evaluation."

"Yessir!"

Beelzebub frowned. "I have a few issues with your responses. First, about your handyman skills."

"What? You think I'm a good handyman."

My boss shook his head. "No, you suck. Except for your immediate predecessor, you're the worst head of Plant Maintenance we ever had."

My immediate predecessor had been Charlemagne. According to Orson, who had worked with the first Holy Roman Emperor for the last ten of his twelve hundred year tenure as Hell's Super, Karl really stank as a Mr. Fixit type. He may have been a great warrior and leader of men back in the Dark Ages of Europe, but he couldn't drive a nail to save his life. Even after death. *Still* ... "Wait a minute. I'm only the third Hell's Super, right?"

"Yeah," my boss said, cracking his knuckles. "So?"

"Prior to Charlemagne, you handled maintenance in the Underworld."

"Well, only for the first thousand years or so. Or was it five? I can never remember." He shrugged. "That was the shakedown period for Hell, and I wanted to keep my eye on the operation. What's your point?"

"Only that you're a genius at fixing things," I said, pointing meaningfully to the ceiling fan that had just sucked all the flies out of the room. "And since there's only been three of us, I'm also the second best head of Plant Maintenance you've ever had."

Beelzebub frowned at the idea then shook his head. "Doesn't matter. You still suck."

He could probably hear the grinding of my teeth. Seemed like it anyway, since a whisper of a smirk flitted across his lips.

"Then there's the issue of your productivity. You don't get one hundredth of the work done that you're assigned."

"Now, that's not fair. This is my eternal damnation. I'm not supposed to be able to keep up with my workload, am I?"

Beezy pulled out a yellow pad. I saw a bunch of random scrawls all over it, but he seemed to ascribe some importance to the doodles. He frowned and put a single check mark next to a squiggle. "Doesn't change the facts."

40

I rolled my eyes, but there was no point arguing with a devil, especially one of the princes. Damned if you do or damned if you don't, as we like to say down here. Sort of a tautology.

"Now, as to your recent special projects, I'll give you points for your initiative on the Escalator and the HVAC jobs." He put two X's next to a badly-drawn horsey. "But let me point out that you did not stop the rebellion on your own. You also didn't defeat Ymir. Bik actually did that."

"But I was the one who figured out who had sabotaged the HVAC system, not to mention climbing that damn mountain and taking on a frost giant."

"Who Bik defeated." Beezy shook his head and placed two more checks next to the squiggle. "In fact," he said, with a raised eyebrow, "you have a habit of getting other people to do your work."

"WHAT? I take my work very seriously."

"Then why do you let other people do it for you?"

"Like who?"

Beelzebub started counting his fingers. "Orson, Edison, Ford, Tesla, Pinkerton. Nightingale and Bik. Even St. Peter, me and Satan. Do I need to go on? If I do, I'll have to take off my shoes." The Lord of the Flies slipped off one of his curly-toed shoes and plopped his foot on his desktop. The room filled with the odor of rotten eggs and a fungal infection.

"No sir," I gasped, trying not to throw up. "You've made your point. You can put your shoe back on." *Please.*

"The real problem here," he said, removing his foot from the desk, "is item number five. You are entirely TOO collaborative to suit my tastes, working so well with all these people." Beelzebub scribbled over the entire page.

41

That's when I noticed he was using a number one pencil. "Hey, no fair! I thought we were only allowed to use a number two pencil on these evaluations!"

As fast as thought, Beezy threw the pencil at me. It lodged in my right eye. "Aagh!" I jerked the pencil from my eye socket. Nearly a minute passed before my vision began to return.

"There is no 'I' in 'Team,' Minion, and if you don't show a bit more respect, I'll poke out your other one!" He lifted another number one pencil from his desk and waved it at me threateningly. "As to the pencil, I'll use whatever I want, and screw the instructions!" He glowered at me.

I glowered back, rebelliously. By now, the vision in my right eye was only a little blurry.

Beezy sighed. "Screw this. Let's wrap up."

I was red with indignation. "Fine by me. So what's your evaluation of my performance?"

"You suck."

"You said that," I grumbled, crossing my arms in disgust. "Three times now."

My boss frowned, as if I posed an unusual problem for him. "You know, human, you have more spine than most of the eternally damned."

"Guess that's because I don't give a damn," I said and looked away from my boss.

I actually did give a damn. Beelzebub was the only devil in Hell I respected. He'd always been a straight shooter with me - unerringly straight, as he'd just demonstrated - and I'd hoped for a little more positive reinforcement from him.

Who am I kidding? This is Hell? Why would I expect a positive evaluation? It's just like Orson said ...

Beezy cleared his throat. "I suppose I should rip that spine out, but I'm not in the mood. Now, if I may continue, you suck at your job and you rely on teamwork too much, but overall, I'd rate your performance as … adequate." He tore the top sheet off the pad, crumpled it and threw it in his trash can. As an afterthought, he threw the entire pad away. This time the flames were a bit higher. They almost reached the top of the desk.

"Adequate?" I said, astonished. "Really?"

He nodded. "As much as it pains me to give any human a passing grade, you get a C. Congratulations, Minion! You are the first human in the history of the Underworld to receive a satisfactory performance review."

Chapter 4

I was too choked up to say anything. The fact that I might have been the first damned human to get any kind of performance review at all was irrelevant. Beelzebub thought I was doing an okay job.

"Now don't get all slobbery on me. I hate that shit. I do have one more thing to talk to you about."

Trying to be discreet, I wiped away the tear that had formed in my eye. "Sir?"

Beezy frowned. "It's your answer to the final question, 'Where do you see yourself in five years?'"

"Well," I said, with a quiet sniffle, "since I'm damned, and to be a crappy handyman is my eternal punishment, I thought I didn't have much choice."

"Ah," said Beelzebub, with an atypical smile on his face. The effect was pretty grisly. He came around the desk and put a hand on my shoulder. "My boy, the world is your oyster."

"What ... what does that mean?" I said, still a little choked up.

"Damned if I know," Beezy replied. "I heard it in an old movie. My point, though, is that you have more options than you think. Options for advancement."

Uh oh. I think I know where this is leading. I glanced around the room, looking for a means of escape. Beezy's grip on my shoulder tightened, and suddenly I had a feeling of being compressed down to a single dot. This had only happened once before. Beezy was teleporting us somewhere.

For a moment, though, I couldn't see where. Then my vision cleared. We were standing on a high promontory above the

Sahara-like surface of Level Eight. Beneath us, a black wound in the sand, was the Throat of Hell.

"Minion, Steve, why be one of the eternally damned when you can be a part of all this? Satan and I have discussed this more than once, and we're in agreement. We want you to become a demon."

Oh crap! They've made the offer official. My stomach felt a little queasy.

For many in Hell, an offer to be made a demon was something to jump at. While it was true that Management had a worker shortage in that area, Satan and the princes were very particular about who they recruited. In a way, it was an honor to be asked, and becoming a demon meant the end of eternal damnation. Though still stuck in Hell, a demon was on the "dishing out" rather than "receiving" end of the punishment transaction.

I'd also get my own pitchfork.

But the cost of these benefits was becoming a demon. First there were certain physiological changes. If I were to take them up on their offer, I would start to grow a set of horns and a tail. And since demons were generally neither male nor female, more profound changes would occur, though I was not sure exactly what they were. Would I grow breasts, I wondered? Female parts? Would I start having periods? That sounded like a new version of Hell to me. And what about my dick? Would it fall off? I shuddered. It had always been there, and I was attached to it. Well, of course I was attached to it, or rather, it was attached to me, but that little guy had given me a lot of pleasure, certainly in life, though admittedly not so much since I'd died. (I don't think urinary tract infections count.) Yet, since Flo and I had gotten involved, things were looking up for my member ...

45

When I thought of Flo, my nausea grew worse. She would never tolerate me if I switched sides. She loathed demons, perhaps even more than devils. Devils, after all, were fallen angels. They may have rebelled against G ... the Supreme Being (SB: not supposed to use the "G" word down here), but they had not chosen, at least not intentionally, to become evil. In fact, I don't think the devils really thought through the consequences of their act of insurrection, though if they had, they might have figured out that those on the side of the SB were by definition going to be the good guys and the angels who revolted would end up as the ones wearing the black hats.

Although, maybe not. One of the main differences between humans and devils is that humans have free will and devils don't. Perhaps they were meant to be revolting. And evil.

Those who choose to be demons, on the other hand, know precisely what they are getting into. With the fall from grace of the rebellious angels, "evil" had been defined on this plane of existence. (There are other planes, but I don't know how things work in those other religions. We don't have much contact with them.) So humans who become demons know exactly what evil is and consciously elect to be one of the bad guys.

That didn't sit well with me either. Perhaps by my being damned to Hell, I was already bad. Yet St. Peter himself had said there was more good in me than evil; I'd just not had enough faith or performed enough good deeds in life to make it through the Pearlies (Gates, not teeth). I was basically a good guy, then, albeit one who had made some bad choices in life. And I didn't relish the prospect of torturing a bunch of poor schmucks like me who had the misfortune to end up down here.

I shook my head. *No.* Becoming a demon just to get out of my own damnation meant consciously electing evil over good, torturing other humans, not to mention losing Flo and changing myself in ways that I found abhorrent. The cost was too high. "I appreciate the offer, boss," I said with care. "I mean, I really do, but I think I'd rather stay Hell's Super."

Beezy's grip on my shoulder tightened, and his claws dug into my shoulder. "Ouch!"

"I can't force you to become a demon. You have to elect to do so of your own free will. Still, I wish you'd reconsider." Those last words seemed to stick in his throat. I think it was hard for Beezy not to get his way, and even harder not to be able to push people around.

I gave him a sickly smile. "Thanks, but no."

The Lord of the Flies gave my shoulder one final squeeze - hard enough to make me see stars - then released me. "This isn't over, you know. Satan is going to want to speak to you himself."

"Give him my regards," Beezy said, pushing me off the cliff, straight toward the Throat of Hell.

"Aaaaaaaaaaaaaaaaaaaaaaaaaaaaaaaaaaaaaaaaaaaaaaaaaaaaa aaaaaaaaaaaaaaaa ... "

Only falling through a single Circle of Hell hardly gave me time to think. Before I knew it ...

"Aaaaaaaaaaaaaaaaaaaaaaaaaaaaaaaaaaaaaaaaaaaaaaaaaaaaa aaaaaaaaaaaaaaaa ... Ouch!"

I did little more than sprain an ankle on landing.

"The Lord of Hell will see you now."

Bruce the Bedeviled, Satan's personal assistant and a recent recruit to the demon corps, stood behind me. His new horns had already broken through the skin of his forehead, and I suspected he had a tail tucked in his trousers.

The double doors to Satan's office flew open. "Come in," said an imperious voice from within.

Great. Now I get to say no to Satan. I doubt he'll take it as well as Beezy did. Still, there was no choice. He was the Boss, and he'd just ordered me inside. Getting off the carpet, I walked into his office.

"What the fuck?"

Satan's office, usually hotter than a furnace, was a pleasant temperature. The space, normally shrouded in darkness, except for a single spotlight that was trained on his desk for dramatic effect, seemed bathed in sunshine. And what I saw in that bright light surprised me even more.

Beneath my feet was the wooden surface of a sailing yacht. In the distance was a lone island with a long stretch of sandy white beach. The water was calm and almost turquoise, like that of the Caribbean. A slight sea breeze stirred my hair; the pleasant tang of salt air filled my nose and settled ever so lightly on my palate.

"Mojito?" said a voice behind me. I turned.

There was Satan, in his customary sunglasses, but dressed in Bermuda shorts, one of those gaudy Hawaiian-style shirts and some flip-flops. The flip-flops were quite the design feat, for they accommodated his cloven hooves. They must have been custom-made, because they fit him like a glove - or a sandal, to be more accurate. In fact, Satan pulled off the whole ensemble really well.

The Lord of Hell took off his sunglasses and smiled, dazzling me with the whiteness of his teeth. He seemed genuinely glad to see me, which was suspicious; since Satan was the original and consummate deceiver, my skepticism was with good reason. "Mojito?" he said again, the smile looking a little strained as he shoved a glass in my direction.

Reflexively I took it. Now, mojitos are not my favorite drink. Why anyone thinks a highball with a bunch of weeds stuffed in it looks chic is beyond me. Still, Satan didn't offer me a beverage very often, and when he did it was invariably excellent. My boss's boss had a glass of his own and was drinking it with obvious enjoyment.

Cautiously, I took a sip through the straw. I'm not fond of umbrella cocktails - you know, those drinks you get poolside that usually have a fake umbrella stuck in them - and generally dislike mint in anything, especially in my drinks. Despite my misgivings, the mojito was excellent.

This was a setup, of course. Satan was never nice to me unless he wanted something, and this was classic manipulation. Still, all I could do was play along. "You wished to see me, sir?" I asked, between slurps of my mojito.

"Yes, my boy," he said, putting a hand on my shoulder. That was the second time in ten minutes I'd been called my boy, so I was pretty sure what this was all about. "But first, come stand with me on the prow of the yacht."

We were a little closer to the island. The white sands looked inviting, and in a few moments, some sunbathers strolled out to enjoy the beach. All of them were women, all in bikinis, all beautiful and spectacularly endowed. A beach full of bimbos. As one, they waved at me. Like any red-blooded heterosexual male, living or dead, would do, I waved back.

Still ... How obvious can you get?

The hand on my shoulder tightened a little, but if Satan was reading my thoughts, he didn't say anything except, "Look how blue the water is." Well, yeah, it was blue. Blue beyond blue, perfect, and as calm as a koi pond. "It's nothing but smooth sailing for you, now, Steve."

He's really much better at this than Beelzebub. I took another sip of my mojito. "Provided I agree to become a demon."

"And why not?" he said. "What's so great about being damned for eternity?"

"I get to stay human?" I posited.

The Devil sniffed as if he'd just smelled something malodorous. "And what's so great about that? Maybe if you were still on Earth, or ... in that other place. In Hell, as a human, you are doomed to torment. As a demon, though, well ... "

"Well, what?" *Man, this mojito is really delicious.*

Satan smiled again, and his eyes lit up. I mean they literally lit up, as if he had little light bulbs in there. He pointed at the mast, and a screen dropped down. A PowerPoint presentation began to run. It was entitled, "Demonhood: the Adventure Begins." The introductory slides showed demons doing all sorts of cool things, like rock climbing, surfing, listening to music in swank bars, soaking in hot tubs. There was usually at least one gorgeous woman involved in each activity.

Hmmm. Maybe Satan would be interested in Orson's idea for a recruitment video after all.

Then the presentation moved to a slide entitled, "Compensation Package."

The first bullet point appeared, using the wipe right feature of PowerPoint. Pretty snazzy. "First, there's the signing bonus: ten, no let's make it twenty virgins."

The girls on the island waved at me again. Without volition, I reciprocated.

Then came the second bullet: "An adamantium pitchfork."

"Hey! I thought adamantium was just a word made up by Marvel Comics."

Satan looked a little sheepish. "Yes, it is. The point, heh heh, is that the pitchfork is made of really hard metal. Here." Satan put his sunglasses back on, conjured up a pitchfork and handed it to me. I set down my drink to examine it more closely.

The balance was perfect in my hands. I swung it experimentally, as if it were a katana. Very cool.

"It can also transform into all manner of objects, depending on the need. Watch." In my hand, the pitchfork turned into a three iron. I took a practice drive with it. *Boy I could really hit a ball a long way with this.* "Hey! Would I get to play golf up on One?"

The First Circle of Hell is a gated golf community. Its inhabitants are good people, virtuous pagans and unbaptized babies, who were either born before the Judeo-Christian franchise was established or who died in infancy in the past two millennia.

"Well, no," he said reluctantly. "The pagans tend to get a bit freaked out by having demons up there, but," he continued with enthusiasm, "we have courses on Two and Three that have been specially designated for devils and demons. They're merely challenging, not torturous to play on, like the ones designed to torment the damned." Satan reached for the golf club; reluctantly I let go of it. With a poof, it disappeared. Sighing, I picked up my mojito again.

"Demons, when they're not on duty, have a wide range of housing options." The presentation showed beach houses, Manhattan-style flats, country manors. "They also eat like kings, food better than anything you could get in the best restaurants of Paris or New York. And demons don't have to wash their own dishes." There was a slide of a very pretty French maid cleaning up the kitchen. She leaned a little too low and ...

The slide changed. We were back to the bullet points. "Three weeks of vacation a year, no, in your case I'll make it four, and you can travel almost anywhere you want."

I choked on my mojito. "Including Earth?"

51

Satan smiled his most charming smile. "Why, of course Earth. Becoming a demon puts you in a very elite group. You can return to your old haunts, or visit all those places you had intended to before you had your brains blown out."

A graduate student murdered me in my office. That was just a week before a planned trip to Tuscany. Bad luck that.

"And the list of benefits just goes on and on. I mean, come on, Steve-o, this is a no-brainer."

It was all so wonderful, so dazzling, so alluring. The word "yes" was practically falling out of my mouth. I clenched my fists in anticipation ... and then remembered Flo and all my friends who would hate me forever if I did this. The prospect of horns, a tail and maybe no penis popped back into my brain too. Swallowing hard, I smiled what must have been a pretty sick looking smile. "This looks great. It's ... it's a wonderful honor to even be asked, but ... " reflexively I flinched, waiting for the blow to come, " ... but I don't want to be a demon."

The grin fell from Satan's face. The room turned to pitch momentarily, and then the lights came back on. The yacht, water, beach and bimbos were gone. Satan was sitting behind his rosewood desk, wearing his jet black business suit. "Suit yourself. I'm not going to beg. Besides, if you're too stupid to take advantage of the best opportunity of your afterlife, then I probably don't want you in the Demon Corps anyway." He frowned. "So get out of here and ... what?"

Satan looked up, apparently listening to something. "Very well. Send it down." A piece of paper materialized above him, and he plucked it out of the air.

"Flyface said a FAX just came for you from Orson." He handed it to me.

Curious, I unfolded the piece of paper. It was a copy of a work order. The handwriting was immediately recognizable. In Flo's elegant cursive was a single word: *"Help!"*

"Lord Satan," I said, looking up at the Earl of Hell. "S ... something's happened to Flo. Do you know ... ?"

"She's disappeared, Minion. And no, I didn't have anything to do with it. Now, if you're not out of my office in three seconds, I will turn you into a thousand grains of sand and sprinkle you on that beach you have just turned your back on."

I was through the door in two.

Chapter 5

"Damn elevator!" I grumbled, fuming. I'd been standing at the doors for an hour, pressing the stupid button to no avail. Without magical assistance, Hell's Elevator was the only way to go up in the Netherworld, except by using the Stairway to Paradise, but it stopped on Level Eight. Satan was very particular about access to or from the Ninth Circle, and a Stairway to his office suite would be like having an open door policy, which he didn't.

Flo was in trouble. That she was immune from harm down here gave me some comfort, but she still needed me, so I was anxious to ...

A swoosh of air almost knocked me flat. With a heavy thud, BOOH, the storied Bat out of Hell, and Satan's courier-in-chief, landed on his perch, which was a large telephone pole stuck sideways into the wall near the Elevator. BOOH was gigantic, with a thirty-foot wingspan, and the ability to carry hundreds of pounds at lightning speeds up and down the nine Circles of Hell. He was also one of my best friends.

Hmmm.

"Hey, BOOH," I said, giving him a high five, which he returned with his customary low five. "How goes it?"

The bat merely shrugged, a typical response from my pal. I never expected him to go into a long monologue about the ups and downs of his day. BOOH was easily as smart as any human I'd ever met, but he didn't talk, except for a frequent "Skree!" and an occasional "Urm." He did however have elaborate body language, and because he and I had spent so much time together, I could read him well. It looked to me that the day so far was fairly typical: ran an errand here, delivered a missive there, did a little hunting, drank a little blood (being a vampire bat, after all). That sort of thing.

After a little chit-chat, I came to the point. "Look, BOOH. I've been waiting for the Elevator forever. Okay," I amended, seeing the skeptical look with which he regarded me, "but for a really long time. I need to get back to the office ASAP. There's some trouble with Flo that I need to check into."

My friend looked concerned. Like most everyone, he liked Flo, and I was pretty sure he wanted to help me, but he shot a quick look at Satan's closed doors.

I sagged. "Yeah, I get it. Satan hasn't given you permission to carry me anywhere. It's … it's okay. You're my friend, and I know you'd help me if you could. I can keep waiting for the Elevator. It's just that," I added in modest desperation, "it's just that I'm worried about Flo and … "

We were in the air before I could finish my sentence.

I worried on the whole ride to Level Five that BOOH was taking an awful chance, that he'd get in trouble for helping me. On the other hand, Satan adored the enormous bat. If the Earl of Hell had a familiar, in the Brothers Grimm "wicked witch" meaning of the term, BOOH would be it. Or a pet. Satan showered more affection on BOOH than any other creature in the Netherworld. And, I thought brightly, he probably hadn't strictly forbad my friend from carrying me.

To think of Satan loving anyone or anything was kind of a marvel to me, but I'd seen his obvious fondness for BOOH on more than one occasion. My friend was operating in a gray area by giving me a lift, but he would no doubt be okay.

In seconds, we were four levels up and in front of my office. BOOH set me gently on the pavement. "Thanks, pal," I said with gratitude, knowing he'd taken a risk for me.

"Urm."

"Yes, I *would* do the same thing for you. Oh, I don't want to push things here, but do you think, if I need you again, you could carry me around a little? I wouldn't ask you when I needed to go down, but it's just so damn hard to go up in Hell, you know what I mean? Well, of course you don't know what I mean, since it's easy for you, but for me it's ... "

"Skree!"

"What? Oh, sorry. You're right. I'm rambling. But, what do you say?"

BOOH stopped flapping and dropped to the pavement. His brow was furrowed; he seemed worried. He looked at me, and then he looked behind him, as if Satan were standing there. I'd never seen BOOH so conflicted, but after a minute, he made eye contact, nodded once then took to the skies.

Damn. He was the best bat buddy I'd ever had. Well, he was the only bat buddy I'd ever had, but he was still the best. And certainly one of my best friends ever.

I would have taken a moment to get all emotional about the jeopardy BOOH could have been getting into, but there was no time for that. Flo's disappearance trumped everything, so I hurried inside my office.

Orson was pacing the floor. The desk was covered with work orders, but my assistant had not bothered to do his customary triage. He looked up at me when the door opened; worry was a tattoo across his face.

"Steve, thank G... I'm glad you're here. You got the FAX I sent to Beezy?"

"Yes," I said, waving my left hand, which was still clutching the paper. "When did it come in?"

Orson bit his lower lip. "Don't know, exactly. It was in a pile or work orders that I was sorting. Maybe a couple of hours ago?"

I nodded. "That's about the time I was traveling down to Eight on the Escalator. Have you gone over to the Hospital to check things out?"

"I tried, but it's cordoned off with police tape."

"What's police tape?"

"You know, the yellow stuff cops use to block off a crime scene."

"Oh, right, like what we use when we're working on a project."

"Yeah."

I grabbed my hard hat. Not quite sure why I did that, but it made me feel more secure. "Come on, Orson. Let's go."

"What are we going to do?"

"We're going to get into that crime scene."

Copying me, Orson donned his own hard hat, and the two of us headed out the door.

The scene at the Hospital was chaos. Well, things in Hell are frequently chaos, that's sort of the nature of the place, but this was worse than usual. Cop cars were everywhere, their sirens roaring, lights flashing so manically they would have put an epileptic into a seizure. Demons in police uniforms crowded around the cars, some with yellow pads out, writing furiously on them. Others had drawn their firearms and were randomly shooting into the crowd that had formed.

Hmmm. How to get in there?

Orson was scratching his beard, obviously wondering the same thing. Then he brightened. "At times like these," he said to me, "I've always found that it pays to be officious."

"Huh?"

"Just follow my lead." With that, my friend plowed through the crowd. His considerable girth helped him knock a few bodies to the side, and I tailed along in his wake. He got stopped at the police line by two demons. "Out of my way!" he bellowed.

"And just who the Hell do you think you are?" said a demon with sergeant strips.

My friend turned me around, showing the cop the maroon "HOTI," I mean, "HOOTI" acronym on the back of my yellow coveralls.

"Big deal," groused the cop. "Two thirds of all Hell works for the Office of the Interior."

"Yeah," Orson said, in his toughest tough guy voice, "but this is Steve Minion, Hell's Super, and he reports directly to Lord Beelzebub."

Oh, so we're going to fake our way in. Got it. "That's right! And I need to get in there stat!"

"What's a stat?" asked a dimwitted demon cop standing nearby. "Oh, I get it. You want to get in someone's pants."

Orson rolled his eyes. "No, you moron. Stat means immediately. It's from the Latin, *statim*, which … "

The demon snarled. "Who you callin' a moron, fat guy?"

The sergeant cut off his underling and looked at me. "Did you say Minion?"

"Yeah," I growled, then realized I wasn't putting on an act. I really was angry. And worried about Flo.

"You're the doll's boyfriend, right?"

I nodded.

"Come inside. The chief wants to talk with you." He grabbed my arm and pulled me through the crowds of police. Orson, seeing his opportunity, followed behind.

The waiting room had been cleared of its regular crew of damned souls. Little Uphir was talking earnestly with a very tall, dark-complected and whip-thin devil in a navy suit. No, it was more like a uniform, and he wore a golden badge, a downward

58

pointing pentagram with the head of a goat superimposed on the star.

This must be the police chief.

As I walked over to the stranger, he turned to regard me. His face was thin, like his body, and seemed composed entirely of triangles. The officer's forehead was broad, his chin narrow. His goatee was closely cropped, but ended just below his face in a point. The devil's black hair was combed back to reveal a deep widow's peak that came down so far on his brow it bisected the space between the thin diagonals that were his eyebrows. In my time in Hell, I'd met many devils who were taller than I, but few seemed to loom over me, as if from a great height. I doubt he was any taller than Beezy in his normal seven foot incarnation, but the new guy seemed like a vulture sitting in a tree far above me, looking down at some carrion he would just as soon rend with his claws.

The devil regarded me in silence, though his eyes burned with a manic fire. His potential for violent anger seemed limitless, though he had hardly moved since I'd first seen him. For some reason he gave me the shivers. Go figure.

The sergeant cleared his throat. "Chief, here's that Minion character you asked about."

Uphir looked at me and sneered. "That's him all right. He comes around here all the time to see Nightingale. Like a dog sniffing up a bitch in heat."

"Hey, watch it! You have no call to talk that way about Flo."

I found myself on the floor, where a lightning-quick slap from the stranger had put me. "Keep your tongue in check, human, around your betters, and especially around me." For the first time, I understood what was meant by the evil eye, because he was certainly giving it to me.

Shit! The guy looks like he wants to kill me! Cautiously, I got off the floor, maintaining a prudent silence.

Uphir turned to the tall devil. "Minion was here this morning. He and Nightingale had coffee together. As far as I know, he's the last one to have seen her."

The devil stared at me with suspicion. Despite my recent dance with the floor, I felt my own temper begin to boil. I would not be intimidated by this guy, at least, not if I could help it. If I could go mano a diablo with Satan, surely I could stand up to anyone. Holding my ground, if silently, I tried to look as intimidating as possible, though university professor types, even ones who have gone through the blue collar school of maintenance, don't tend to scare anyone but undergraduates submitting late assignments.

Yet, despite my resolve to maintain a brave face, this particular devil scared the crap out of me in a way that only Satan ever had. He was evil, certainly; that was part of the definition of a devil. More, though, he apparently had a bubbling hatred for humans inside him. The dark stranger was silent, but his ruby eyes seemed to bore right into my skull.

Finally he spoke. "Minion. I've heard of you. You're not the most popular human among the Devil and Demon Corps."

That was true. I had a deserved reputation for my smart mouth. Also, on at least two occasions, when on special assignment for Satan, I'd used my position to push around more than a few demons, though not, to my knowledge, devils. Well, maybe Laverne, the devil in a blue dress, who worked up in Glutton's Gap. I'd had BOOH intimidate her into helping me. That counted, I guess.

The longer the chief stared at me, the more nervous I got, until all of my bravado deserted me. "I guess ... I guess, sir, that

I've antagonized a few of your brethren at times, but I've only been doing my job."

The chief's hands formed into tight fists, so tight that his dark skin whitened around the knuckles, yet somehow he managed to control what looked like an urge to put me back on the floor. "I see," he said at last then turned back to Uphir. "Can anyone else corroborate that Minion was with Miss Nightingale shortly before she disappeared?"

"Oh, me! Me!" said a small voice from the corner of the room.

The little imp who had spied on us in the broom closet stepped forward. "Flo and Steve - I can call you Steve, can't I...?"

"No."

That must have offended him, because he threw his tiny pitchfork at my leg. I was grateful, though. If he hadn't done that, the chief probably would have decked me, since even this little perv was one of my "betters," and I'd just shown him some minor disrespect. Wincing, I pulled the pitchfork out of my thigh and tossed it back to him.

What an irritating shrimp of an imp.

"Flo and *Mr. Minion*," he said, turning a frosty look in my direction, "were feeling each other up in a broom closet along that hallway." He pointed in the direction of the coffee shop.

"We were not, you little pipsqueak!" I said heatedly, feeling my face turn red with embarrassment. "We were just kissing," I continued, after pulling the pitchfork out of my other leg. I almost returned his weapon a second time, but not knowing what part of my body he'd target next, I pocketed it instead.

The imp jumped up and down like a toddler who'd been deprived of his favorite toy. He pointed at me, a huge (for him) pout on his face, and turned to the police chief, hoping, no doubt, for him to intervene.

61

"Give it back," the chief growled.

No matter who this guy was, I was now thoroughly pissed off. It doesn't ever pay to show anger to a devil, but I have more guts than brains, and when I get mad, my mouth takes over. "He's just going to throw it at me again, so why should I?"

A whip that appeared in the chief's hand took me across the chest, and once again I crumpled to the floor.

"Because I said so."

"Yes sir," I gasped, taking the pitchfork from my pocket and offering it to the imp, who wrenched it from my grasp, shoved its tines into my palm then raced to safety between the legs of the police chief. The shrimp-imp grinned evilly then stuck his tongue out at me.

I looked up to the chief. There was something about this tall, hate-filled fiend that I found very intimidating. For either a devil or a demon to unnerve me was unusual. Uphir, for instance, didn't scare me. He and I had gone head to head on more than one occasion, and I gave at least as good as I got. Asmodeus, the Prince of Lust, didn't intimidate me. Nor did the maître d'evil at Red Square, a nightclub on Level Five. Even Digger, a very powerful demon - easily twice the size of the police chief - who ran the sulfur mine down on Six, didn't scare me. Of course, Digger was an idiot, and I could outsmart him any day of the week.

That was another one of the reasons for my discomfort; aside from his obvious hatred of humanity, this devil was clearly no dummy. His eyes bore right through me every time he looked my way, which he did just then. I found myself shivering.

"Where did you last see Miss Nightingale?"

"Here, in the Waiting Room, just before I took the Escalator to see Beelzebub."

The chief rubbed his goatee in thought. "Did you ride down with anyone?"

"Well, no, but … "

"Then you have no alibi for the period during which Miss Nightingale disappeared."

Intimidating or not, this guy really bugged me. "No I don't, at least not for the few minutes it took to ride down to Eight. However, I spent almost all of the time since I last saw Flo with Beezy, uh, Lord Beelzebub, and with Lord Satan. You can check with them if you'd like. Besides, I have no motive for kidnapping her. I love her."

This third time, Orson helped me up from the floor, where the double whammy of Hellfire and coconut cream pie had put me. Red whelps began to form on my face from my coconut allergy. Having nothing to wipe the cream off my puss, I used my sleeve.

The devil looked at me appraisingly. "That last comment at least is true, I suppose. But whether or not you have a motive remains to be seen."

Orson stepped forward. "Sir, I can vouch for this man's character."

For some reason, the devil found this amusing. A thin smile formed on his lips. It creeped me out. "One damned human vouching for another is not the most persuasive endorsement I've ever heard."

A surprising voice came to my defense. "Oh, Minion didn't do it," Uphir said. "He's a pain in my butt, but Satan and Beelzebub trust him. Besides, he really does care for Nightingale."

"Thanks, Uphir," I said, surprising myself. "Look, chief, I want to help. I've done a little detective work before."

The big devil rumbled. I think it was a laugh. "You're referring to the Hellions? From my perspective, you were played for a fool during that escapade. Besides, you had Pinkerton's help, as I recall."

"Well, yes. Allan Pinkerton is a friend of mine. But I deduced who the leaders of that group were on my own. I also figured out who sabotaged the HVAC system the other day."

The chief looked thoughtful. "I hadn't heard that," he said slowly. After a moment of reflection, he frowned, as if he didn't like the conclusion he'd reached. "Very well," he said, reluctantly, "I'll let you help, provisionally, at least." The devil reached in his pocket and pulled out a laminated ID card. He handed it to me. The card said, "Steve Minion, Consulting Detective."

"Ooh!" Orson said, examining it as I used the accompanying clip to fasten it to my outer pocket. "Just like Sherlock Holmes. Can I get one of those too?"

Now it was my turn to help Orson off the floor.

The chief glared at him and me both. "Insubordination seems to run in the Plant Maintenance Department. So, Minion, why should I let the fat human help?"

"Uh, Orson is my assistant. We generally work as a team."

"Fine." The chief reached into his coat and pulled out another badge, which said "Orson Welles, Assistant to the Consulting Detective."

"Always the assistant," Orson grumbled, fastening the badge to his pocket.

"What was that?" the chief hissed.

"Nothing, sir," Orson whispered. His face glistened with sweat, a very natural and healthy reaction to this devil, in my opinion. "Nothing at all."

The police chief took out a small pad, jotted down a few notes then snapped it closed. The tablet disappeared in the very large palm of his hand. He looked to Uphir. "We're done for now. Tell Minion and his assistant what you told me."

"Yes sir," Uphir said with unusual deference.

"And Minion," the chief said, turning to me, "keep me informed about your activities."

"How will I find you, uh, sir?"

"Don't worry. I'll find you." The chief looked around the room and randomly blasted one of the damned with Hellfire. A look of manic glee flashed across his face, and a tiny bit of spittle ran out of one side of his mouth. Then he disappeared.

I swallowed hard. That guy gave me the willies.

With the chief's departure, all the tension seemed to slip from the room, except in the case of the imp who, deprived of his hulking protector, gave me a wide-eyed look, stuck his tongue out a final time and scurried out of sight.

Orson and I looked at each other; we both shivered. "Man," my friend said, "that guy gave me the heebie jeebies."

"If you're talking about the chief instead of the squirt, me too."

"With good reason," Uphir said. I turned to him in surprise and saw that the little demon looked a bit rattled himself.

I frowned. "The only other creature in the universe I've ever had that kind of reaction to has been Satan himself. Who is that guy?"

The demon physician's eyes looked nervously in both directions, as if just answering my question might get him in trouble. "Azazel," he said breathlessly.

"Oh, crap! No wonder he scares me shitless."

"Well, we demons have a healthy respect for him too." Uphir was sweating, which I found interesting. I didn't think demons could sweat. "He may not be a prince of Hell, but he might as well be, as powerful as he is."

There are various stories surrounding Azazel, some canonical, some apocryphal. In a way, he is like Beelzebub. Many believe Azazel to have once been a Canaanite god. Another story, from Leviticus 16, has Azazel as the recipient of a goat that has been invested by the high priest, Aaron, with all the sins of the Israelites. That would make Azazel the original scapegoat. It might also explain the goat head on the devil's cop badge.

But there's a third tale about Azazel that, at least down here, is the most commonly accepted. Most believe that Azazel was a leader of the original fallen angels. There are even some who say it was he and not Lucifer who fomented the rebellion in Heaven and tempted Eve in the Garden of Eden. That would put him on nearly equal footing with Satan.

Obviously the Lord of Hell won the war of beliefs, and he probably didn't take kindly to having Azazel as a competitor. Instead of making him one of the princes down here, he put Azazel in a middle-management job. If this last story was the true skinny, he would be almost as powerful as Satan, perhaps even more so than Beelzebub, but without the perks. That wouldn't make for a very happy camper.

I frowned. No wonder he scared me. He was dangerous … and disgruntled. "Uphir, what did Azazel want you to tell me?"

The demon shrugged. "What I know about Nightingale's disappearance, which isn't much. I've always had a good sense of where she is, at least here in the hospital. I'm not always monitoring her, but if I think about her, I can tell you within three feet her location."

I'd seen him perform this little trick many times. "Do you have any sense of her now?"

"That's what I was telling Azazel. A little while ago, I was aware of her being in the waiting room. Then I got distracted, performing a colonoscopy. It was a fun one too," the little puce creep said with enthusiasm. "I always love pushing the camera up an anus, especially now that I've upgraded to using one of those big mothers like you find in local news rooms."

"Please spare me the details," I said, trying to contain my revulsion.

"You sure? Oh, okay. Well, anyway, after I'd finished, I wanted to tell Nightingale about the procedure, but she was nowhere in the hospital."

"Perhaps she just stepped out for a minute."

"Doubt it," Uphir said. "Nightingale almost never leaves the building until she goes home at night."

I considered visiting her apartment. She was unlikely to be there, but the trip would have to be done sooner or later, if only to look for clues. "Do you know anything about this?" I asked, showing him the copy of the work order that I still had clutched in my hand.

He stared at it briefly. "No, but that's her handwriting all right. I'd recognize that disgustingly neat penmanship anywhere."

Except for Orson's ill-advised comment to Azazel, my assistant had generally stayed quiet since we'd entered the hospital, taking in first my conversation with the police chief then this brief exchange with Uphir. Now Orson spoke. "Is there anyone else who keeps tabs on her like you do?"

Uphir snorted. "Well, there's Tinkle."

"What? Who's that?" The name was unfamiliar to me.

"He's the little drop-kick devil who poked you with his pitchfork. He has a crush on Nightingale that may even rival yours, Minion. Tink's constantly sneaking around, watching what she's doing. He's the only one other than me who could possibly know where she is. Well, other than Satan, but I doubt you'll get much help out of him."

I thought back to my recent visit with the Earl of Hell. "No, you're right there."

"Nightingale has been a thorn in my Lord's side since she decided to come down here." Uphir paused. "But of course, I'm crazy about her."

"What?" Orson said with surprise. "I never really got that impression."

"Why sure! She's my favorite sparring partner. She makes things so much more fun around here. Her reactions to some of my surgical procedures are priceless, just priceless," he finished, chuckling.

"Then," I said slowly, "you wouldn't have kidnapped her."

"Is that what you think happened to her? Hmm. So does Azazel. But, anyway, no. I'd never do anything that would take her out of the hospital."

I think he's serious. And probably not a suspect. "So, then, maybe I should go talk to Tinker Bell."

"Tinkle," Uphir corrected. "Good luck with that. You didn't exactly get off on the right foot with him."

My palm still itched where the little guy had stabbed it. "No, I suppose I didn't. Do you know where he might be?"

"Probably in the cafeteria, getting a Slurpee. He's addicted to those things."

"Okay. Thanks, Uphir."

Hell's demon physician sniffed. "Please don't mention it. It's not my practice to help you humans, but I want Nightingale back as soon as possible. Get cracking." With that, Uphir left.

"Come on, Orson. Let's hit the cafeteria."

Chapter 6

The staff cafeteria was nearly empty when we got there, except for a few demon doctors in one corner, slamming down coffee as if they were fiends, which they were, and chain smoking.

I hated the cafeteria. The coffee shop, where Flo and I had met earlier that day, was merely sterile. By sterile I don't mean the literal sense of the word, that is, antiseptically clean. A "germ-free" Underworld would be laughable. The coffee shop was sterile, though, in that the décor was without character, uninteresting, a chrome and plastic blankness. The cafeteria, in contrast, had lots of character, but it was character of ill-repute. The cafeteria was primarily for the demonic workers of the hospital. It was a filthy place with scratched wood paneling, old area rugs so badly stained that if there had ever been any patterns to their designs they long ago had been obliterated. The furniture was ripped, chipped and tawdry. The windows were grimy, and the air was full of cigarette smoke and no small amount of sulfur. In short, the staff cafeteria was like the faculty lounge of a badly-funded high school.

In the back of the room was a counter, where diners could select from the salads, entrees, veggies and desserts that sat behind panes of glass. Damned food service workers would serve it up with as much enthusiasm as those dowdy, middle-aged ladies in hair nets did back on Earth. As with all cafeterias, there was a long railing along which the diners could slide their plastic trays as they accepted little dishes and bowls the counter staff would slop the food into.

At the register, standing on his tiptoes to receive a Slurpee the size of a conga drum, was Tinkle.

"Hi," I said in as friendly a fashion as possible, which wasn't easy considering he'd recently stuck me three times with that damn pitchfork of his. I was inclined to kick him across the room; instead, I squeezed out a reasonable facsimile of a smile.

When Tinkle saw me and Orson closing on him, he backed into the counter, nearly spilling his Slurpee. His eyes were wide with fear, though why a devil would fear a human was beyond me. Even considering his small stature, he was probably powerful enough to mop the floor with both of us, but spending your existence staring up at everyone probably resulted in a fierce inferiority complex. That was good. It might make it easier for us to reason with the little twerp.

Tinkle set his Slurpee carefully on the floor - I noted with approval that he had gotten grape, which was also my favorite - then pulled his pitchfork, waving it at the two of us.

"Hey!" I said, holding my hands up in surrender. "We don't want to fight."

"That's right, Tinkle," Orson agreed.

"Don't call me that!"

"Sorry. That's what Uphir said your name was."

The little guy eyed us suspiciously, gave one more threatening poke and put away his pitchfork. He picked up his Slurpee and took a drink. "Well, it's not. Or at least not exactly. It's pronounced TNK-el."

Orson arched an eyebrow at me. We couldn't hear much difference, except for the curious lack of vowels in the first syllable and the emphasis on the "el" instead of the "TNK."

TNK-el walked over to an empty table, barely managing to place his drink on its surface, then hopped up into a vacant chair. "Humans and demons alike should show me more respect," he said haughtily. "I used to be an angel you know, not some sleazebag like Uphir, or you two for that matter."

70

"Really?" I said, feigning interest and sitting down next to him, while Orson went to get us a couple of coffees. I knew this, since all devils were former angels, but pretending to give a damn about the imp seemed a good way to break the ice.

"Yeah," he said, his chest swelling with pride. "A cherubim. You know, that's the second highest order of angels, after seraphim."

"Forgive me for saying, but aren't you a little sm… "

As fast as thought, TNK-el whipped out his pitchfork again. "Don't say it. Just don't."

I kept my lips pinched shut and did a little thinking. All those European paintings by the grand masters. They represented cherubs as adorable winged babies. Perhaps he used to be one of them. "Oh, of course. I've seen paintings where … "

TNK-el rolled his eyes. "That's a bunch of Baroque crap, the product of some overactive human imaginations. Those figures are putti, not genuine cherubs. I get that all the time. Putti are dinky and not even real. Cherubs are, well, we're puissant," he said with obvious pride.

"Then why … " I began and slammed my mouth shut.

The little devil's temper flared, and he poked both thumbs.

"Ouch!" I pulled my hands off the table and out of harm's way.

"If you *must* know, I'm this small because," he looked a bit forlorn, "well, I've been sick."

"Oh," I said, sucking on my fresh wounds. *Damn! That stings.* "Sorry to hear that. How long have you been sick?"

"Since," he sighed, "since the Fall. Not one of my better career decisions, I suppose."

No kidding. That was like leaving upper management at Apple and taking a job as cashier at an IHOP. "You said you've been sick. What's … what's wrong with you?"

TNK-el screwed up his face into an impressively hideous frown. "Did you ever play pile-on as a kid?"

What boy hadn't? "Yeah."

"That's sort of what happened."

The little devil got quiet for a moment. "Long I fell," he whispered, "and far. Unfortunately, I wasn't alone. When we landed, I had the misfortune of being at the bottom of the heap, with about fifty of my brethren on top of me. I was thoroughly smooshed and have never really recovered. But!" he growled, "I'm still a devil, through and through. Which makes me higher in the pecking order than any demon. And certainly any human!"

"What are we talking about?" Orson asked pleasantly, as he set a coffee in front of me and took a couple of spare seats.

"Cherubs," I said.

"Oh. Are you a former cherub? That would explain Ow!"

"How does that explain 'ow?'" I said mildly. "Stings, doesn't it?"

"No shit," he grumbled, rubbing at his new wound.

"Cherubs are actually very high-ranking angels," I explained, trying to show I'd been listening. "Fascinating story, really. Tell you more about it later. But for now … " I turned to the little guy, who was sucking on his straw. His mouth was now painted purple. "Look, TNK-el, I feel like we got off on the wrong foot."

"No shit," TNK-el said, mimicking Orson's voice perfectly. *"Mr. Minion."*

"Please, call me Steve."

"Why can I call you Steve now, but couldn't before?"

"Well," I stalled, trying to come up with a reasonable explanation then brightened when it came to me. "We didn't know each other before, but we do now. I would be … I would be honored if you would call me Steve."

A look of disgust drifted across his face. "Suck-up. Maybe I'll just call you Minion, minion."

I sighed. "Whatever you prefer. Listen, though, I wanted to talk about Flo's disappearance. You know I care about her. Uphir says you do too."

When I mentioned Flo's name, TNK-el became visibly upset. He set down his Slurpee and wiped at one eye. He made a purple mark on his cheek that made him look like a crying Pagliacci. "I ... I do. I don't know why, but I think she's just wonderful!"

"Probably because she's the hottest woman in Hell," Orson murmured.

TNK-el leapt to the table top, brandishing his pitchfork. "You watch what you say about Miss Nightingale, fatso!"

"Hey, calm down," Orson said smoothly. "I meant no offense. Besides, we all know it's true. She's beautiful."

"Yes, yes she is," the devil agreed, sighing, as he sat back down. "Both inside and out."

Angels know a thing or two about beauty, and devils are just angels who, as TNK-el said, made a bad career decision. No devil in Hell could be unaffected by a beautiful woman like Florence Nightingale, and I was convinced that he really did care for her. Which meant, I reasoned, that after we finished all this trash talk, he would probably help me, if he could.

"Uphir says that you sometimes keep tabs on her." I stared up at the ceiling when I said this, since what Uphir really meant was that TNK-el was a pervy little stalker. "Did you see what happened?"

TNK-el took a huge draw on his Slurpee. He had nearly finished it. "Yeah. Not sure I should tell you, though. I ... I didn't tell Azazel."

"What? Why not?"

TNK-el screwed his face up into the shape of a pretzel. Not quite sure how he pulled that off, but he must have been very malleable. Anyone who could be squished down to the size of a garden gnome during a game of pile-on had to be. "Because Azazel didn't ask me. Not to mention that I don't like him."

"Really, why not?" Orson asked.

The little guy made the sound of the raspberry. Or maybe he farted loudly, because a new scent now wafted among the cigarette smoke and sulfur fumes. "Oh, he's a former seraphim, and all of those characters think they're superior to cherubs."

"Does it really make that much difference?" Orson was interested in angel lore.

Tink, I mean, TNK shook his head. "No, it doesn't. Catholic theologians make a big deal about this, but did you know that Lucifer was of the cherubim also?"

That surprised me. "No, I didn't."

"Yeah, well look it up," he said, finishing his Slurpee. "Anyway, Azazel walks around like a big bully, but he can't really do anything to another devil. He doesn't scare *me* ... very much."

"Well, would you tell me what happened to her, even though you didn't tell Azazel?"

TNK-el got a troubled look on his face. "Okay, or I will as best I can, since I'm not entirely sure. I was, ahem, I was following Flo after you left. First, she went to Dermatology and chased off some demons with Brillo pads."

Orson frowned. "Why would she have Brillo pads?"

"Not her, stupid," the imp said, rolling his eyes. "Them. The demons had the Brillo pads."

"Oh."

"Anyway," TNK continued, giving Orson a warning look, "then Flo made a stop at the main nurses' station. There was a

74

note for her there. She read it and, well, from my perspective, which is a little on the low side admittedly, she look surprised. She folded the paper and put it in her pocket. Flo wrote a note of her own, stuck it in an envelope and dropped it in the mailbox near the station. Then grabbing her coat, she hurried to the exit."

Orson frowned. "Wonder what she read that got her moving so fast?"

I shrugged and turned back to the little devil. "Then what happened?"

"Flo rushed out the doors. She was moving so fast I could hardly keep up. I was staring through the glass at the front of the hospital when I saw it happen."

"Saw what happen?"

"She just froze on the pavement. Then there was a bright flash of light. It was blinding, even to me, and I turned away briefly. When my vision cleared and I looked back, she was gone."

"Just like that? Flo disappeared in a flash of light?" Orson turned to me. "What does that mean?"

"It means that something supernatural is going on," I said grimly.

"Really, genius?" TNK-el sneered. "What was your first clue, the supernatural flash of light?"

"Hey, you don't need to be sarcastic. And this is actually more helpful than you'd think. It means that no human kidnapped her."

Orson stroked his beard in thought. "True. There are several people in Hell, like Shemp and the rest of the Stooges, who might not appreciate her having helped you in the past, but ... "

75

"… they couldn't have conjured up a bright flash of light. Besides, I don't think any human in Hell really has it in for Flo. She's almost universally beloved."

"Yes, except by Satan," Orson pointed out.

I frowned. "I don't think he really dislikes her. She's just an administrative problem for him. And remember he has no power over her."

"If Lord Satan himself can't affect Flo," TNK-el interjected, "who could?"

"Humph." I sat back in my chair. "Now that is a very good question."

"Well, you ponder that, Minion, ah, Steve," he amended. TNK-el hopped off his stool and headed for the exit of the cafeteria. "As for me, I've gotta run. With Flo out of the hospital, the raid on Dermatology is back on. Duty calls. I have to head up there and pop a few zits." He looked at the floor, frowning. As if he'd made some sort of decision, he nodded to himself. "If there's something I can do to help find Flo, let me know."

"I will. Thanks."

"Tsk. Typical devil," Orson groused, after TNK-el had left.

"What do you mean?"

"He didn't throw away his Slurpee cup." My friend scooped it up and carried it to the nearest trash can. "Funny thing. Trash cans in Hell are almost always empty."

"Yeah. Go figure. But TNK-el doesn't really seem to be a bad guy, as his kind goes, though he has a serious case of SDS."

"What?"

"Small Devil Syndrome. It's like Small Man Syndrome, but with horns."

Orson chuckled. "And a tail."

"Yeah, that too. Oh, and a really dinky, uh, pitchfork." We started laughing, but a dirty look from a demon doctor shut us up.

Still, the laughter had felt good. It helped loosen the knot in my chest. The tension I'd been carrying around since I'd found out about Flo's disappearance was threatening to give me high blood pressure.

"Let's go back to the office and think this through," Orson suggested.

"Good idea, but before we leave, maybe we should break into the mail box and see what Flo mailed."

My assistant pulled a crowbar from his tool belt. "Sounds like fun."

We dumped our coffee cups on top of TNK-el's Slurpee container and left the cafeteria. The main nurses' station was at the end of a labyrinthine series of corridors that put us somewhere in the middle of the building, as far away from the patients as possible. I usually got lost trying to find my way there, so I tied a piece of string to a doorknob across from the cafeteria and played it out as we walked. After about ten minutes and more than one wrong turn, we finally got there.

Most of the nurses were demons in drag; they were no help at all. There were, however, a few humans whose eternal damnation had them working at the hospital. They were a pretty timid lot, but after some cajoling, we managed to get them to talk to us. None of them had seen the note Flo had received or had any idea why she'd rushed off.

"Okay," I said, finally giving up on them. "Thanks anyway. Oh, where's your mailbox? We have it on good authority that Flo mailed something just before she left."

An elderly woman who looked like she'd faint at the sight of blood shook her head. "Too late. The mailman emptied the box twenty minutes ago."

"Of course he did," I said with a sigh. "Thanks for your help."

Not that you provided any.

As we walked, I gathered up my string. Someone had moved its end to the bottom of an open elevator shaft, but we only fell to the second basement so hardly got more than a few bruises. It actually worked out pretty well, because on landing, we knew where we were. We went out through the parking garage and headed for our office.

Chapter 7

"So what do we know?" I asked Orson, pouring some sludge from the Mr. Coffee.

"Not much," he replied, sipping on his own brew. "Flo disappears in a flash of light. Many of Hell's inhabitants could pull that off. Heck, I could do it with a bright flash and a couple of thugs."

I frowned. "So are you saying that we have to consider the possibility that humans are suspects too?"

He shook his head. "Not really. While it's possible for humans to find a way to produce some bright light, the staging would have to be perfect to fool TNK-el. Do you know about Occam's Razor?"

I nodded. "The simplest solution is most likely the correct one."

"Yes, so, as you said in the hospital, more than likely someone with supernatural powers did it. Not that that narrows things down a great deal around here, but it's a start."

The door to our trailer flew open. Standing in the threshold was a wild-eyed Scotsman, wearing a leather apron. "Och, mon! Ah just heerd!"

We rolled our eyes. "Hey, Allan," I said by way of greeting. "Good to see you. Come in and pour yourself some coffee."

"Yeah," Orson seconded, "but please lay off with the fakeo Scottish brogue. It's too exhausting."

"Fine, fine,"Pinkerton grumbled, as he grabbed one of our spare mugs - the one that said "I WENT TO HELL, AND ALL I GOT WAS THIS STUPID MUG" (in very small type) - and poured himself some coffee. "I've come to help, if I can, with the Flo situation. You don't need to be rude."

"He's not being intentionally rude, Allan. It's just that your affected brogue gets old pretty fast."

Allan Pinkerton, a close friend of ours, and one of the greatest detectives in history, was indeed a Scotsman, but he had spent so many years in the United States during the last half of the Nineteenth Century and then a century and a half in Hell hanging out with Yankees that he had long since lost his accent. He often affected one though, because he thought it was funny.

We didn't.

"We really *are* glad to see you, Allan," Orson said. "We have a bit of a mystery here and could use your help."

"That's why I'm here, of course," he said, looking for a place to sit down. There were only two chairs in the office, mine and Orson's stool, so Allan made do with a nearby stack of work orders. "Surprisingly comfortable," he commented. "Florence is a very old friend of mine, as you know, so as soon as I heard, I rushed from my workshop to get here."

"So we see," Orson said. "You didn't even take time to remove your apron."

Allan looked down in surprise. He reddened slightly then merely shrugged.

I suppose everyone has a crush on Flo.

"The Elevator did not cooperate," he continued, tossing out a colorful but appropriate Gaelic obscenity, "which is why it took so long for me to get here."

"So when did you hear about the kidnapping down on Seven?" I asked.

Allan blew across the surface of the steamy black brew in his mug, trying to cool things off before he took his first sip. "Within minutes of the occurrence. I've always told you the grapevine down here moves like a bat out of Hell, no disrespect to our mutual friend, of course."

He meant BOOH, and I waved away his concern. "Why was this such big news that the grapevine picked it up?"

"Are you kidding?" Orson chimed in. "Flo is the only human who ever came to Hell by choice, except the J-man, of course, during the Harrowing."

"Not to be contrary or anything," I interjected, "but there are a fair number of people down here who sold their souls to the Devil, so they're sort of here by choice."

Orson's eyes narrowed. "You're just splitting hairs. That's not the same thing, and you know it."

He was right. I *was* splitting hairs. As a former university professor, I'd been trained in the fine art of knit picking. Grinning sheepishly, I signaled for him to continue.

"Thank you!" Orson huffed, trying to contain his irritation. "As I was saying, Flo's special, and her disappearance would cause ripples across the entire Underworld."

Allan nodded. "Just so. Now, what do you have for me?"

We told him what we'd learned at the hospital, and about our encounters with Azazel and TNK-el.

He whistled. "Azazel, eh? Never met him, but I know him by reputation. Not someone you'd want to cross."

Orson and I looked at each other and shared a shudder. "We have no intention of crossing him," I said. "He's a pretty intimidating character, with a hard-on for torturing humans."

My assistant agreed. "And crazy as Hell. But in this situation, we have a common goal."

Allan scratched his beard. He looked skeptical. "Don't know about that. Why should Azazel care if Florence has disappeared?"

That was a good question. "I don't know, but he *is* the chief of police down here."

81

"So what?" Pinkerton continued, taking his first sip of coffee. "Hell's police force functions primarily as a dispenser of misery down here, as you well know, writing traffic tickets, beating up little old ladies, stealing donuts, those sorts of things. They don't ever actually solve crimes, at least not that I have heard."

"Perhaps," Orson ventured, "he's doing it as a favor to Uphir."

Now both Allan and I looked at Orson with skepticism. "Why would anyone do a favor for Uphir?" the Scotsman asked. Orson shrugged. "However," Allan continued, "even if you were right, the next logical question is, why would Uphir care about Flo's disappearance?"

"That one's easy," I said. "Nothing gives Uphir more pleasure than tormenting Flo with all the outlandish things he does in the hospital. She's his best audience."

"Not to mention being easy on the eyes," Orson added.

I hadn't considered that Uphir might find Flo attractive. While devils, being former angels, are instinctively drawn to beauty, demons, most of whom had started their existence as humans, are not necessarily. "So you think Uphir is attracted to Flo?"

"Could be. I've seen him look at her sometimes when she isn't aware of it. He's not always leering at her, you know. At times, he seems like a lovesick puppy."

The three of us looked at each other, revulsion plain on our faces. Uphir was about four foot six, with a blotchy brownish-purple complexion, like his entire body had been worked over by a crowbar-wielding thug and was badly bruised as a result. His skin was pitted, as if by smallpox or terminal acne, and punctuated here and there with random, oozing pustules. Uphir was unhealthily thin, fairly common for a demon, and dirty, not to mention having horns and a pointy tail. The thought of him being attracted to Flo was too repulsive to contemplate.

"Very well," Allan continued, after our moment of mutual disgust had passed. "So he wants Flo back in the hospital. That still doesn't answer why Azazel should want to help Uphir, who is essentially a second-class citizen down here. What's in it for a devil to help a demon?"

"Damned if I know," I replied grudgingly.

"Damned if you don't," Orson added.

"True."

"There's something else going on here," Allan concluded, "but we don't have enough information about Azazel or his role in all of this to puzzle things out. However, no matter his motives, I think he bears watching."

"He thinks the same thing about us." I showed Pinkerton our consultant badges. "He deputized us, sort of, but I think that was mainly to keep tabs on us. We are now obligated to tell him anything we discover."

"And what have you discovered?"

Orson and I told Allan about what TNK-el said, including the bright flash of light and Flo's subsequent disappearance.

"And you believe him?"

"Yeah," I said, frowning. "Devils are not known for their forthrightness, but in this case, I think he's telling the truth. Azazel may be a bit of a mystery to me, but TNK-el is an open book."

Very few devils and almost no demons are able to fool me. Satan tricks me all the time, as does Beelzebub on occasion, but few others seem able to pull it off. That's because of my highly accurate bullshit-o-meter. This is one of the reasons, I think, that my bosses wanted me to enlist in the Demon Corps.

"So Flo has magically disappeared." Allan frowned. "That doesn't make sense."

"Why?" Orson asked.

"Because she's supposed to be immune to anything Hell can throw at her."

I grabbed an orange, peeled it and shoved a slice in my mouth. For added measure, I took a sardine from an open tin and ate one of those. Oranges and sardines were consumed by all of Hell's damned; we didn't want either scurvy or rickets. After I swallowed - and gagged a bit - I nodded. "It's true. Flo has a sort of aura - I call it the FloZone - and she seems able to walk through Hell without anything serious happening to her. She can be offended or even emotionally hurt by the atrocities she witnesses down here, but, physically, she's as invulnerable as Superman."

"Superman?" Allan scratched his head. "You mean that fellow Nietzsche wrote about?"

"Not really," I said.

Associating with people from different time periods, who share some but not all of the same cultural references that you have, is one of the quirkier aspects of Hell. Since I'd been dead for over fifty years, I'd occasionally get stumped myself, like when someone who died in the Twenty-first Century waxed eloquent over the joys of tweeting.

Pinkerton tapped thoughtfully on the side of his makeshift chair. "Then I don't see how someone could have made her disappear."

"I suppose," I said slowly, "she could be physically grabbed and carted off. It's not like she has super strength."

"Just invulnerability," Orson added.

"I feel as if you two are discussing something about which I have no ken, but never mind. All we have is a bright light and

84

her disappearance. The light was probably supernatural in nature, but her disappearance doesn't have to have been."

From a large roll we kept in the corner of our office, Allan tore off a piece of butcher paper. Other than work orders, butcher paper was the only thing we had to write on. We also used it to wrap up dead rats, skunks and other vermin that materialized periodically in our office before tossing them in the dumpster. Allan draped the sheet across my desk. "I believe, then, as you think of suspects, you're going to have to consider humans as well as devils and demons."

Orson brought up the Occam's Razor bit again. "Probably," Pinkerton agreed, "but let's not do any slicing with it just quite yet."

"Great," I grumbled. "That really narrows down the old suspect pool."

Pinkerton patted my shoulder companionably. "Patience, my friend. I didn't mean all humans. Let's confine ourselves to people who might have a personal grudge against Florence."

"That shrinks the list down to almost no one," Orson said. "Flo is universally beloved down here."

"I doubt the Stooges are particularly fond of her, considering the help she gave us during the Escalator Escapade. Especially Putty Face." Allan knew that "Putty Face" was my pet name for Shemp Howard.

"Agreed," Orson said. "In fact, Steve and I had already thought of them."

Allan wrote down Shemp's name as a proxy for all the Stooges. "Who else?"

"Well, there's Asmodeus," I said. "He would have good reason to be mad at Flo."

"Why?"

"Because she spurned his advances at a cocktail party recently." Asmodeus was the prince of Hell whose particular purview was Lust. He'd been trying to get into Flo's knickers for some time, with no success.

"And you have to add Lilith," Orson said, as Allan was writing down Asmodeus.

Allan glanced up from his sheet of paper. "Lilith? Which one? There are 666 of them you know, not counting the original. Steve, why are you blushing?"

Lilith - the one I knew, anyway - was the personal assistant of Asmodeus. She was also a succubus, that rare demon that has a specific gender. In Lilith's case the gender was most definitely female. She was a beautiful, scorchingly sexy redhead, with a spectacular body, which I had more than a passing familiarity with.

Nothing beyond first base, I swear. Well, okay … second base. But that's it. Really. I think she hit a triple with me once or twice, but I hadn't reciprocated. Anyway, that's my story, and I'm sticking to it.

Regardless of our respective batting averages, Lilith definitely had the hots for me, and she was really jealous of Flo. Reluctantly, I explained all this to Allan. When he finished laughing, he wrote down Lilith's name. "Anyone else?"

"Satan, I suppose, but he said he didn't do it."

"And you believe him?" Orson said. "Prince of Lies, remember?"

"I remember, I remember. Yeah, put him down too, I guess, though I don't know how we'd be able to prove or disprove his involvement. He's also the Deceiver, you know. He can fool anyone."

Allan wrote him down. "Anyone else?"

Orson held out empty palms. "Fresh out."

"Me too."

"Well, don't worry too much," Allan said, as he rolled up the butcher paper and handed it to me. "We don't know where Flo is, but as you've mentioned more than once, she can't really be hurt. We want to find her, of course, but she'll be safe wherever she is, and ... "

The screeching sound of the PA system almost deafened us. I guess it wasn't broken after all. "What the HELL is going on up there?" said Beezy's voice. "I'm getting calls from all over Hades about the work orders that you two are not taking care of."

I looked over at my desk. We had ignored all incoming jobs since Flo's disappearance. My wire inbox was now overflowing, and hundreds of work orders had tumbled to the floor.

"We've ... we've been investigating Flo's disappearance," I said, deciding on honesty, since devils can spot a lie faster than a cat goes for string.

"And when did that become your job?" Beezy hissed.

"Since," Orson interjected, "since Azazel made us consulting detectives on the case. He even gave us badges!" he added.

"Azazel? DID YOU SAY AZAZEL? Oh shit." There were a few moments of silence on Beezy's end. I guess he'd had his share of run-ins with Azazel. "Okay," he said reluctantly. "I don't know why he'd do that, but if Azazel put you on the case, you're on the case. I guess."

Wow? Did Beezy just back down? I've never heard him do that with anyone, except maybe Satan.

"But," he continued, "that doesn't mean you can ignore your work orders entirely. Go through them and fix the stuff that absolutely has to get taken care of. Got me?"

"Yessir!" Orson and I answered in unison.

"And you, Pinkerton. Why in all the Underworld are you on Five instead of in your workshop building your crappy barrels?"

Huh? How did he know that Allan is here? I wondered again if Beelzebub had some of the mind powers Satan had. He never showed them in an ostentatious fashion, but every once in a while my boss demonstrated too keen an understanding of what was going on in remote locations of Hell.

"Lord Beelzebub," Allan said deferentially, "I thought I could help with the investigation."

"And do you have a badge also?"

"Well ... no."

"Then get the Hell back down to Seven. You haven't met your quota for today, and I'll draw and quarter you if you don't get it done."

Draw and quarter. Good choice of torment for a Scot. Braveheart and all.

"Righto, Beezy, ah, Beelzebub. On my way," he said, scurrying toward the door.

"Fine. Beezy, uh, Beelzebub out!" The screech returned, and our eardrums shattered.

"You'll have to figure out motive, means and opportunity by yourself, Steve," Allan said, dabbing the blood from his ears with his apron. Being leather, though, it wasn't particularly absorbent; all my friend managed to do was smear the red ooze into his sideburns.

I grabbed a cloth from a desk drawer, wetted it with my coffee and cleaned him up. He winced whenever I came close to an ear. "Thank ... ," he began when I was done, but I silenced him with a gesture. Last thing we needed was a flying pie.

"No problem. I'm sure your ideas will be helpful," I said, trying to avoid expressing any gratitude on my own part.

He winked. "Understood. If you come up with something I can help with, let me know. Damn, that hurt!" he said, holding a hand over one ear as he closed our office door.

Chapter 8

"What a mess!" Orson exclaimed. He and I were crawling on the floor, gathering up the hundreds of work orders that had come in since Flo's disappearance.

"Maybe this is not as bad as it looks," I said hopefully, beginning to rifle through the papers in my hand. "This one here, for example. Constantine's desk drawer is stuck. That seems like a good thing, from the perspective of Hell anyway. Beezy would probably approve if we ignored that one."

Constantine was spending all eternity as night watchman for one of Hell's largest CPA firms.

You might think that the ruler who made Christianity the official religion of the Roman Empire and who brought together the first Council of Nicea would have earned himself a place in Hea... - that other place - but these things are always more complicated that you'd expect. First, well, he killed a lot of people. You know, Franks and Goths and folks like that. He was a bit of a despot. Actually, a major despot. Also, he suffered from the mortal sin of Pride. I mean, anybody who renames an already-existing city after himself must have thought he was the bee's knees. In any event, from my perspective his action bordered on the criminal; Byzantium sounds way cooler than Constantinople.

"Maybe we can ignore Constantine," my assistant agreed, "but this one we gotta do." Orson showed me, and I groaned. Another three bulbs had burnt out on the Sign above the entrance to Hell.

"How about this one?" I asked. Orson did most of our work order triage, so I trusted his judgment more than my own.

"A plumbing leak in Westmoreland's bathroom? No way." My assistant rapidly flipped through the remaining work orders in his hand. "No, no, no, no, no, no ... Oh, here's one we need to do."

"Who's John Hancock is on the work order?"

"Harry Houdini."

"The escape artist? I didn't know he was down here. Wonder why?"

"I don't know," Orson said with a shrug, "but we have to handle this."

"Why? He's only human. As I think about it, we probably ought to concentrate on orders from devils and demons."

"That would make sense, if we had any. Work orders from devils and demons, I mean, not sense, though I sometimes wonder about that too. " Orson was getting caught up in a grammatical conundrum of his own making, which made me smile. Usually, he was pointing out my mistakes. He shook his head. "All of these, except for the bulb business which was sent by Beezy himself - probably why he gave us such a hard time just now - are from humans. Houdini's, though, merits special attention."

"Why?"

"He's playing the Palace."

"Crap," I muttered with disgust. The Palace, located in Hell's all-gold replica of ancient Rome up on Level Four, was a favorite venue of Hell's management. The parade of acts that went through that place was a veritable *Who's Who* of entertainment history. Spartacus, Barnum and Bailey, Sarah Bernhardt, Bill Cody, Bill Cosby, Wild Bill Hickok, Annie Oakley, Charlie Chaplin, the Kings of Comedy, if you could name a damned entertainer, that person was likely to have played the Palace. If Houdini was there, the devils expected him to perform, and if the work order

90

related to his act, we'd need to take care of it. "What's Harry's problem?"

"His Chinese water torture cell has sprung a leak. Until it's fixed, well, his act doesn't hold water."

"Bad pun," I grunted.

"No worse than any one of yours!" Orson said with mock outrage. "Anyway, considering the audience of the Palace, we've got to handle this one."

"Yeah," I sighed. "The show must go on."

"Hey, it's show business, and we know there's no business..."

"Like show business."

"Like no business I know. I'll get the monkey wrench." With considerable grunting and groaning, Orson got off the floor and headed to our tool closet. He took out his hammer and replaced it with a bright red wrench. Being much weightier than the hammer, it pulled heavily on his tool belt. If he were wearing trousers instead of coveralls, I would have seen the quintessential handyman butt crackage.

Ugh. Not a pleasant thought, especially where Orson's concerned. Hell, someone could fall and get lost in there.

Orson placed the two work orders, the one for the Gates to Hell, the other for Houdini's glass box, on my desk. The others he added to one of the large piles of ignored paperwork in the corner of our trailer. "What are you snickering about?" he said, noting my eyes on his rear end.

"Nothing. Just daydreaming about the Grand Canyon. Let's go get some light bulbs."

We walked the few hundred yards to the Parts Department. The building was about fifty feet farther from our office than usual. The Parts warehouse was getting skittish again, and I would not have been surprised if it soon went off on one of its periodic jaunts in the Netherworld, as it sought to hide from me and Orson. In its escapades, the building was aided at times by devils and demons, who moved it when we weren't looking. I never had been sure what motivated the periodic disappearance of the building. This was nothing unusual - it happened all the time - but it *was* irritating.

Once, about five years ago, Orson and I even saw the building sprout legs and take off at a gallop to parts unknown. Poor Dora. She was inside at the time, and we heard her screams echo across the Fifth Circle as Parts ran away with her. It came back only hours later, but to this day, Dora refuses to discuss the incident.

I particularly didn't want to contend with a building relocation at that moment. Searching the nine Circles of Hell for an itinerant Parts warehouse when I was dealing with a normal workload was one thing, but every spare minute was needed to look for Flo.

Orson and I closed on the entrance to Parts, which, like I said, was a warehouse, though painted in camouflaged colors just to make things especially difficult for when the building decided to go on the lam and hide from us. Before the entrance, we saw a butt the size of a watermelon covered in a black skirt. Beneath the skirt were two fireplugs pretending to be legs. They were mostly covered by high, black combat boots. Attached to one ankle was a thick chain, to which a small safe was attached.

Dora was almost never seen outside of Parts. I don't know if she slept in there or if she snuck in when no one was looking. I had recently seen her at the Temple of Mammon, up on Four, so her chunky legs and Jacob Marley accessory were not really a surprise to me, but I don't think Orson had ever seen the compleat Dora. Oh, he'd seen the chain before, because she'd shown it to us once, but not the leg to which it was attached. Or the other one either. Not to mention the capacious ass. He looked appropriately revolted.

"Hey, Dora," he called, as convivially as he could make the greeting sound. Dora may have just grossed him out, but she and her department were essential to him, and he always tried to stay on her good side.

The old broad looked over her shoulder at us. She had a lighted cigarette in her mouth and horror in her eyes. Quickly, she opened the door to her department and scurried in, like a rat trying to escape a couple of toms, or a hermit crab crawling back into its shell. The big behind, the skirt, the boots, and most importantly, I think, the chain and safe disappeared from view. All that was left to be seen of Dora was her top half, complete with bleached blonde hair, skin like rotting leather, horn-rimmed glasses and leopard print blouse.

"What's up?" Orson asked as casually as he could, but I could tell from his wide eyes that he was still in shock from seeing the full-on Dora.

Behind her office door, the head of Parts looked less vulnerable. She certainly *acted* more in control, because she released a string of invective that I didn't think she was capable of. Everyone in Hell swears - it's a compulsion that Satan puts on all of us when we get here - but Dora was never very good at it. She impressed me this time, though.

"Shit, Dora," I said. "Why are you so mad?"

A few curses later, she finally grumbled, "The PX was out of menthols. I only have two cartons left and, well, I don't like my stash to get that low."

Though Dora was a chain smoker, not for a minute did I believe that was the cause of her outburst. For a long time, I'd suspected she had a crush on my assistant. This wasn't much of a surprise, for despite his weight, Orson, with his iron gray beard and thick head of hair, cut a striking figure among Hell's damned. Dora must have known that, as unattractive as her upper parts were, her lower extremities were even less fetching, and I think she had never wanted Orson to see them. Not that I could blame her. If I had a butt that big, I wouldn't want anyone to see it either.

You never could tell about Dora; she was unpredictable. Sometimes she could be like an obsequious grandmother, a bleached blonde, heavily wrinkled, boozer of a grandmother, but still like one, and when she was in that mode she just oozed concern. Other times, she was a bitch. This was one of those other times. We could only hope she'd mellow out

"What do you need, Big Nose?" Apparently, Dora was going to be unpleasant to the end.

"The usual," I said with a sigh.

Dora took another drag on her Kool. "What do they do with all those bulbs? Eat them?"

Orson, having recovered his composure, started to pour on the charm. I guess he was aware of Dora's feelings for him after all. That would explain the occasional sweet-talking he'd do with her. "It's worse than usual, luv. Three have burned out at once."

"What!" she spluttered. "That's all I have left, and it will be days before I get a new shipment."

My assistant flashed his most ingratiating smile. "I'm so sorry, but we have little choice."

Dora stared at him for a second, speechless, apparently dazzled by his pearly whites. "Well, okay. I'll get them." She disappeared for a moment into the recesses of the warehouse. One at a time she brought out the bulbs. She set the final one on the counter constructed atop the lower half of her two-part door. "Sign here," she said, a tear forming in her eye.

A common characteristic of the greedy, or the avaricious if you prefer, is an unwillingness to let something go once she or he gets his or her (to be politically correct) hands on it. Greedy people tend to be hoarders, and Dora was no different. She hated parting with her parts, which was why she was head of the department to begin with. Every supply order she filled was a spear to her soul.

I penned my name and lifted a bulb from the counter. "Where do you get these monster bulbs, anyway?" I asked with mild interest. The sign used five megawatt red compact fluorescent bulbs. They seemed like a fairly specialized product.

She shrugged. "Holland? How the Hell should I know? I send my requisition to Procurement, they cut a purchase order - usually fuck it up too - and I eventually get what I need. Emphasis on the eventually. Remember that insect repellent bulb you tried a few months ago?"

"How could I forget?" I said, rubbing my forehead. We'd been out of the big sign bulbs, and Dora had talked me into trying the yellow insect bulb. I'd managed to get it to work by using some aluminum foil and holding it all in place with duct tape. Unfortunately, in the process I also managed to short out the Escalator.

"Well, I got them in the first place because of a Purchasing Department screwup. I'd ordered rappelling bolts. They sent repellent bulbs instead. Whoever works that department has some serious deficiencies in clerical accuracy."

"Why didn't you just send them back?" I asked, suspecting I already knew the answer.

She laughed. "Duh! I'm a hoarder, you schmo! I never send anything back. I just reorder. Besides, you never know when something will come in handy."

"Whatever. Thanks Dora." We turned to go.

"Wait a second, you two." Dora looked at us with atypical concern. "I hear Flo's been kidnapped."

Orson and I became suddenly serious. "She's disappeared all right," my assistant said. "That's all we know for sure. As you say, though, it might be a kidnapping."

"Then why are you wasting your time doing work orders, when she needs your help?"

I thought again about how almost universally beloved Flo was in the Underworld. That someone would wish her harm was almost inconceivable. "Beezy says we have to keep up on our workload, even if she *is* missing."

"Yeah," Orson said. "But he agreed to let us mix in some investigative work with our normal duties."

"Well, that's good." Dora lit another Kool with the dying embers of her previous cigarette. "Wonder why he was so accommodating."

Orson showed her his badge. "Because Azazel deputized us."

Dora's eyes widened when she heard the name. "Azazel? Azazel? Watch out for him boys. He's bad news."

"What do you mean?" I asked.

"He's a killer. Wiped out whole towns of early Semites back in the day, or at least so I've heard, just for fun. All of the devils are afraid of him." A nicotine hack took possession of her. She spat an iridescent green goober on the pavement behind us then wiped her eyes with her blouse. "Even Beelzebub, I guess."

"That's hard to believe." Beezy had never even shown fear of Satan. I didn't care how powerful Azazel was. I was pretty sure our boss could handle him.

"Well, believe it. And I don't trust Azazel either. For all I know, he could have kidnapped her himself."

Orson's head snapped up in surprise. "What? Why do you say that?"

"Because the rules mean nothing to him. It doesn't matter that Flo is supposed to be untouchable. Azazel does what he wants. That's what people tell me, any-who."

"Who tells you all this stuff?" I knew almost nothing about Azazel and wondered why she was such an expert.

Dora reared back as if I had offended her. "Listen, sonny. I supply parts to devils, demons and humans from all over the Underworld. I hear things. Just watch out for him. And find Flo. Make sure she's okay, okay?"

"We're as worried about her as you are," Orson said, "but she can't really be hurt down here. She's a saved soul, and immune to harm."

"Maybe," she said doubtfully. "But couldn't someone trap her in a hole or something? She wouldn't be harmed, but she'd be imprisoned forever."

I hadn't thought of that. My chest, always where I felt my tension, knotted up.

"And remember what I said about Azazel. He breaks rules. Any rule."

"Okay," I said, mentally adding Azazel to our list of suspects.

Orson and I picked up the three bulbs and headed toward the office.

"You make sure you find Flo!" Dora shouted after us. "Damn! I love that lady."

There was a red light, a clap of thunder, the smell of brimstone and a whizzing sound, followed by a big splat and a loud thump. Dora was nowhere to be seen, but curses were coming from inside the Parts building.

As we returned to the office, I turned to my assistant. "What's Dora's poison?"

"Grasshopper pie."

"Oh. That makes sense."

"Right."

Whenever I speak too fondly to or about another, I get popped with a coconut cream pie. Orson gets lemon cream; he hates lemon. A Grasshopper pie, for those who have never had one, has mint as a major ingredient, as do menthol cigarettes.

Flo smokes menthol cigarettes, but that's only because she's not allowed the regular kind. Still, as a chain smoker for most of her life and all of her afterlife, she is so addicted, she has to smoke something. Since she hates the taste of menthol, and mint, that's what she gets.

And that's about as concise an example of the way things work here in Hell as I can conjure up.

Chapter 9

Orson and I were standing in our office, looking down on the three massive light bulbs we'd placed on the linoleum. "So how are we going to get these monsters and the ladder up to Gates Level?" I grumbled.

My assistant frowned in thought at the glass squares, then he brightened. "I know! I can make a harness for you and attach the bulbs to the harness. You could easily bear the weight."

I looked dubious, but nodded. "You're right. It's not that they're so heavy, but they're each about as big as a block of ice and awkward as hell to carry. Go ahead."

Orson found a clothes line in the parts closet and proceeded to make a noose in one end. Then he made a second noose about two feet down the line from the first. Orson slipped one loop over my right shoulder then the second over my left, with the span of clothes line between them forming a nice, snug fit across my shoulder blades. He then pulled another stretch of rope across my chest and tied it to the two loops.

"Good design," I said in approval. "If you'd tied it around my neck, I might have choked to death."

"Too late for that anyway. You're already dead, in case you hadn't noticed."

"Har, har. Please proceed."

Orson cut three pieces of the remaining clothes line, tied them to the necks of the light bulb, then had me sit on the floor, while he connected the three lines to my harness. "Here, let me help you stand up."

The weight was fine, though the corners of the bulbs dug into my privates and other parts of me around the midriff region. I looked at myself in our mirror.

"What do you think?" my friend asked.

"I think I look like a badly-decorated Christmas tree, but this works okay. Let's go."

Orson got our ladder from the tool shed outside, then he and I began our trudge toward Hell's Elevator. I clanked with each step, like the Tin Woodman.

"Man, I wish BOOH were here," Orson huffed as he alternately carried and dragged the heavy ladder along the pavement.

I didn't want to call on BOOH any more than necessary, but I had to agree with my friend. "Me too. He'd have us Gates Level in two shakes."

"Skree!"

"BOOH?" I asked looking up, just as the giant bat settled on the concrete beside us. "What are you doing here?"

BOOH placed a claw in front of his lips in the universal "Shhh" gesture.

"Uh, why are you wearing sunglasses?"

BOOH looked quickly in both directions. "Urm."

"Oh."

"What did he say?" Orson asked.

"He's not really supposed to be ferrying me around without specific permission from Satan, so he's trying to do it on the lowdown." I didn't have the heart to tell BOOH that the sunglasses, if anything, made him even more conspicuous, though I suppose a bat the size of a dinosaur really can't be inconspicuous, no matter what he does. I let the matter drop.

With a slight clank, I climbed on top of BOOH's shoulders. Then the bat leapt in the air, grabbed Orson with one claw and the ladder with the other and headed for Gates Level. As we flew, the bulbs bumped lightly against each other making a tinkling sound that was actually soothing to the ears.

Great. Now I'm a giant wind chime.

On reaching Gates Level, BOOH barely crested above the Mouth of Hell, hugging close to the ground, or what functioned as ground there. I think he was trying to stay hidden beneath the clouds that covered the surface of GL. As a result, he scraped up the ladder a little bit, as well as Orson, if the grunt I heard was any indication. I slipped off BOOH's shoulders as gracefully as I could, taking care not to break the bulbs draped around me.

"Thanks, BOOH," I whispered.

The Bat out of Hell raised his sunglasses fractionally, winked at me, let them drop back to his face and made a hasty retreat back through the hole.

"Was that BOOH wearing those sunglasses who brought you up here?"

I almost jumped out of my skin. St. Peter had slipped up on me with nary a sound. "Ah, no," I said hastily.

Peter eyed me with suspicion. "It sure looked like BOOH to me."

Of course it was BOOH, you supercilious saint! Is there another Bat out of Hell that I don't know about? What I said was, "Couldn't have been. BOOH doesn't wear sunglasses."

Peter merely snorted - his favorite noise - and walked back to his desk to process some more of the recently-dead.

With a groan, Orson climbed to his feet. "Did you just lie to a saint?"

I grinned. "At first I was worried it might be a sin, but then I realized that a damned soul really doesn't have much more to be concerned about in that department."

Orson nodded. "True enough. So, let's get these light bulbs installed."

"Righto." My friend helped me out of my harness, and we placed the bulbs on the ground. I followed S.O.P. - that's Standard Operating Procedure, not something weird like Sulfate of Potash (potassium sulfate) or anything like that - and taped off the area before the Escalator to give us some working space.

Hell's Escalator is surrounded by three normally brightly-lit signs. The small ones on either side were relatively unimportant, but the big one on top had the famous quote from Dante: you know, the old "Abandon all hope" line. At the moment, though, the text couldn't be seen, since the bulbs were burnt out. Even a single dead one would take down the entire sign, like a bad bulb on an old strand of Christmas tree lights. As was his practice, Orson hung an out-of-order sign on a cloud hovering in the vicinity, while I consulted the small panel Beezy had installed to let us know which bulbs were burnt out.

You'd think that after doing this nearly every day for fifty or sixty years, seventy in Orson's case, we'd have replacing a bulb on the sign down to a science. No such luck. Every time we performed this little bit of routine maintenance, we had a new challenge. Today that challenge was our very own ladder.

It was our big one, the kind that's really two ladders in one - like Certs is two, two, two mints in one - where one set of rungs slides into the other. Two ladders in one: that makes it twice as heavy and twice as much trouble. The damn thing was stuck, and we had a devil of a time pulling the inner rungs out in order to extend the length enough to reach the burnt-out bulbs. Even spraying it down with WD-40 didn't help much. With Orson straining against one set of rungs and me pulling in the opposite direction on the other set, we made slow headway. Then suddenly, for no particular reason, our truculent tool decided to cooperate, and with a WOOSH! that threw us both to the ground, the ladder let go. It almost came apart on us, which would have given us two ladders, neither one long enough to reach the sign.

Grumbling, we adjusted the thing to the proper length and locked the rungs in place, then we leaned it against the sign. Since Orson wasn't allowed to do any of the actual bulb changing, he steadied the ladder while I climbed up with the first of the bulbs. That's when the latches on the rungs decided to give way, but I was expecting it, so I didn't fall when my ten foot ladder suddenly shrunk four feet. I did break a hand however.

Orson's, when I stepped on it, but I didn't get away scott free either. I scraped a knuckle.

Hey. It really stung.

Since Orson was more badly hurt than me, I allowed him a little therapeutic cursing under his breath, though that's generally frowned upon on Gates Level, while his hand healed. Then we went back to fighting the ladder. When we had it the proper length, we again set the latches. My assistant was not satisfied, however. He took his screwdriver - the flathead I believe - and savagely drove it between the rungs. The ladder squealed as if he had stabbed it then just lay on the ground docilely. Satisfied, we again leaned it against the sign.

The rest of the job went pretty smoothly. The bulbs were installed within minutes and

ABANDON ALL HOPE etc.

once more blazed above Hell's Escalator.

The only good thing about changing bulbs on Gates Level is that I could make St. Peter sign off on the work order. This wasn't actually required. I mean, getting work orders signed upon completion *was* required but usually by a denizen of Hell. Gates Level, the DMZ of the eternal realms, usually didn't have a demonic or devilish attendant. Satan preferred to leave the concierge activity to Peter and save Hell's workforce for tormenting the damned. Usually Beezy made an exception to departmental policy and signed off on the sign, so to speak, himself.

Yet today I thought I'd get Peter's John Hancock. *Perhaps he knows something about the Flo situation.*

Orson pulled his screwdriver from the ladder, and we collapsed it with little difficulty. While my assistant removed the out-of-order sign and the duct tape that blocked off our work area, I went to talk with Pete.

At the moment, the saint was without any customers. He stood behind his podium-like desk, twiddling his thumbs in boredom. I guess he wasn't bored enough, though, to enjoy the diversion of a talk with me. Peter sighed when he saw me coming.

"What do *you* want?"

I handed him the work order. "Sign here, please."

"Why do I have to sign sometimes, and other times I don't?" he said, scribbling his name in the completed box.

I shrugged, and Peter snorted.

"Hey, why are you annoyed with me?" I hadn't done anything to particularly irritate him recently, at least not to my knowledge.

Peter gave out a loud harrumph. "I don't particularly like being lied to."

"What are you talking about?"

"Who," he corrected.

"Okay, who?"

"BOOH, that's who, so why?"

Oh. "Plausible deniability?" I said with a shrug.

"What?"

"Okay," I said, correcting myself. *Now we're back to what.* "How about implausible deniability?"

"Why are you intent on insulting my intelligence?" he grumbled.

"Because ... I don't know." This was beginning to sound like an Abbott and Costello routine. "Listen, it was for a good cause."

"Well, I don't care." Yep, definitively Abbott and Costello. "You still lied. And anyway, BOOH looked stupid in those sunglasses."

"He's trying to maintain a low profile."

Peter smoothed his robe. "Good luck with that. Now, what do you want? Are you going to tell me today or wait until tomorrow?"

I started laughing. *And that's the whole baseball team.*

"What's so funny?"

I almost burst a gut. "If I have to explain it," I said, still chortling, "it wouldn't be funny."

"Go away, kid. Ya bother me," Peter said in an offhand manner.

I looked up, startled. *Maybe he's following this after all.* "Seriously, St. Peter. I was hoping you could give me some information."

He looked at me with suspicion. "What do you want to know?" he said in a way that indicated he was still peeved.

"There's been an incident in Hell."

"So what? There are always incidents down there. It wouldn't be Hell otherwise."

I did my best to look patient. "This is more serious than most. Apparently, Florence Nightingale has been kidnapped."

"What?" Peter clutched the sides of his desk. "That's against the Accords!"

"What Accords?"

"The ones that govern the interrelations between Heaven and Hell. Nightingale is a saved soul."

"I've been meaning to ask you about that. How come no one from Hell can enter Heaven but someone destined for Heaven can come into Hell? You know that really pissed Satan off, don't you?"

Peter didn't answer my question. Instead, he said, "No harm may come to her. Satan knows that."

"I talked with Satan, and he says he didn't do it."

The old saint frowned. "He's probably lying."

"Could be. He lies all the time, but he said that he didn't do it, and this time I believe him."

"Which probably makes you a chump." Peter stroked his beard. "Still, Satan, though I know he doesn't like having Nightingale down there, can't hurt her."

"Can anyone down in Hell?" I asked, fear clutching my chest. "I mean, if Satan can't, who could?"

"I don't know," he said slowly. "Why do you ask?"

"Well, I've recently run into a devil I've never met before, and, I have to say, he scares me."

"What's his name?"

"No, not What. It's Azazel."

"Azazel?" Peter eyed me with suspicion. "Did you say Azazel?"

"Yeah. He's the chief of police down in Hell."

"Now that's a name I haven't heard in a very long time." Peter was silent for a moment. "Azazel's the police chief?" he said at last. "That seems like an odd job for him."

"You know this guy?"

Peter looked at me speculatively. Then, as if he'd made some sort of decision, he nodded. "I'm not really supposed to talk to humans about devils, but yes, I know Azazel. Bad customer. Very bad customer. As bad as they come."

"As bad as Satan?"

He nodded. "Every bit as bad, and every bit as powerful."

"Really? Why isn't he a prince of Hell then?"

"Long story, but I can tell you he's trouble. In fact," he said, pausing slightly, "he ought to be your primary suspect."

"But," I said weakly, holding up my badge, "he deputized me and Orson, so we could help find Flo."

"He probably did that just to keep an eye on you two."

Yeah, that's what we thought too. Crap. "Why is he so much trouble?"

"Well, he's angry. All devils are angry. Guess I can't blame them, particularly."

"Why do you say that?"

Simon Peter rested his elbows on the Book of Life and cradled his jaw in his hands. "It all goes back to free will. You know devils don't have it, right? Just we humans do."

Sometimes I forgot that Peter hadn't always been a saint. He'd once been just like me - with better hair, though.

"Think about the ramifications of not having free will. It is said that Satan - and the other devils - lost God's grace when they refused to pay obeisance to Adam. And then they fought a war against YAHWEH, which they lost pretty quickly, by the way. But tell me this, if they had no free will, how could they have chosen not to obey God?"

My ears were ringing a bit. I wasn't used to hearing not only the "G" word, but the "Y" word, the true name of "G." True names, as any fantasist can tell you, are incredibly powerful. They shape reality. I shook my head to clear it from the confusion of TRUTH, and tried to answer the question.

"Well, by ... " I stopped. "Hey, that's right. How could they have rebelled against G ... the Creator's will?"

"The answer is they couldn't. It was God's will that they become devils, creating the evil side of the equation and making free will relevant in the first place. That they became devils was all part of the Divine Plan. They really had no say in the matter. Only humans can choose."

"Devils have always hated humankind for having free will when they could not," he continued. "They resent having been made the bad guys, yet, having no free will, they couldn't choose to be good no matter how hard they tried."

Peter's explanation cleared up a lot for me. "And Azazel?" I prompted.

"Azazel has a particular reason for hating humans. You've heard the expression, 'scapegoat,' right?"

"Yeah. I also know the story from the B ... , the Book, about Azazel being the first scapegoat."

"Then think about it for a minute, Minion," Simon Peter said. "Azazel not only has to be evil, without any say in the matter, but at least in the Old Testament Bible, he was forced to carry the sins of the Jews."

A light bulb turned on in my head. "Kind of like J ... the J-Man."

"Yes, but Jesus chose to do that. Azazel had no choice. No free will, remember?"

Peter continued. "This is why all devils dispense damnation with a vengeance. And to get their hands on a virtual saint like Florence Nightingale, someone who isn't supposed to be punished, who isn't supposed to even be in Hell in the first place, well, tormenting her soul would give any devil great pleasure."

I frowned, trying to process all that he'd told me. "And you think Azazel more than most."

"Azazel more than any of them," Peter summarized. "As I said before, put his name at the top of your list of suspects."

"O ... okay," I said, turning to go. "Thanks."

"Don't mention it," he said over his shoulder, a clear dismissal if ever I heard one. A line had begun to form in front of him, and he got back to work. "Next!"

Chapter 10

Orson and I were standing on the metal treads of Hell's Escalator, along with a fairly large crowd that had queued up during the period we were replacing the light bulbs. The two of us each had a hand on the ladder, since it was pretty heavy for a single individual to manage for very long. Our other hands were firmly grasping the black plastic of the Escalator's handrail. This did not in and of itself provide assurance that we would not fall. The handrail would periodically cease to form a straight line, becoming more of an undulating critter, like a sine wave.

That's the undulating part. The critter part would be a snake.

Being old hands, so to speak, at dealing with the Escalator, my assistant and I expected this and had no trouble. The same could not be said for the poor unfortunates in front of us. About halfway down to Level Three, the railing abruptly started its twitching serpent routine; one of the recently damned - a poor slob still stunned by not making it through the Pearly Gates -- was caught unawares and pitched forward against one of his peers. He knocked the woman over, and she in turn knocked over the person in front of her. Like dominos, about thirty people toppled, and it was only with some effort that they regained their footing.

Orson just shook his head. "Rookies."

"True, but the same thing happened to me once, and probably to you as well."

"Yeah," he admitted grudgingly. "But I didn't cause it. I was in the middle of one of those pileups. You wouldn't believe how many people fell that time."

"Yes I would," eyeing the girth of my rotund friend.

"Har, har. You never tire of the fat jokes, do you?"

"Hey, I didn't make a joke."

"Never mind," he grumbled. "What's next?"

"The Handcuff King, I think." We had just reached the Fourth Circle and stepped onto the golden cobblestones of the Via di Saint Gregorio.

The Fourth Level is the heart of Greed in Hell, and Mammon, the prince of Hell who is most closely associated with that particular deadly sin, fancies the idea of a city laid out completely in gold. He patterned his principality after ancient Rome, and being fond of ostentatious displays of wealth, decreed the whole city must be made of the yellow ore. Didn't make the streets any better, though. The golden cobblestones jutted up in slapdash fashion from the surface of the road; we tripped on them more than once as we made our way slowly uphill.

Our destination was Hell's analogue to the Palatine Hill. The Earthly version is where the original inhabitants of the city of Romulus and Remus lived. Caesars had palaces there and, in fact, the word "palace" has as its etymological source the name of this very hill.

The Palace at which Harry Houdini was to perform was a golden replica of the residence of Tiberius, with some interior modifications, like a ginormous stage and seats for all the devils and demons who wanted entertainment on a grand scale.

For an even grander venue, all they have to do is walk down the Hill to Hell's Anfiteatro Flavio Colesseo, or the Colosseum as we Yanks call it. There, the devils and demons can watch humans fight each other or get eaten by lions, and play the thumbs up/thumbs down game. Unsurprisingly, thumbs down is almost always how the D&D's like to play it.

However, if you want to experience an aria screeched by a famous soprano, or a knife throwing act gone gruesomely awry, or the failed human pyramid of some acrobats, you go to the Palace.

Still lugging our ladder, we stepped inside. The demon bouncer stopped us briefly, but I showed him the work order, and he waved us through.

There were at least a thousand devils and demons in attendance. Going up and down the aisles were some of the damned, offering the audience members cigarettes, beers, hotdogs and, predictably, rotten tomatoes. One of the human vendors had a thick mop of black hair. He glanced at me and frowned.

Shemp Howard. Putty Face. Still as angry as ever, I see, and still one of the few eternally damned who might have an axe to grind with Flo. We'll need to look him up later.

"We have a wonnerful shew for you tonight, just wonnerful," said a devil onstage, doing a crummy impression of Ed Sullivan. He did have the arm-crossing right and the skinny tie, though, so I guess he was mostly okay. "In a little while, Topo Gigio will perform, and of course the featured act tonight: the Beetles. Yaaay!"

"Ugh." Orson almost spat on the floor. "He's not talking about the Fab Four, but a quartet of giant cockroaches who mime to rock music as they dismember some poor unfortunates."

"How do you know that?" I asked marveling.

"Show business is my life."

"Oh."

"Besides, I saw them perform once at Red Note." Red Note is a nightclub that caters to the damned down on Five. "Pretty revolting."

"Now, give a big hand for Mr. Television himself, Uncle Miltie!"

Milton Berle walked on stage wearing a dress and high heels. He had makeup on and looked pretty much like he always did when he was alive and in drag. There was a little complication, in that the stage floor was made of mud, of the consistency one might wrestle in, if one were inclined to do something like that. Uncle Miltie had to slog his way to center stage. He did it manfully, sort of, and that was in four-inch spikes, which I thought deserved a round of applause on its own. I'm not too sure very many women could have accomplished the same feat.

"Uh, it's great to be playing the Palace," he said tentatively through the microphone. Before he could get out another word, he was pelted by about a hundred rotten tomatoes, which pummeled him into the mud, to much demonic delight and loud applause. Orson and I just shook our heads and slipped backstage.

It didn't take us long to find the world's greatest escape artist. Houdini was sitting on a wooden crate next to a large glass box that was reinforced, top and bottom as well as on the corners, by steel plating. The great escape artist, looking pretty depressed, dangled an open set of handcuffs from his fingers.

Harry Houdini was a short, swarthy Hungarian-American with an impressive mane of dark, kinky hair, frosted at the temple. He was dressed only in a leopardskin Speedo, which showed off his impressive build. He was pretty chipped for a guy in his early fifties. That's about how old he was when he let a college student pop him one in the stomach, which ruptured his - unbeknownst to him - infected appendix. He died of peritonitis about a week later.

Orson and I leaned the ladder against a nearby wall. "Mr. Houdini?" I asked politely.

"Yes?" he said, looking up from his handcuffs.

"I'm Steve Minion, Hell's Superintendent of Plant Maintenance, and this is my assistant, Orson Welles."

A proper gentleman, Mr. Houdini got off his crate and stood to greet us. After a round of handshaking, I said, "We got your work order."

He nodded. "Thank you for coming."

"What seems to be the trouble?" Orson asked.

Houdini pointed to the glass enclosure. "My act doesn't work."

I walked around the prop. "But I thought the Chinese Water Torture Cell was your greatest stunt."

The man frowned. "It is, but the tank won't fill. See?" Houdini walked over to the glass chamber and depressed a small chrome lever. In the distance, I heard a loud flush, and water began to flow into the tank, only to drain out almost immediately. After a while Houdini released the lever and the tank, discouraged, stopped all attempts to fill itself.

"Hmm."

Orson and I made a couple of circuits of the tank. On the second circumnavigation, we noticed a tall, thin bit of PVC pipe in the corner of the tank that stretched the entire height of the chamber. Around the bottom of the tube, resting on the steel floor, was a hard plastic disk.

"Flapper?" Orson suggested.

"Probably. Let me double-check."

One of the nice things about our ladder, when it wasn't being contrary, was that it was very versatile. We pulled the two sets of rungs completely apart from each other, then fastened them together, forming an inverted V-shaped ladder, much like what a painter would use, only taller. With a little maneuvering, we were able to drop the legs of one side into the glass rectangle. I was up and over the side of the chamber in seconds. On

114

reaching the bottom, I lifted up the plastic float and looked beneath it. "Yep. Flapper."

"What?" Orson mouthed. The glass was muffling our voices. I held up my hand, asking for patience and climbed out of the chamber. "Yep. Flapper," I repeated. "Mr. Houdini … "

"Please call me Harry. Or Erik. That was my birth name."

"Any preference?" Orson asked.

"Harry, I suppose. I've gotten used to it over the centuries."

"Okay, Harry. Oh, and please call us Steve and Orson."

"Certainly."

"Anyway, where's the Men's Room?"

"Huh?"

I shrugged, a little sheepish. "I'm nowhere near the Parts Department, and I don't want to take the time to go there and get what I need. I think I'll find a suitable substitute there."

Orson wrinkled his nose. "Oh, gross."

"No, it should be okay. The part, I mean. Not the bathroom."

Harry had no idea what we were talking about, but he pointed to a door about thirty feet away. "I don't go in there very often. It's pretty disgusting."

"What else would you expect of a public toilet in Hell?" I said, as I wended my way to the door of the Men's Room.

A toilet in Hell is really a pointless fixture. None of us needs to pee or take a dump or anything like that. That would be a waste of ectoplasm. Well, I say none of us has to, though we do when the situation is appropriate. Occasionally, we'll get really bad cases of constipation or diarrhea or a wicked bladder infection as a random form of punishment. When that happens, we'll spend hours in the bathroom, enduring abdominal cramps, filth and a stench that is worse than any sulfur pit in Hades. The bathrooms are also useful to the D&D Squad. Sometimes one of them will grab some poor human and shove his head in a crapper, making him choke on toilet bowl water and human waste. Demons often tell me that Men's Rooms are really quite useful to them, if not much fun for the men who end up using one.

In fact, a skinny, be-pimpled demon, who I imagined was a stagehand, saw me go in and followed. He grabbed me by the scruff of my coveralls, preparing to stuff me in the john, but when he saw the HOOTI acronym on my back, he knew I was one of Beelzebub's own and let go. Straightening my collar with as much dignity as I could muster, I turned my back on him and headed for the nearest stall.

The tile floor was strewn with wet wads of used toilet paper. The gasket at the bottom of the toilet was leaking, but I ignored it, since my work boots were usually pretty waterproof. I turned off the water at the wall then flushed the toilet. It was clogged, of course, but that only meant that it overflowed. Not the most pleasant thing for me, but it accomplished my purpose. Removing the porcelain top, I stared into a now-empty tank.

In its center was a short version of the PVC pipe we'd seen in Harry's glass chamber. Lifting up the plastic float, I uncovered the red rubber flapper that automatically sealed off the drain. It was in good shape, as if someone had just gone to Home Depot and gotten it for $14.99. There was a little sediment buildup on the flange thingies - Hell's water is not exactly known for its purity - and that made removing the flapper a bit of trouble, but in about a minute, I had it off. My rubber prize in hand, I trotted back to Harry and Orson. "Got it!" I said triumphantly.

"What's that?" asked Harry.

"The part that's going to fix your tank."

"Where'd you get it, I mean, other than the bathroom?"

"You don't want to know," Orson said.

I started up the ladder.

"What do *you* do?" Harry asked Orson.

"Nothing," my friend grumbled. "Not allowed to."

"Ah," Harry nodded, understanding.

"Well, you *could* steady this for me." Our demonic ladder was beginning to act up again. It was rocking back and forth on its four metal feet, threatening to pitch me to the floor.

"Oh right." Orson grabbed the ladder with one hand and planted a foot firmly on the bottom rung. His four hundred pounds took the fight out of the metal beast, but just for added measure, my assistant pulled out his awl. "If you don't settle down," he hissed, "I'll stab you again, this time with something that will leave a mark." A sound like a snarl came from the beast, but the threat was effective. The ladder froze in place.

"Thanks," I said, going over the top of the tank then back down the rest of the rungs to the chamber floor. I knelt, lifted the float from the steel, removed the old, flawed flapper and snapped the new one in place. Then I stood.

That was the easiest repair job I think I've ever had.

I reached the top rung and had one foot over to the other side when the ladder bucked violently, sending me to the floor.

Except for that last part. I groaned, climbing off the ground.

"Bastard!" Orson yelled and with a flourish plunged his awl deep into the metal of the ladder's side. There was a loud screech.

"I warned you, didn't I?" he said savagely then yanked the awl out of the side of his antagonist. We pulled it out of the tank, folded the ladder up and set it against the wall, where it lay, whimpering.

"Try it now," I said, rubbing my hands on my pant legs.

With a shrug, Houdini went over to the chrome lever and depressed it. The tank began to fill immediately, and in less than five minutes the black float around the PVC pipe reached the top of the chamber, turning off the water. Harry pushed the lever again, and the water drained out. "Seems to work like a charm," he remarked.

"Don't say that too loudly," Orson whispered. "That will usually cause something to break again."

Houdini frowned. "Maybe, but probably not this time. The audience *wants* to see me do this, and there's at least one prince of Hell watching."

"Oh? Who?"

"Mammon. He's not here of course, but he usually has that live feed of his going when I perform."

I whistled. "I heard you were good, but I didn't know you were *that* good!"

Harry sighed. "I used to be good, but now they won't let me be."

"Do you mean they won't let you be good or they won't leave you alone?" That was Orson all over. He was always a stickler with grammar.

"Both," Harry said, dejectedly.

"Sign here, please." The escape artist signed off on the work order and returned it to me.

"HARRY HOUDINI!" yelled a voice through a PA system. "TWO MINUTES!"

"Ah, and just in time ... The show must go on," he added, without much enthusiasm.

Harry walked behind the chamber and started to push. The contraption was on wheels and, with an enormous effort, he got it moving toward the stage. Orson and I hurried over to help him. "Thanks," he panted, "but no. It's part of my damnation."

"Oh, okay."

"Well, have a nice day," Orson added.

"Yeah. Sure."

Things got a little harder for Houdini when he reached the stage. The mud flooring made pushing the chamber more difficult. The long hose, which must have been the water source, didn't help things; he kept tripping over it.

"And now," said the announcer, "let's give it up for the great Harry Houdini, performing his classic Chinese Water Torture Cell escape trick."

"Let's stay and watch," Orson whispered. "This is supposed to be amazing!"

"Emphasis on the 'supposed to be,'" I muttered, but I was curious too, so we watched from offstage.

Four muscle-bound demons came on stage carrying the metal lid to the chamber. Harry stepped on the lid, and the demons locked him to it by his ankles. A rope with a hook on the end dropped from the catwalk above the stage, and one of the demons grabbed it, burrowed beneath the mud and hooked it to the underside of the lid. With a jerk, the lid and Harry were lifted in the air, and the escape artist dangled upside down a few feet off the ground. The demons produced a pair of handcuffs and locked Houdini's wrists together. Then the rope raised him about fifteen feet in the air. In seconds, still upside down, he was inside the glass chamber. The demons scrambled to the top of the cell and latched the lid in place.

The emcee walked over to the glass container and, with a flourish, flushed Harry. The tank began to fill with water. Immediately Harry started working on removing the handcuffs.

It has been said that Harry Houdini could hold his breath for more than three minutes. Good thing that, for his head was submerged in under a minute. I noticed with admiration that he had the handcuffs off during that time. Then I also noticed, with some horror, that the cuffs, as if animated, locked themselves back on his wrists. Upside down, Harry looked at us with wide eyes then went back to work.

At three and a half minutes, the cuffs finally decided to cooperate and stay off his wrists. Frantically, Harry groped for the locks around his ankles, but by then he had run out of air. I saw him reflexively suck water into his lungs. His eyes were huge by now. He grabbed his throat and drowned. In seconds, his body bloated up, as if he had been in there for days.

The applause was thunderous.

"Uh," Orson said, as we turned our backs on the horrific scene, "now I wish we hadn't stayed."

"Yeah. To drown again and again doing a trick you could manage in your sleep, and knowing this was going to happen with each performance ... *that's* Hell."

"For Harry it is." Orson shuddered.

"Flush!"

We turned back to the water chamber, which was rapidly draining of water. Houdini's eyes, which had bugged out of their sockets after he drowned, shrank back to normal size. His pale and bloated skin returned to its normal color, tightening up against his muscular frame. Even through the glass, I could hear him sigh while he unlocked his legs from the shackles holding him. "Ow!" In the final indignity of the performance, he fell to the bottom of the chamber. Now the audience was howling with laughter.

The demons pushed the chamber and its occupant offstage. As Houdini rolled by us, he made eye contact.

"Sorry," Orson and I mouthed.

He just shrugged. "Three more shows tonight!" he shouted, though the thick glass muted his voice.

Wheee.

"Steve Minion! Well, I'll be." said a gravelly voice.

120

A demon in a yellow hard hat was walking toward me. It was Karnaj, the demon who staffed the entrance to Hell's Sulfur Mine down on Six, and he had a few friends with him. "Actually, I don't 'be,' at least not since I died, but you know what I mean."

"Oh, hey, Karnaj." This particular demon was okay, a bit officious, but he rarely gave me trouble, so I put him in the "okay for a demon" column.

"My friends and I have been invited to the owner's box for a drink. Come join us."

"Ah, thanks, but … "

"I insist," Karnaj said, throwing a not-to-be denied arm around my shoulder.

"Uh, okay."

"Excellent!" He began to lead me away.

"I'll be out as soon as possible," I said to Orson over my shoulder. "Meanwhile, keep an eye on Putty Face!"

Chapter 11

The owner's lounge of the Palace was the entire front section of the first balcony. This was Mammon's town, and so the owner was titularly the Lord of Greed himself. However, since he never left his version of the Pantheon, Mammon didn't personally use the lounge.

This is actually a pretty common thing with owner's boxes, whether they be at theaters or arenas or stadiums - stadia, I suppose, since this after all was a facsimile of Rome. But owner's boxes are usually used for business purposes, entertaining a client, displaying the wealth of the owner, etc. Mammon's box was no exception.

One of the demons, a fellow named Nabob - "Bob to my friends, so call me Bob," he said - turned the polished brass knob on an ornately carved mahogany door and opened it. Karnaj steered me through the entrance.

I gasped. The entire room was paneled in the same wood, even the floor, though there it was laid out in a parquet pattern and covered in part by an exquisite Persian rug. The other exception was the wall facing the stage. That was glass, from floor to ceiling, extending the length of the room. I whistled. "This is the biggest piece of glass I have ever seen! How it doesn't collapse under its own weight is beyond me."

"Mammon's will," Karnaj said. He had continued to keep his arm around my shoulder, as if he was my best friend. It was pretty creepy, but I tried hard not to show my revulsion. Instead, I stared down at the act on the stage. The Flying Wallendas - or some of them anyway, those who had died but not made it to that better place - were performing a high wire act. Three of them were on the wire: one stood in the middle, balancing as best he could while the other two destabilized the wire by walking toward him from the opposite ends. All three of them were blindfolded, not uncommon with a Wallenda performance, but a bit of a disadvantage when they had obviously been set up on a collision course.

"The glass slides back into the wall to remove any barrier between the box and the performers ... "

"Swell."

"Or wood paneling can be closed to seal off the box entirely."

"Really?" I said a bit over-earnestly. "Man, I'd really like to see that."

"Sure, pal," Karnaj said. At a gesture from him, one of his buds pulled on a sconce mounted to the wall near the door through which we'd just entered. From recessed compartments, mahogany paneling slid silently into place, covering the glass.

"Why can I still hear the performance?" My face was damp with sweat.

"Oh, there are speakers in here. I suppose you'd like them turned off?" Karnaj asked, clearly amused.

"Uh, yeah, that would be great."

Karnaj nodded, and someone killed the speakers, but not before I heard an "AAGH!"

My new demon best friend pivoted toward the bar at the far end of the room, and since I was a virtual appendage to his right arm, I pivoted with him. In lockstep, we approached the bartender, a handsome and clean-cut young demon in a crisp white shirt and perfectly tied black bowtie. He may have had trousers on as well, but I couldn't tell. I certainly hoped so, though since Hell's health rules as pertained to bars, restaurants and similar establishments were understandably lax, there was no requirement for him to wear slacks.

"What's your poison, Steve?" Man, Karnaj just would *not* let go of my shoulder.

"How ... how about a martini?"

"Very good, sir," said the demon barkeep. "Would you like it dirty?"

"No thanks." Back on earth, I loved a bit of olive juice in my martini, but down here, well, who knew how they might dirty it?

"I'll have the same," Karnaj said. "What about you boys?"

"We'll have what Steve's drinking!" they shouted in unison.

With great efficiency, the bartender mixed five martinis in rapid succession. I got the first one.

"Go ahead, Steve," said one of the other demons. "You don't want it to get warm."

"Okay." This was the moment when the Persian rug usually would be pulled out from under me, the glass would break, cutting my hand, or the demons would pull out their pitchforks and begin working me over. Yet none of these things happened. I took a tentative sip of my drink, my eyes widened in surprise, and I slammed back the entire martini.

It was super, even better than the one I'd had with Flo at the Red Note, though the company certainly wasn't as pleasant. Still, the four demons were doing their best to entertain me.

Karnaj chuckled as he finally released his grip on my shoulder. "I guess he liked it. Better make him another one, Roger, so he'll have something to drink with the rest of us."

"That ... that was the best martini I ever had." Crisp, clean on the palate. Potent. Very potent, for I could feel a little buzz. This was a bit of a marvel to me, since alcohol doesn't generally affect humans down here. Oh, there are exceptions of course, like for Carrie Nation and other temperance movement leaders, some Salvation Army folks who weren't holier than thou after all, but generally alcohol has zero effect on the damned.

"You know," Karnaj said casually, as I enthusiastically took possession of my second martini and began to sip on it, "martinis for demons are the best anywhere. Why," and then he whispered in my ear, "a demon martini can even get *you* drunk!"

Now it has never been my ambition to get drunk, but the occasional high spirits that accompany a good cocktail are part of the experience. Drinking a fine alcoholic beverage without experiencing a slight buzz leaves the imbiber feeling dissatisfied.

And that includes all you wine snobs who claim, "I drink wine because I like the taste." Baloney. You might as well have a milk shake every evening if taste is your primary concern. Or drink non-alcoholic wine. Oh, there isn't any of the alcohol-free stuff that tastes good? That's because they don't have any alcohol in them! Admit it, oenophiles everywhere. Alcohol *is* part of the experience.

"So," I said slowly. "This is actually something completely different from what a human normally gets down here, right?"

"Of course!" Bob said, indicating an untouched spread of finger food on a nearby table. I saw lobster tail, fine cheeses and breads, fresh fruit, egg rolls. Oh, and those little meat balls that I could never get enough of at receptions I attended during my lifetime. My mouth began to water. "Demons get the best of everything, and since you're practically a demon already … " Karnaj tried to unobtrusively kick his colleague, but the sudden hiss of pain from Bob blew the cover on that.

Ah. Now I get it. "Thanks for the drinks," I said, putting my half-finished second martini on the bar, "but I really need to get back to work."

Karnaj's steel-like grip was back on my shoulder. "Oh, stay just a few more minutes. Uh … please?" He swallowed hard, as if he'd just eaten something unpleasant.

Since Karnaj was one of Beezy's own, Beelzebub must have been behind this effort to schmooze me. Besides, if this had been Satan's doing, it would have been handled with more finesse. And guile.

Karnaj guided me to a nearby table, while Bob grabbed my drink from the bar. In seconds we were all sitting at a round table topped with green felt. I thought of the painting of the poker-playing dogs. "You know," I began, "I didn't actually agree to … "

He cut me off. "Don't be hasty, don't be hasty, Steve. There's no need to rush to a decision. We just wanted to tell you how great it can be as a demon."

"Yeah. I really like it," Bob said.

"Me too!"

"Me too!"

"Me too!" yelled Roger from the bar.

I rolled my eyes.

"We know you're undecided," Karnaj continued, "but think of all the great things about the life of a demon!"

"Like horns and B.O.?" I asked, taking another sip of the martini. *Damn!* It was so good.

"No," he said, his grip reflexively tightening on my shoulder until I yelped. "Sorry. Don't know my own strength. I meant like the lifestyle, being part of the team and not the downtrodden."

"Not to mention the women!" Bob enthused.

At that moment, as if on cue, the door opened, and a stunningly beautiful woman entered. She had a figure like a young Anita Ekberg, only more voluptuous, and a face that would have made Ann-Margret, one of the heartthrobs of my

126

pubescent years, look plain. Her wavy red hair tumbled over one shoulder. The other was bare. The tightly-fit dress, or what there was of a dress, was a nude shade, scant on fabric, huge on architecture. Or maybe it was just the owner's own spectacular physique that made her breasts gloriously present themselves.

Lilith looked a little flushed. She must have just gotten word to high-tail it up here.

Lilith: my favorite succubus, the nicest demon I'd ever known and, other than Flo, the only woman in the Underworld I found attractive. Naturally, both Satan and Beelzebub knew this, so it made complete sense that she'd been conscripted into the recruitment campaign.

Not that she was unwilling. As a succubus, she loved seducing anyone. But she had me convinced that she actually had feelings for me, and recruiting me to her side, and away from Flo, would be a job she'd love.

The thought of Flo reminded me of her predicament, if indeed it was a predicament. She was simply missing, I knew. *Perhaps nothing has happened to her at all.*

I took another sip on my drink, feeling a little lightheaded.

"Lilith!" Bob enthused. "What a delightful surprise!"

I bet. But I took yet another sip.

Lilith flashed her most fetching smile, which, being a succubus, was enough to fetch an entire military platoon. "Oh, I was just in the neighborhood and thought I'd stop by."

"Would you like a drink?" Karnaj asked.

"Why, yes," she said, taking the seat one of the other demons had place next, and very close, to mine. "Don't mind if I do. I'll have … "

I had not been able to take my eyes of the sumptuous redhead since she entered the room. "She'll have a crackhead slammer."

127

"Oh, Steve, you remembered! How sweet!" she said, taking my hand, which, despite my better judgment, I didn't withdraw. I noticed that Lilith hadn't broken eye contact with me either, and she was giving me a come hither look that Mae West herself couldn't have matched.

A crackhead slammer is Lilith's favorite cocktail, a fact I learned on our first date, that is, at our first meeting, only a few days earlier. The slammer was made with cinnamon schnapps, peppermint schnapps and Dr. Pepper. Yeah, I know it sounds revolting, but she's fond of anything with cinnamon in it.

Roger walked Lilith's drink over to our table. I was relieved to see he had on slacks, though he wasn't wearing any shoes. His toenails were sharp and curled up toward the paneled ceiling.

"Oh, look at the time!" Karnaj said, staring at his wristwatch. I was almost certain it hadn't been there a minute ago, but this was Hell, magical, blah blah. You get the idea. Also, the watch was a convenient prop at the moment, so its sudden appearance was no surprise. "Gotta go!"

He and the other demons hastily rose from their seats, and I started to copy them. "No, no!" Karnaj said. "You and Lilith finish your drinks. See you later, pal."

I grimaced.

"You too Lilith!"

"Goodbye, boys," she said, coyly, though she still didn't take her eyes off me. Feeling a bit like the blue plate special, I gulped involuntarily.

The demons almost ran out the door, including, I noticed, Roger. In seconds, I was alone with the most alluring woman I'd ever known.

Lilith leaned forward and planted a soft kiss on my lips. "You didn't call me."

"Uh, it's only been a few days."

She pouted a little. "But guys always call me. Right away, too."

At this I smiled. "Like that would surprise me?"

"Did you like the candies?" she asked, drinking some of her slammer through a small red straw.

This made me smile even more. "Yes. They were very good. I finished them, I think, that very night."

"Haha! I knew it!" she said triumphantly, as she jiggled suggestively in her chair. "You like cinnamon, just like me. We are so much alike!"

"Except you're a demon, and I'm one of the damned," I added, getting straight to the point.

Lilith took my hand and placed it on one of her breasts. "But it doesn't have to be that way," she whispered seductively. She knew I was a breast man and that touching her magnificent mammaries sent me into such a deep state of rut my brain practically shut down.

It hardly worked this time, though. We only spent about five minutes sucking face and generally feeling each other up before I surfaced for air. Usually it was more like ten. "So you're trying to recruit me too, huh?" I finally managed to say.

"Well, why not?" she panted. "You know I'm crazy about you. If you were a demon, we could spend lots of time together. Just give me a chance. The sex would be wonderful, I know it."

"Yeah, but then I'd be a demon. Tell me, how long would it be before my dick fell off?"

"Oh, a few years," she said casually, "but we'd have lots of fun until then."

"What?" I'd been kidding. "If I have to lose my penis, I *know* I don't want to be a demon."

Demons are neither male nor female, as I believe I've told you before. Not having a penis, though, is unthinkable for a guy.

"I was kidding, just like I know you were, silly! You'll always have your penis. It's just that, as a demon, well," she blushed slightly, "another opportunity would open for you."

"Yuck!" I started to rise, but she pushed me back in my seat.

"Besides," she said hurriedly, "Lord Satan has already anticipated you would be reluctant to, ah, part with your part, or at least add a companion to it, and he's willing to make an exception. He's promised to leave you completely male."

"Then I'd be an incubus?" An incubus was the only demon I knew of that was completely male.

"No, no, then *I* would be unhappy. I want you all to myself. You'd just be Steve, a male demon who is not an incubus. You'd be unique."

"And why would he do that for me?"

"You know, I really don't know, except you're very special. All of us know that. Particularly me." She blushed.

"Me? I'm a nobody. Just another damned soul trying to make it through the afterlife."

Lilith looked down in her lap, chewing on her lip as she decided whether or not to say something. Finally, she whispered, "And just about the only human Lord Satan has ever respected." Quickly she looked around, half-expecting the Earl of Hell to materialize at any second. "Please, don't tell him I told you that. He'd have me seducing sumo wrestlers for the next two hundred years if he found out."

"He probably already knows." I pointed at my skull. "Mind reader, practically omniscient. Remember?"

Lilith looked horrified.

"Don't be concerned," I said. "I'm sure he knew you were just trying to help him recruit me."

She relaxed a little, but her face quickly resumed a worried expression. "It's more than that, Steve. I, I think I love you."

130

"Come on, Lilith, are succubi even capable of love?"

My dishy girlfriend - yes, I knew she was a girlfriend, no point denying it, even though Flo would always be first in my heart - was quiet for a second. Then, in a very small voice, she said, "I never thought so, but then I met you."

Which was just about the most flattering thing I'd ever been told. Needless to say this lead to another five minute session. It was very heated, and so was I. Parts that should have known better wanted to misbehave on their own, and Lilith wanted to help them. She reached for my lap ...

And I pulled away, gasping. "Lilith," I panted, "You're confusing me and ... and I can't do this right now. I've ... I've got to find Flo."

At the mention of Flo's name, Lilith frowned. "Her again, that scrawny human!"

"She's *hardly* scrawny." Flo was really built. I told you that, didn't I?

"Compared to *me* she is!" And she grabbed my hand again, placing it on her backup breast. Being right handed, I tended to naturally reach for her left one, but her right was just as pleasing. And she was correct. While Florence may have been the more beautiful woman, and with a rack that would drive any man crazy, Lilith was even more buxom.

With my last ounce of self-control, I stood. "Look, you're both gorgeous, voluptuous women, but right now, that's the last thing on my mind." That was of course a lie. Plenty of things in my brain were lined up behind comparing these two sexy women, but there was something more important I needed to think about. *Now, if I can just remember what it is.* I shook my head. *Oh, yeah.* "Lilith, I'm worried about Flo. She may be in trouble."

131

Like a teenager who had just been grounded for a week, Lilith crossed her arms and stared at the ceiling, pouting. Finally she said, "Okay, what kind of trouble is she in?"

She really had a good heart, amazing for a demon, but she was a succubus, that rare breed of demon who was born to be one. And while her mother was the Lilith of Jewish lore, her father (and the father of all succubi, by the by), was an archangel. That meant there was substantial good in her that could not be excised, not even by Satan. I had yet to see much bad, though she had to have some of that too.

The same could be said for all of us, I suppose, no matter how good we think we are. Shit, I thought I was a fine person in life, and look where *I* ended up?

I sat back down. Lilith tried to take my hand again. "Please, Lilith, not now."

To my surprise, she simply nodded. "Go ahead. I'm listening."

"Florence is missing, and there is some evidence to suggest she's been kidnapped."

The redhead's startling blue eyes widened. "You're kidding. I thought she was untouchable."

I shrugged. "Me too. And I don't think she can be hurt but … but maybe she could be held against her will."

"Would the Powers on High even allow that?" She looked up at the ceiling again, gesturing at it with her thumb.

"St. Peter seemed to imply that it was possible. Especially with Azazel involved."

"Azazel? I've heard the name before, but I've never met him."

I rubbed my chin, trying to decide how much to share with her. "He's a very powerful devil who once was in line to have Satan's job."

132

"You're kidding!"

"No, I'm not. I don't have all the details, but I know Satan won, and Azazel was given a job in middle management."

"You got all this from St. Peter?"

"Most of it, yes."

"And you trust him?"

"He's a *saint*, Lilith. I don't think he's even capable of lying."

"If you say so. I haven't even met the gent."

I smiled ruefully. "Consider yourself lucky. Oh, he's very good at his job, and certainly holier than thou, but he's a bit prickly and full of himself."

"Oh," she grinned. "I know that type. I guess they're everywhere, even in the High places. But anyway, do you think Azazel is involved?"

"Haven't a clue," I said with a shrug. "Maybe. There aren't very many suspects."

"Humph. Yeah, the famous Florence Nightingale, beloved by everyone."

"Well," I said slowly, "maybe not everyone. Your boss for instance was pretty humiliated by her sudden departure from his reception."

"Boy, isn't that the truth? He screamed bloody murder at me after you two left. I think he's still determined to get her in the sack."

"Which could be a motive for kidnapping her. Provided of course that she's been kidnapped at all, and not just wandering through Hell admiring the sights." I thought for a moment. "I'd like to talk with him."

Lilith sniffed. "You should talk with me too. I have just as much motive as he does."

"What do you mean?"

"She's a barrier between you and me. I'd *love* to see her fall off the face of the Netherworld."

"That would put her in Chaos."

"Figure of speech."

"Oh." But she was right. I *did* need to question her about this, though it couldn't be now. If I spent much longer in her presence, I might finally lose control, and join her in making the two-backed beast.

"Can you get me in to see Asmodeus today?" I asked, pulling the discussion in a safer direction.

"Let me see." Lilith's iPhone was in her hand - where it was before, I have no idea, certainly not in that dress of hers, unless she'd parked it in her cleavage - and she was staring at her calendar app. "He has an opening in a couple of hours. Now me," she said, arching her eyebrows, "I have an opening for you anytime." She shifted back in her chair. How she could appear to be lying down while still seated seemed like magic. Maybe it was. She parted her legs, and I could almost see ...

"In fact, why don't you just put it to me right now?"

"Oops!" I said, glancing at my wristwatch, grateful to have gotten the idea from Karnaj. "Look at the time! Sorry, but I can't stay longer." I stood.

"Fine, fine," she said irritably, and sat back up in the chair, crossing her arms again in disgust.

"Don't be mad at me, please?" Trying to resist the irresistible was hard. "What about after I meet with Asmodeus?"

Lilith was thoughtful then got a crafty look in her eyes. It made me nervous. "Okay, but I'm taking the rest of the day off, so you'll have to come to my place." The succubus grabbed a napkin and scribbled an address on it with a pen she'd also managed to secret away somewhere.

"But ... "

"If you want to eliminate me as a suspect, you're going to have to talk to me. It's there or nowhere."

I sagged, defeated. "Okay, pretty lady. You win."

She smiled at the compliment. "I always do," she said with satisfaction.

Chapter 12

I closed the door to the owner's box, leaving a very frustrated succubus behind me. With my sleeve, I wiped the sweat from my brow.

Boy! That was close. Another few seconds and …

"Steve!" a voice hissed from the stairwell. It was Orson. "Looks like Shemp is getting ready to clock out. If we hurry, we might be able to get ahead of him and catch him unawares outside."

"Lead on, Macduff."

"Did you know," Orson said, as we hurried down the stairwell, an ornately carved structure of the same mahogany that the owner's suite was made of, "that no one ever said that in 'Macbeth?'"

I gasped. Very few actors would refer to "Macbeth" as, well, "Macbeth." They'd call it "the Scottish play." Calling it by its true name was considered bad luck. On reflection, though, I decided bad luck was irrelevant in a place defined by misfortune.

We grabbed the ladder, which was leaning against a wall near the stage exit. "Of course someone said it," I replied.

"No, it's a misquotation. Macbeth says 'Lay on, Macduff,' meaning 'let's fight.' Don't worry, Steve, it's a common error."

"I'm sure you're wrong," I repeated, as we shoved the ladder through the door and took the stairs down to the alley behind the Palace.

Orson glowered at me. "Did you know, Steve-o," which was something he never called me unless he was irritated, "that in 1948 a famous director did a screen adaptation of Macbeth? In fact, said famous director directed and starred in it."

"Really?" We stashed the stupid ladder behind a rusted dumpster. "No I never knew that."

"Well, I did."

"How did the movie do?"

Orson grimaced. "My timing was not the best. It came out about the same time that Olivier did his 'Hamlet.'"

"Ooo. You're right about the timing."

He frowned. "I also made the artistic decision to have all the characters speak with a Scottish brogue."

"Sounds interesting. Pinkerton would like that."

"Maybe, but the studio execs didn't." Orson pouted. "Neither did the audience."

I patted Orson's shoulder. "Well, great art is not always appreciated in its time."

My friend looked thoughtful. "Thing is," he said slowly, "I never intended to make a great film. I wanted it to be a good one, but my primary objective was to do a film on time and under budget."

"And did you succeed?"

"Yes. We filmed in twenty-three days, and the movie only cost $800,000 to make."

"You're kidding!"

He leaned against the dumpster and began removing the dirt from beneath his fingers with a toothpick. "It even made a small profit."

"Not bad."

"You know what?" he said looking at me intensely. "The studio executives forced me to rerecord the dialogue without the brogue. But years later, my original, Scottish burr and all, was restored, and the film has grown in critical acclaim!"

I smiled. "On time, on budget, and a good film too. Good for you."

He blushed. He knew he was being his own apologist, but my praise seemed to mean a great deal to him.

"You continually surprise me," I said.

"What do you mean?"

"Don't worry. I intended it as a compliment." *Who knew? Orson Welles* was *capable of bringing a project in on time and on budget.* He could put his ego aside and just get the job done. Orson was condemned to an eternity of being an assistant, not ultimately responsible for anything. I wondered how Plant Maintenance would run if our roles were reversed. True, he was, if anything, a worse handyman than I, but he was a better manager. Orson would probably do a good job as Hell's Super, or as good as anyone could, since fixing things in Hell was a no-win situation. *But he'll never get the chance. Kind of a pity.*

"You surprise me too," he replied, in an awkward but sincere attempt at reciprocation. We were lucky not to get slapped with a couple of pies. "Now, let's try to surprise Putty Face."

"Good idea." We hid behind the dumpster and waited for Shemp's shift to end.

No one had bothered to put up lights in the rear of the building; all of those had been saved for the garish signs marking the entrance to the Palace. As a result, the alley was a muted scene, the images obscure and colorless, an artist's study in grays. The pillars at the back of the Palace, marking the stage door exit, cast long shadows, like the trunks of massive trees, onto the way; the black silhouette of our dumpster seemed a hulking thing, a metal monster ready to pounce on any passerby who was brave enough to navigate the narrow lane running between the replicas of the palaces of Tiberius and Domitian. The whole effect was forlorn: helpless, hopeless and threatening.

In a few minutes, a sliver of light appeared at the back of the theatre. A door was opening, and for a moment the lone figure standing in the jamb looked like a shadow trapped in a golden box. Then the box shrank, returning to a sliver before disappearing altogether.

With a halting gait, Shemp descended the stairs to alley level. He moved slowly, as if he were carrying a heavy burden. Though Shemp had only been sixty when he died, he looked like an old man, a tired old man. No, more than tired. Defeated, like he carried the weight of Eternity on his back. Which he did, I guess.

As he passed by the dumpster, Orson and I stepped out to greet him. "Hello, Shemp. It's been a while." Despite wanting to make this a neutral conversation, there was an edge to my voice. I had had two alley encounters with him before, and they had resulted in violence. Both times, Shemp and his goons had been the perpetrators and I the pigeon. They had taken me by surprise with the first one, and I'd suffered for it, with my legs broken by two of Shemp's bat-wielding thugs, not to mention a wicked headache from being repeatedly slapped in the noggin with a rubber chicken. The second time Shemp and his henchmen ambushed me, though, I'd been ready and sicced BOOH on them.

So the score was tied at one to one. I didn't particularly want to hurt Shemp this time. I just wanted some information, but it was hard to put aside the bad memories. The feeling must have been mutual, for when he saw me, Shemp's exhaustion vanished, and his ugly puss pinched up like he'd just sucked on a grapefruit. "Minion!" he hissed.

"Yeah. Minion."

"And me, Welles," Orson added, cracking his knuckles.

Shemp raised his hands in the universal gesture of surrender. "Two against one. Look, I don't want no trouble. Besides, haven't you done enough to me and my brothers?"

I put a hand on Orson's shoulder. "Back off, Orson. We don't want any trouble either. Just some information."

Shemp looked at me with undisguised hatred. "Why should I give you any information? You ruined everything."

With his words, all of my anger drained away. I sighed and sat down on a nearby cinderblock. He was right. I did ruin everything for him. Shemp, the rest of the Stooges and about ten thousand other damned souls collectively called the Free Hellions had plotted to use the Stairway to Paradise to escape Hell. I'd stopped them, and they hated me for it. I couldn't blame them. "You're right, I did," I said at last. "If it's any consolation, I've felt bad about that. You have to understand, though, that I was just doing my job."

He frowned. "Oh. You were just doing your job. Well, big deal. Like I care."

"You know, don't you, that Satan and Beelzebub didn't give me much choice."

He frowned again. Man, he was an ugly cuss when he did that. "Maybe so, but you're still a traitor to the community of the damned."

"Now that's uncalled for," Orson protested.

"No, it's okay, Orson. Look, Shemp. Let me try to explain," I said, taking his arm.

He brushed me off. "There's nothing to explain, I ... "

"Just shut up for a second and listen, okay? So ten thousand of you tried to escape Hell. Do you know that if you had succeeded, Satan would have made the other thirty billion of us suffer for your hubris?"

"Hubris, huh? That's a pretty Park Avenue word."

"Maybe, but do you know what it means?"

"Yeah. I ain't no idiot." He paused. When he spoke again, his voice was less sure. "Do you … Do you really think Satan would have tightened the thumbscrews on the rest of youse guys?"

"I know it for a fact." Well, I didn't know it for a fact, but I couldn't imagine any other outcome. "And that's not all. Every one of you was officially damned, just like me, and escaping Hell would have been as much an affront to the Big Guy upstairs as it would have been to Satan. The Hellions were messing with nothing less than the divine order of the universe."

"Yeah," Orson chimed in. "You know, or you should if you had any sense, that the Hellions are hardly unique down here. None of us likes being damned."

Shemp bit off a shard of torn fingernail. "Seems to me that you two at least have it pretty good."

Orson and I stared at each other in disbelief. "How do you figure that?" said my assistant finally.

"You have such cush jobs, and you report to Beelzebub directly."

"And you think that's fun?" I laughed savagely. "Oh, and guess what else is fun? All the times Satan makes me jump down the throat of Hell to meet with him in his office suite."

The Stooge looked shocked. "You've done that?"

"Yeah, four times now. Once, because of you and the rest of the Hellions, I had to do it all the way from Gates Level. How many bones do you think I broke when I landed?"

"Uh … "

"All of them! You have no idea what a misery it is to be Hell's Super."

"Or his assistant!" Orson added with indignation.

"Hey!"

141

"Nothing personal," Orson said, trying to mollify me. "I wasn't talking about you. I was talking about the job. Shemp, do you know how many thousands of work orders pour into our office every day, or how much grief Hell's management gives us because we can't keep up with our workload? Do you know what it's like to have Beelzebub mad at you?"

"Well, no."

"Then before you assume we have such 'cush' jobs, remember that, just like with you, Satan devised these positions for us because they would result in nothing but misery. Our afterlife sucks!" Orson was so exorcised, he kicked the dumpster, then began to hop around on one foot. "Damn it! You made me break my toe!"

"Walk it off," I said quietly. "So you see, Shemp, Hell is not a walk in the park for us either."

Shemp rubbed the dark stubble of his five o'clock shadow. He must have had a very long shift. "Okay. I guess you don't have things so good either. So what is it you want to know?"

"It's about Florence Nightingale."

Putty Face's eyes grew large. "I heard about that. Is it really true she's missing?"

"Yeah. I thought maybe you might know something about it."

"Me? Why?"

"Well, she did help me on the Escalator job, so indirectly she's one of the reasons you didn't escape Hell."

"And you thought we held a grudge against her, huh?" He laughed softly. "That's rich. Rich, but wrong. Look, Minion, I don't know a single human in Hell who would want anything to happen to Miss Nightingale."

"Really?" Orson said. He was no longer hopping, but walking toward us with a slow limp. "Even the Stooges?"

"Even the Stooges. Especially the Stooges, in fact. Do you know that after Beelzebub threw us all down the stairs and back to our own special spots in Hell, she came to visit us? Well," he added, "I don't know if she visited all ten thousand of us would-be escapees, but she visited me and my brothers, also the Joes, and Marx, Lenin and Trotsky. Some of us were pretty banged up from the fall - I guess crossing a major devil will do that to you - and she bound our wounds, those that hadn't healed yet, anyway. She also let us know how sorry she was for the part she played and that she understood why we wanted to get the hell out of Hell in the first place."

I smiled softly. "That sounds like Flo." Well, not those exact words. I imagine she put it more delicately than that, but it was characteristic of Flo to nurture the downtrodden.

"Moe, Curly, Larry and I had heard stories about Nightingale, but we'd never been on the receiving end of her kindness. That's one classy dame!" He smiled, as did I. Kindness is so rare in Hell; a damned soul could not help but be touched by Flo's generosity of spirit.

"So," I said, "you don't think a human, Hellion or otherwise, would be involved in this?"

He shook his head. "Not intentionally. Look, the Hellions still keep in touch ... don't tell anyone!" he said, looking around as if he expected infernal retribution at any moment. "I wouldn't want Satan or Beelzebub on our butts again."

"I suspect they already know and don't care. You can't really hide much from Satan when he has a mind to know it."

"I suppose that's true." He frowned again. *He really should stop doing that. When he frowns, he makes himself even uglier, if that's possible.* "Anyway, let me put out some feelers, see if any of the Hellions have any skinny about this. I'll let you know."

"You'd do that? Gee, thanks!"

"Not for you, Minion. I guess I understand now why you stopped us on the Stairway to Paradise, but I'm not ready to make all nicey-nice. Still, I'll do it for Nightingale."

"That's good enough for me."

Shemp nodded and turned his back on us. As he limped slowly down the alleyway, he seemed to get smaller and smaller, until he was only a tiny black shadow that faded into the gloom.

Chapter 13

We left the Escalator when it reached the Fifth Level, then made our way back to the office, lugging the ladder. My arms were aching from supporting its weight for so long. The thing seemed to have gained fifty pounds since we'd started with it, which struck me as entirely possible. After all, it had been uncooperative ever since Gates Level. I think it was mad at us, especially Orson, because he seemed to be struggling with his end of the ladder even more than I was with my own.

"Man!" my assistant said, as he closed the supply shed door. "That ladder is the right tool for changing those bulbs up on One, but in future, let's not drag it along with us on other jobs."

"Agreed," I panted. "Wouldn't have done it this time either, if we weren't trying to speed things up so we could carve out a little time to hunt for Flo."

Orson headed for the rickety steps of our trailer. The treads creaked as he climbed to our office door, and I wondered for not the first time how they even managed to support our weight without collapsing more than about once a month. "Yeah, and having the ladder with us on Two actually paid off. It was useful on the Houdini job, and going directly from the Gates Level put us at the Palace at precisely the right time. An unusual streak of luck," he said in wonder, all luck being a bit of a marvel down here. "By being there when we were, we were able to run into Shemp. Oh bother!" he said, as the office doorknob came off in his hand.

"It must have been expecting me to reach the door first. Here. I'll handle it."

"That's okay." My friend shoved an elbow through the glass - fortunately it was his, not one of mine - then reached through the hole and opened the door with the inside knob. "Ow! That stings!"

"I usually use my hammer," I said, trying to be helpful.

"I thought if I was fast enough, not very many pieces would lodge in the fabric." From his tool belt, Orson retrieved a leather work glove. He slipped it onto his left hand and brushed the glass off his elbow. "I was wrong."

"What you said about Shemp, though, was right on the money. Now we have a few thousand extra eyes looking out for her."

Orson, finished with his sleeve, took off his glove, only cutting one finger on his right hand in the process, then sat down on his stool. "You mean twenty thousand, don't you? Ten thousand Hellions times two eyes a Hellion."

I frowned at him. "Well, there might be someone who only has one eye or is blind altogether, but yes, that's what I mean. You don't have to be so damn precise."

"Bite me." Speaking of biting, Orson was using his teeth to work the shard out of his finger. Anyone could see where that was heading. He winced when he cut his lip then spat the offending glass to the floor.

I pulled out my desk chair and sat down, making note of the large number of work orders that had come in while we'd been out. The pile, higher than my wire inbox, was beginning to topple, so I straightened it. As I did so, one work order caught my eye. It was a dirty gray, one written on the old paper stock, the type we used before we'd changed to the new bile-colored ones. Whoever sent in the order was either too cheap or too lazy to order new work forms. I pulled it from the middle of the pile. "Lazy."

"Beg pardon?"

"It's an order from Belphegor." It was not directly from him of course. Prince Belphegor was the patron devil of Sloth. Since he was as lazy as the sin he patronized, he would never fill out his own work order. Some underling must have done it for him.

"The usual?"

I winced. "Yeah."

"Crap. Okay, I'll get the ropes and pulleys."

In the distance, an eerie music began to play. It reminded me of the theme song from 'The Twilight Zone.' A wisp of whirling black formed in the air before us, growing in size until it was a perfect circle of smoke, three feet in diameter. I whistled. Whoever was creating this had impressive control over his black magic. "Minion," a voice rasped. "Report."

It was Azazel. "Hello chief."

"None of your insolence, Minion. Call me my Lord."

I swallowed hard, but he wasn't my boss, and he wasn't one of the five princes of Hell, six counting Satan, so I decided to uphold the social etiquette of the Underworld. "I'm, I'm not sure that's appropriate."

"You will call me Lord Azazel," he said in a low voice, "or feel the lash of my whip."

I shrugged at Orson. So much for Miss Manners. "Yes, my lord."

"I said Lord Azazel."

Great. A stickler for detail. "Yes, my Lord Azazel."

"Better, Minion. Now, that report."

"Yes sir, I mean, my Lord Azazel." This was going to get old very quickly. "Well, as you know, Miss Nightingale doesn't have many enemies, so obvious suspects are few."

"But we have identified some!" Orson added hurriedly.

"Silence, underling! If I wanted to talk to an assistant, I would have addressed you directly. Leave this conversation to your betters."

Orson was purple with outrage.

That made me mad. "Now, wait a second," I said, rising from my chair. "Orson is *my* assistant, not yours, and I value his opinion ... "

The talking end of a whip darted from the wheel of smoke, catching me across one cheek. Orson darted forward to help me, but, biting down hard on my lip to block the scream that threatened to erupt from my mouth, I waved him away. This devil frightened me, but equally he pissed me off. Still, no one ever wins a fight with a devil, so I just held my ground in silence.

"Good," said Azazel. "You have some guts but know when to hold your tongue. No wonder you're Satan's little pet."

"Hey!"

"Want a matching scar on the other cheek?"

"No, not particularly," through gritted teeth I added, "my Lord Azazel."

"Then control your temper and finish your report. Who are your suspects?"

Swallowing a grumble that was about to escape my lips, I answered his question. "Our initial suspects were the only individuals who we knew had any personal grudge against Flo ... Miss Nightingale."

"You mean other than Satan and all the other devils in Hell," Azazel said, mockingly.

"Yes," I said, clearing my throat, "but they seem only to have a general objection to her. The individuals I have in mind could each have a specific axe to grind."

"Very well. Continue."

"There's Asmodeus, of course. He wants to get in her ... "

"I know what he wants. Another conquest for the petty, pretty prince of Lust. That makes sense. Her recent rejection of him would offend his pride. Reasonable. What about his assistant?"

Azazel seemed remarkably knowledgeable about the goings on all over Hell. Perhaps his police force doubled as a spy agency, or maybe he did his own surveillance. However he got his information, his interest in the doings of others reminded me of J. Edgar Hoover's. The image of Azazel in a dress flitted briefly across my mind, and it was only with effort that I banished it. I decided lying to the devil police chief was bad policy, even though I didn't like the idea of publicly declaring Lilith to be a suspect. "It's possible ... my Lord. You see, Lilith ... "

"Wants to get in your pants as much as Asmodeus wants in Nightingale's. I'm aware of that too and also find her a reasonable suspect. Continue."

"Yessir." I was sweating like a fat man in a sauna. He seemed to know everything I did. "Well, there are the Free Hellions."

"Ah, I wondered when you'd get to those morons. And ... "

"I just met with Shemp Howard. He assures me the Hellions hold no grudge against Flo because of her involvement in the Elevator Escapade."

"Do you believe him?"

"I think so, sir." I glanced at Orson, seeking confirmation. He nodded.

"Why do you believe him?"

Can he see me through that black disc of his? I realized that I'd been waving my hands at it as I talked. That was probably wasted effort, so I tucked them in my armpits. "Because Flo has spent much of the last three months visiting the Hellions, binding their wounds, talking with them about their frustrations and generally comforting them." This was a bit of

149

embellishment, but knowing my lady love, for her to act that way would be completely in character.

The smoke spun more rapidly. I think Azazel was getting impatient. "Be careful what you say to me. I know when someone is lying ... or embellishing."

Uh oh. Do we have another mind reader here? I could feel the goose pimples rise on my arms.

"However, I accept your assessment. Provisionally."

Whew. "Shemp is going to put out the word among the Hellions. Uh, he still keeps in touch with a few of them."

"You mean all of them."

"Well, yeah," I agreed reluctantly, hoping this admission didn't get anyone in trouble with the police. "Anyway, they will keep their eyes out for anything relating to Flo, uh, Miss Nightingale and let us know if they find anything."

"So you've recruited ten thousand damned souls to the cause of finding her. Hmmm. Admittedly, the Hellions could have chosen brighter leaders than the Stooges, but the organization seems to follow their lead. Very well," he said, as if he'd made a judgment. "That was also well done. What else?"

"That's all I have for now."

"WHAT? It's been hours since I assigned you to the case."

Orson and I again made eye contact, then we both looked at the mountain of paperwork that was growing on my desk. "Well, I'm sorry, but Beelzebub said we have to keep up on the work orders and only do our sleuthing as time permits."

"Beelzebub, you say? Do not worry. I'll tell the old fat one to release you from your regular responsibilities until Nightingale is found."

Orson looked at the black disc in shock. "And he'll listen to you?"

The whip lashed out again, and Orson had a gash on his face that was twin to my own. "Did I not tell you to keep silent?"

My friend nodded as he held his hand to his cheek, lips pressed tightly together. A tear gathered in one eye.

The wheel of smoke began to spin more rapidly, and sparks started to fly from it. "Beelzebub will listen to me if he knows what's good for him!" Azazel laughed savagely.

Now I didn't much like him threatening my boss, who, on a certain level at least, I liked - as much as one can like a devil, of course. On the other hand, I didn't relish tasting the lash again. In this instance, caution trumped outrage. Besides, Beezy was a big boy; he could take care of himself. "It would ... it would be helpful to have more time to look for Flo, but this particular work order," I said, waving the gray one in front of the disc, "we have to do, in any event."

"And why would that be?"

"It's from one of the princes of Hell."

"Which one of the *princes*?" Azazel's sarcasm was thick.

"Belphegor."

"Ah. AH AH AH!" He was laughing. Apparently. On him it sounded creepy. Guess he didn't think much of Belphegor. "The Lord of Laze himself. What does he want you to do? Blow his nose for him?"

I shrugged. "Something like that."

"Then by all means take care of this important task. By the time you do, Beelzebub will have released you from your regular duties. Then you will be all mine. Ah. AH AH AH!" The smoke disc collapsed upon itself and was gone.

"Nice guy," Orson grumbled, heading for the supply closet.

And just as quickly reformed. From out of the black haze, a heavy boot emerged. Azazel gave Orson a quick kick in the ass, sending him sprawling.

I kept my mouth shut. This devil really enjoyed his cruelty, and I didn't want to be on the receiving end just because I made one of my patented snide comments. Good thing he couldn't hear what I was thinking, the jerk.

Without a beat missed, the devil police chief spoke. "And don't think I can't pick thoughts from your brain as easily as Satan can. *Jerk*! Azazel out!"

The disc disappeared, and I began to shake uncontrollably. "A mind reader. My go … shit! He's a mind reader for sure, just like Satan."

Chapter 14

Orson got off the floor. His face was a mask of fear. "Is that what you were thinking?"

I gave a bobblehead nod, as my friend placed his bruised butt carefully on his stool. "I didn't know anyone down here but Satan had that power. I've sometimes thought Beezy could do it, but he's never given me irrefutable evidence. Azazel just did."

"Do you," Orson began, then swallowed hard. "Do you think Azazel is as powerful as Satan himself?"

I shrugged. "Dunno, but he seems to be one of the strongest devils I've ever encountered. He must be. He's not even afraid of the princes of Hell, or at least, so it seems."

We sat quietly for a few minutes, nursing our fears. Finally, Orson got to his feet and stepped to the supply closet. He pulled out two lengths of thick rope and some pulleys. "Let's go. Better to work than to worry."

"Right," I agreed, getting out of my chair and heading for the door.

The Escalator deposited us near the sulfur mine. As far as we could tell, there was no activity at all, no hand carts coming out of the wide entrance to the mine, no damned humans scurrying like so many ants around the place, no demons in hard hats riding the miners. It was very curious. Every other time I'd been here, the mine was bustling with activity.

"Odd," Orson commented.

"Yeah, it is. If we had more time, I'd make up some excuse to go inside and see what's going on."

"At least it explains why Karnaj and his buddies could spend so much time enjoying the pleasures of the Palace."

There was a river beside the mine, where barges normally floated, waiting to be filled to the brim with some of the output of the mine for carting off to one of the main sulfur distribution centers about ten miles downstream. Like the mine, the docks were abandoned. We looked at each other and shrugged then made our way to the bridge a few hundred yards beyond the loading area. Once across the bridge, we continued upstream along a road that paralleled the water.

Our destination was about a mile away, a compact but bustling walled metropolis with the ironic name of Sloth City. All humans who spent a life of indolence were sent there upon death. At the entrance to the city, they were issued heavy medallions, made of lead, hanging on leaden chains. These were placed around their necks. All the medallions were the same, round in shape, and with the pseudo-word "tuit" stamped into the metal. On Earth, all of them put off or completely neglected life's tasks, forever saying they would eventually get "around to it." Well, now they each had one, and their procrastination was at an end.

As we reached the gate, a demon stopped us, while his fellow brought out two round tuits. Orson pointed to himself and simply said, "Pride," which was the cardinal sin my friend committed in life. "Ditto," I added, pointing to my own chest. The two demons nodded and waved us through.

Since everyone inside had, in life, been guilty of the sin of sloth, in death they were forever doomed to activity. Couriers peddled along the streets at top speeds, carrying useless parcels and meaningless missives from one end of town to the other. Bricklayers built walls at a phrenetic pace then tore them down only to build them over again. Foxholes were everywhere, being dug, being filled in. Rinse and repeat.

154

There were tall skyscrapers in Sloth City. We watched a team of window washers racing up the side of one, hoisting themselves up on scaffolding supported by cables. They seemed to be in competition with another group of washers on another side of the building. They probably were, and whichever team lost most likely got pitched from the roof to the pavement below.

There was no trash anywhere. A scrap of paper wouldn't even have time to hit the ground before a sanitation worker snatched it from the air. The city's main park was perfectly manicured by all the gardeners perpetually cutting the grass, trimming the hedges, pruning the trees.

In the center of the park was a large, bare hill. The hill was reserved for Sisyphus, who Belphegor wanted to relocate from Level Two to Sloth City, where the ancient Greek king could be an inspiration to all the indolent who inhabited this corner of Hell. Funny thing, though. Belphegor never seemed to get around to it; he hadn't for two thousand years.

Every structure in Sloth City was tarted up with bright colors, like South Beach, though the hues were brighter, more garish, more "energetic" than the pastels of the hotels along Miami Beach. Painters were vigorously attacking every structure in town. We saw one man finish a hand railing along the sidewalk and then immediately start painting it again. It was like Disneyworld.

Except nobody was smiling. The looks of fear and misery on everyone's face depressed me. I knew they had to maintain their frantic pace around the clock. There was no quitting time in Sloth City.

As we approached the far edges of town, activity slowed, colors became more muted, until everything was gray, grayer than gray. Humans disappeared from view, and the din of their

155

activity was left behind. Silence reigned everywhere. The few individuals on the streets, demons or devils all at this point, walked at a preternaturally slow pace, as if traveling through molasses. We slowed our own pace to match.

Our destination was a large, single story building on the edge of town, on a patch of land abutting the river. The structure seemed to have no color at all, as if its occupant couldn't be bothered with issues of hue. We walked straight to the front door - there were no stairs in this place - and let ourselves in.

A number of demons were inside - few devils chose to wait on Belphegor personally, for reasons that will become obvious soon enough - but each dozed quietly in one of the numerous alcoves built into the walls of the large antechamber. The room was dusty - so were the demons for that matter. No one bothered to clean Belphegor's mansion. He didn't care, so why should they?

Orson went over to one of the sleeping staff members. Using his finger, my friend wrote something in the dust on the demon's chest. Orson stepped away and grinned, showing me his handiwork. "Wash me," he'd scrawled. I just sighed.

In the center of the anteroom was a jowly demon sitting in an overstuffed chair. Propped on his ponderous belly was a laptop. He was snoring. With the toe of my boot, I tapped his foot. "Sleepy," I whispered, noting with amusement, and not for the first time, that he shared a name with a Disney dwarf. "Wake up."

"Wha … ?" He cracked an eyelid.

"It's me, Sleepy. Hell's Super. I've come about the work order."

Sleepy blinked slowly, finally managing to get his eyes open enough to look at me. Recognition seeped into his consciousness, and he fumbled with the laptop on his gut.

"Yesss. Minion. Welles. Go in. He's waiting for you." With that, he closed his eyes and went back to sleep.

Speaking of eyes, Orson rolled his, not too vigorously, though. He didn't want to draw attention to himself, but he communicated his contempt quite effectively to me.

We slow-walked our way through the chamber to the double doors on the far side. These were panel doors, and we drew them apart slowly and quietly, revealing a very large bedroom, a monstrous bed and a huge and repulsive devil lying on top of it.

Belphegor, the devil prince most associated with Sloth, was fatter than even Beelzebub, and Beezy was the patron prince of Gluttony. I doubt that Belphegor ate as much as our boss, who would consume anything, rump roasts, flies, toads that happened to be hopping by, MoonPies, RC Colas, buffalo turds, hotdogs. Even calamari and beets. But Beezy was very active and burned calories all the time, during his walks across the Eighth Circle of Hell, turning himself into a sand demon and spinning across the desert or blowing himself up in a thermonuclear explosion. Belphegor loved to eat, too, as long as it wasn't too much trouble, which was why there was a feeding tube within inches of his mouth, but he hated to move, much less exercise.

So he was big, I mean really big. He was bigger than Beezy would be if he'd just swallowed Orson. He was shaped much like a slug, like Jabba the Hutt, though Jabba looked like he'd been on Weight Watchers, at least, compared to my client, who was now lazily eyeing Orson and me.

"Here we are, Belphegor. It's been a few years."

"Yes," he said with an effort. "I'd like to stare out my window now." He winced.

"Bedsores bothering you, sir?" Orson asked.

"Yes."

"We'll get right to work, then."

"Not too quickly."

"Of course not," I added. "We'll keep the activity level, and the noise, down as much as we can."

He blinked once in acknowledgment.

Belphegor was the laziest creature in the universe. He was lazier than Matthew McConaughey's voice, lazier than Christmas lights left on a house all year to keep from having to put them up again next holiday season. He was lazier than second-day mascara, an ignored typo, wilted grass, acronyms.

You get the idea. "He was as lazy as a slug." No, that's wrong. That's a simile, and Belphegor was too lazy to use similes. All those extra words, you know. "He *was* a slug." See? We got that description from seven words down to four, just by switching from a simile to a metaphor. He'd like that.

For all that, I got along with Belphegor better than most other devils. In fact, all the devils under his control were pretty easy to work with. They were just too lazy to give a shit. That's why, as disgusting as he was, I treated the Lord Devil of Sloth with respect. I could have been nasty, I suppose, because Belphegor was likely to find it too much trouble to punish me, but it's not like me to be gratuitously mean anyway. Oh, I'll be mean for a reason, if for example someone has treated me badly, but generally I believe in live and let live, or in this situation, live and let die, or maybe just leave me alone.

Orson handed me a pulley and one of the ropes. We then crawled on top of the bed, me near Belphegor's head, Orson near his tail. In this way, we could reach to the ceiling, where two hooks we had mounted years ago were still in place. Each of us attached a pulley to a hook, then threaded it with a length of rope. Kneeling beside the devil, I gently slipped an end of my rope under his torso, while Orson slid his line under Belphegor's butt. I almost shuddered when I touched his skin. It was squishy and sallow, as if the prince had a terminal illness.

Orson and I tied together the ends of our respective ropes, forming two loops supported by the pulleys. Then we got off the bed. Near the headboard was a lever we had installed about forty years earlier. I pulled the lever, and the bed dropped about two feet into the floor. Belphegor was now suspended in the air by the ropes. With a little bit of muscle, Orson and I turned the monstrous devil a hundred and eighty degrees. He was now facing the window instead of the door. I winced when I saw the huge red bedsores on his right side. Three years lying in the same position would do that, I thought with distaste.

Orson looked with barely-concealed disgust at the filthy linens on the bed. "Uh, would you like us to change the sheets or flip the mattress as long as we have you up?"

"No," he said. His voice was labored, as if the ropes were constricting his lungs. Or maybe it was just Belphegor being Belphegor. "Too much trouble. Just get me resettled."

"Yes sir." I pushed the lever back in place, which raised the floor, and the bed, back to its normal height. Then, still careful to move slowly, we crawled back on the bed. We had the ropes off Belphegor, the pulleys off the ceiling and ourselves off the mattress as quickly as we dared.

"There you go." I reached in my pocket and pulled out the work order. "Sign here, please."

"Have Sleepy do it." And then the Lord of Sloth smiled.

Now this probably seems like an unnecessary expenditure of energy on his part, and it was. But on the few occasions when Belphegor showed any facial expression at all, it was likely to be a smile instead of a frown, for as we've all been told, it takes forty-two muscles to frown and only seventeen to smile. This has been studied, apparently, by university scientists, and it shows two things: Belphegor would prefer smiling, because it takes less energy. It also shows research faculty should have their teaching loads increased.

But back to the smile. The Lord of Sloth smiled, and then he said, "It's good to see the river again. Pretty."

I looked out the window. None of Sloth City could be seen. That was all behind us. All that was visible was the river, and its green banks. For Hell, it was an unusually pleasant view. "Yes, it is, sir."

"No activity."

"None that I can see."

Belphegor sighed. "Good. Earlier today, lots of noise … coming … from mine. Curious."

Orson looked at me with surprise. Belphegor wasn't usually so chatty. "We noticed that something funny was going on there too," my assistant said.

"Or rather, nothing was. It looked deserted."

Belphegor panted. "Sounded like everyone left quickly this morning. … I hate quick. Some … one should investiga …" The devil was nodding, and we took this as our cue to leave.

As we neared the door, he spoke again. "Before you go, my tube … " These final words took the last of his strength, it seemed. He was asleep in moments.

We moved the feeding tube so it was close to his mouth again then slowly and quietly exited the room, pulling the doors closed with nary a bump when they touched. In the antechamber, we woke Sleepy. With an effort, he signed off on the work order. Then we left him and the rest of the staff to their slumber.

Chapter 15

We crossed the bridge, still carrying our ropes and pulleys.

"Man!" Orson declared. "Have you ever seen Belphegor so talkative?"

I looked down at the river, a churning canal of gray liquid that looked more like Diet Coke than water. "No I haven't. I think he was trying to tell us something." The wharf was still deserted. Orson and I were the only two creatures in sight. "This really is odd."

"Yeah. I've never seen the mine closed down."

"Me neither. If I didn't have an appointment, I'd check it out."

"Appointment?"

I nodded. "With Asmodeus and then," I added, blushing, "with Lilith."

"Oh ho! You've been holding out on me."

I gave him a playful shrug. "Stop it. You know they're both suspects. I have to talk with them."

He laughed, giving me an affectionate squeeze across the shoulders. Hours before, Karnaj had done the same thing, but the demon had creeped me out. Orson brotherly hug, in contrast, warmed my soul. He punched my arm gently, then said, "How are you going to get up to Two? Wait for the Elevator?"

I shook my head. "Can't. That could take hours. I'll get BOOH to give me a ride me again."

Orson looked worried. "I hope he doesn't get in trouble for this."

"Me too, but he agreed to help, and I don't have many options." With that, I whistled loudly.

Scant seconds passed before BOOH flew out of the Throat of Hell. He landed on the rocky landscape near us. He was sporting a floppy hat in addition to his sunglasses. There were two holes poked in the brim for his rather substantial ears.

Orson did his patented eye-roll, but I whispered to him. "Come on. He's trying his best." In a louder voice I said to BOOH. "Hello. Do I know you, sir? You seem familiar, but I can't place the face."

"Skree!" yelled the bat.

"BOOH? Is that you? I didn't recognize you. Did you recognize him, Orson?"

My friend rolled his eyes again but played along. "No. Not at all. That's a really good disguise, BOOH. No one will *ever* catch on that it's you."

I shoved an elbow in Orson's ribs, all the while smiling at my batty friend. "Thanks for coming. I have an appointment soon with Asmodeus, and I don't have time to wait for the Elevator. Could you take me up?"

"Skree!"

"Thanks. Oh, and," I added, looking at my assistant, who seemed distracted. He was scratching his beard, deep in thought. "Could you drop Orson at our office on the way?"

"No, that's okay," Orson said. "I think I'll look around the mine a little, see if it's really deserted and, if so, why. I'll take the Elevator when I'm done."

"Good idea." I climbed on BOOH's shoulders. "Meet you back in the office. Be careful."

"You too," he cautioned.

"Yes, Asmodeus is a pretty dangerous character."

He chuckled. "It wasn't Asmodeus I was talking about."

"Oh."

"Lilith's got the hots for you. One slip of willpower, and you're done for."

I was a little offended. "But I love Flo, not Lilith."

"I know, but don't kid yourself. If Lilith is determined enough, you don't stand a chance."

I swallowed hard. "You're right about that." A human heterosexual male against a succubus. Not an even match.

Orson turned toward the mines, as BOOH and I took to the skies.

The rim of BOOH's hat flapped lightly in the breeze as we flew. The felt dug into my private parts, making me wish I'd let BOOH carry me in his claws. I didn't enjoy traveling carrion-style, but it beat having my nuts squeezed.

We passed through the four circles in dizzying succession. Through it all, I could see little, basically just whites and blacks, as I was alternately blinded by the comparatively bright skies of the air between each level or by the dark of a ring's interior. BOOH, who flew this route many times a day, was completely unfazed, though as a bat he did have the advantage of echolocation - bat sonar - to guide him, no matter the visibility.

My friend dropped me at the entrance to Lust Unlimited, the twenty story office tower in the middle of town that was the Prince of Lust's headquarters. Then BOOH took off like a bat of hell, which was to be expected, but especially so today, since he didn't want to be seen with me.

As I approached the lobby elevator, running feet scraped along the marble floor behind me. "Milhous!" I warned, without turning around. "If you slap that stupid 'Out of Order' sign on the elevator again, I'll hit you with my hammer."

The former president skidded to a stop. As was his fashion, or his damnation, I was never sure which, he was dressed in a bellman's uniform, complete with the organ grinder monkey cap. "Hey! It's my job. It's a stupid job, but it's still mine. Besides, I could get in trouble if I let you use the elevator."

This was a dilemma for the old guy. I wouldn't call it a moral dilemma; those aren't supposed to exist down here. Besides, I'm not sure Milhous completely got that 'moral' adjective anyway. The threat of diabolic retribution was real, though. I gave the situation a little thought then brightened. Perhaps I could help. "Look," I said, brandishing my hammer, "you *might* get hurt if you let me use the elevator, but I guarantee you will get hurt if you don't."

"Good point," he said, scratching his nose with the sign.

"Besides, I have a legitimate appointment with Asmodeus. Lilith made it for me."

"How convenient. It just so happens Lilith is off today. You could be lying."

I thought about everything I knew of Milhous, his involvement with the House Un-American Activities Committee, and his critical role in the Alger Hiss case. "You see conspiracies everywhere, don't you?"

He shrugged. "I always have. During my life, it stood me in good stead."

"Except for that Watergate thing."

"Yes, except for that," he agreed, looking sheepish. "But still, I'm not and never was a crook."

"You told me that before. You told all of us that before. Now, if you don't mind," I said, reaching around him and pressing the button. There was a ding and the door opened.

Milhous threw his hands up in disgust. "Next time," he threatened, and scuttled back to his alcove to wait for another victim.

"Ding" went the elevator again as it opened on the twentieth floor. The front office was empty - not even a Kelly girl to sub

164

for the vacationing Lilith, something I would have expected of Asmodeus. Not that he really needed a secretary. If he wanted to, he could probably run the whole Lust operation by himself, but a prince of Hell needs an assistant - it's a status thing - and a sexist pig like Asmodeus would want someone called a "Kelly girl" instead of simply a "temporary worker."

But today he had neither, and I wasn't sure what the protocol was. Generally, it isn't a good idea to just barge into a major devil's office; they tend to be a bit testy when you did that. On the other hand I had an appointment, and according to the clock above his office door, I was right on time. With a bit of trepidation, I turned the door knob and stepped inside.

The office of Asmodeus was a very large room lit only with candles. Curtains of damask hung on the wall, behind which were numerous alcoves supported by thin stone columns. In each alcove sat a woman, scantily clad, on a cushion of red silk. The room was dominated by a gigantic bed; it was enveloped by a translucent lavender veil that hung from the ceiling. On the bed lounged a naked Asmodeus, his enormous phallus and tail in what were probably perpetual states of erection. On each side of him lay a succubus, also nude. All three had a blush to their bare skin, leaving little doubt as to what they'd just been doing.

"Excuse me," I said, clearing my throat. "I'm here for my appointment, Lord Asmodeus." I didn't particularly like this guy, and since we had some history, he probably didn't care much for me either. Still, he was a devil prince, I'd stepped into his office unannounced, and I caught him with his pants down. Well, actually, completely off, but you get my drift.

"Minion? Is it that time already?" Asmodeus climbed out of bed. The clothing of an Arab sheik, complete with turban, formed around him. He shooed the succubi from his bed. "I was just taking a break with a couple of my assistants before getting back to work."

"Oh? An afternoon of meetings?"

Asmodeus grinned wickedly. "Of a sort. I have a theme going today. I've gathered up all the feminist activists in Hell, and I'm proceeding to, euphemistically speaking, have my way with each of them." He gestured at all the women in the alcoves.

"These are all damned feminists?" I said in astonishment.

"You bet. Of course, many women's rights advocates went Upstairs, so I can't get at them, but there are enough down here for me to work with."

My blood begin to boil. I was born in the mid-1950s, and I became socially and politically aware in the Sixties, which is when the so-called second-wave feminism –focusing on issues of gender equality, reproductive rights, legal equality and workplace rights - began. Many of my female friends in college identified themselves as feminists, and while I did not agree with them on everything, I considered myself a supporter, even going so far as to work as a volunteer for passage of the failed Equal Rights Amendment in the late seventies. Torturing feminists by forcing them into acts of sexual submission was abhorrent to me, but right up Asmodeus's alley.

On the other hand, I was dealing with the Devil Prince of Lust, who could fricassee me with a glance. So I had to choose my words carefully. "But, but feminists were just seeking equality. Surely they weren't damned for that. This just seems cruel."

Asmodeus looked at me with derision. "Of course it's cruel, you idiot! Not to mention ironic and unjust. So what? I'm a devil."

I smacked myself in the forehead, like I was the stupidest creature in Hades. "Sorry. That's pretty obvious. Still," I said, sweeping my arm broadly to indicate the women of his makeshift harem, "they can't all be victims of the Cardinal Sin of Lust, can they?"

He shrugged. "No, though a surprising number of them are. Usually not sexual lust. Susan B. Anthony for example - oh, some pretty nice ta tas on that one - had a lust for power. Her pal, Elizabeth Cady Stanton, who only wanted justice for the members of her sex, ended Upstairs. Anthony, though, wanted social and political power. She had no interest in belly bumping."

"Another euphemism for sex, I suppose. How many do you know?" I asked, curious.

"Oh, thousands," he said, warming to the topic. "In English alone I know four or five hundred, like dipping the wick, bisecting the triangle, churning butter, that sort of thing." The face of Asmodeus lit up with an unexpected enthusiasm. "I know, give me a letter of the alphabet, and I'll give you a slang term for coitus that starts with it."

"Okay." The fact that he was degrading these women still infuriated me, but I also love the language. I was interested to see how good he was. "I choose the letter S, but it can't be one of the standard ones, like sex or screwing or ... whatever," I said, suddenly blanking on other possibilities.

He looked at me quizzically, then grinned like a mischievous boy. "How about 'shampooing the wookie?'"

I laughed. "You're kidding."

"Nope. That's a Star Wars reference, you know."

"I remember. How about C?"

He snapped his fingers. "Easy: caulking the tub, checking the oil, completing the jigsaw puzzle, and about fifteen more."

"Wow!" Despite my aversion to his 'feminist' domination theme of the day, I was impressed. "Who comes up with all these?"

"Guys mostly."

"Well that would figure."

"Yes," Asmodeus said with enthusiasm. "I am compiling a book of all these phrases. It's one of my hobbies. I'm going to call it *The Coitus Compendium*."

"Keen."

The Prince of Lust, who up until now had been all smiles, looked at me with suspicion. "Are you being sarcastic, human?" he said with all the dignity of one of Hell's rulers.

"Not at all, my lord," I said hurriedly. "Everyone should have a hobby, and yours seems particularly appropriate, considering your responsibilities here in Hell."

"Precisely. I'm very good at my job, and I try to be thorough." He gestured toward the women in the alcoves. "Look at all these feminists."

"I am, and I have to confess," I said quietly, not wanting the women to hear, "I didn't realize that so many of them would be quite this attractive."

He leered at his prey, and more than one shuddered at his glance. "They aren't normally. As with most damned souls, their true appearance is more or less the same as that when they died, which for the most part is pretty repulsive. For all these women know, that's how they look now, old, sickly, fat, whatever. I don't see why I should have to polish my porpoise on an unattractive old hag, though, so I transformed them back to their youthful best. Some of the feminists were quite beautiful when young, like Gladys over there. Others, well, not so much. With the latter, I performed a few enhancements for my own pleasure."

168

"Sounds pretty sexist."

Asmodeus looked at his nails and polished them against his robe. "So? It's who I am. It's what I live for. ... Oh, wait, I forgot my pitch!"

"I beg pardon? You mean your pitchfork?"

"No, my pitch. I promised Satan." The Lord of Lust cleared his throat. "You know, Minion, as a demon, you'd be allowed to boff, boink, bone, etc., whoever or whatever you wanted."

Whatever? I guess he thinks I'm into farm animals or something.

"There are many, many privileges to demonhood," he added. "You shouldn't let this opportunity slip away from you."

I just shook my head. "So even you are trying to sell me on becoming a demon. I can't believe it."

He snickered. "Yes, well don't let it turn your head. I only pointed this benefit out to you as a favor to Satan."

"So, it's not true that I can have my way with any woman in Hell?"

"Oh, that's *completely* true, but I couldn't care less if you became a demon. As I said, I'm only doing a favor. But enough of this. I just have a few more minutes before I have to get back to work, so ask me what you came to ask."

"Okay." I cleared my throat. *How to proceed? Maybe just with the direct approach.* "Did you know Florence Nightingale has disappeared?"

"Of course! It's all over the Underworld."

I stared down at the Persian carpet that covered his office floor. "I don't suppose you know anything about it, do you?" Surreptitiously I glanced up at him.

Asmodeus was stroking his beard. He really was a handsome devil. "Meaning did I have something to do with it, of course.

Minion, this is the second time in a week you've accused me of foul play."

"My lord," I said hurriedly. "No disrespect intended."

He laughed. "And none taken. In fact, I'm flattered. What devil wouldn't like to be blamed for something evil, and what could be more evil than absconding with the only thoroughly good human in all of Hell? But no, I had nothing to do with it. Why would you think so?"

"I … I thought maybe you were angry with Flo, Miss Nightingale, for leaving your reception, and you, so abruptly the other day."

"I was, briefly," he admittedly through pursed lips. "But that faded quickly."

"Why's that?"

His eyes lit up. "Well, I enjoy a challenge, and I haven't had a real one, like what Miss Nightingale poses, in over a thousand years."

"If that's so, why wouldn't you kidnap her so you could 'have your way with her?'"

He snorted, reminding me of St. Peter at his condescending best. "And where's the challenge in that? No. Mark my word. I *will* have Nightingale eventually. She will come to my bed of her own free will."

Not if I have anything to do about it.

What I said was, "That will certainly be a challenge. Flo is a very strong-willed woman."

"No doubt, no doubt, but who can resist the Lord of Lust?" He conjured up a mirror, looked at his handsome visage and smiled broadly. He tossed the mirror in the air, and it disappeared.

"My lord, forgive me for doubting your word," though as a devil, perhaps he liked people believing he routinely lied. He did of course, lie that is, they all did, but who knows when one will take offense? Devils, every horn-headed one of them, are prickly characters. For that reason, I was trying to ask my questions carefully. "Do you have any evidence of your whereabouts for the past several hours?"

Asmodeus indicated the many women in the alcoves. "How about all of these witnesses? They've been in my office for the past day, watching me wave my wand in many chambers of secrets. I'm sure they'll vouch for me, right ladies?"

As one, the women nodded. I couldn't imagine any of them daring to contradict Asmodeus, but I felt it was useless to press the point. Besides, he was probably telling the truth. He'd want to feel the rush of seducing Flo, rather than forcing himself on her.

"Thank you, Lord Asmodeus. There are very few inhabitants of Hell who have any motive for harming Flo in any fashion, and I promised Azazel that ... "

"Azazel?" Asmodeus said with surprise. "Azazel? He's the one who has you checking up on Nightingale's disappearance?"

"Yes," I said, showing my consultant's ID. "He sort of deputized me."

"Interesting, interesting," the devil said to himself. "I'd be cautious around him, if I were you. A dangerous customer, that Azazel."

I frowned, looking at him to provide some further bit of information. He disappointed me, though. "So I'm beginning to understand," I said at last.

"Well, consider yourself warned. Now, if you'll excuse me, I have a schedule to keep." His sultan outfit transformed itself into the gold command uniform of a Star Trek captain, or the shirt part anyway. The bottom was unencumbered by the inconvenience of clothing. "Yeoman Rand!"

171

A young, short brunette emerged from one of the alcoves. Her features were striking, and strikingly familiar as well. With a shock, I realized where I'd seen her before. A photo from her later years adorned a paperback copy of *Atlas Shrugged* that I'd owned back during my lifetime. It was Ayn Rand.

Rand wore a short, red dress that I recognized immediately. It was the most sexist of all the women's uniforms in all the incarnations of the Trekkie franchise. "Aye, captain?" she said, her voice quivering.

"Take your station."

With a sob, the woman got into the bed. For a moment, our eyes met. I did not see fear in them, but humiliation. And outrage.

He arched an eyebrow at me. "Not exactly a feminist, though some people think she can be interpreted that way. Frankly, I don't care. I just really wanted to work her into today's theme. If you'll excuse me, I'm now going to violate the Prime Directive, if you know what I mean."

"Good one," I said, though my stomach was queasy.

"Prepare to be boarded, yeoman."

"Aye, sir."

"Open the pod bay doors." Asmodeus crawled into bed.

I couldn't watch and turned my back.

"Doors ... open ... sir."

"Docking in five, four, three ... "

I hurried out of his office as the theme song from 'Star Trek' began to play in the background. They were using the melody from "The Next Generation" instead of the one from the original series.

I slammed the door behind me in disgust.

Chapter 16

Outside Lustland's corporate office, I whistled at a passing cab and was awestruck when it stopped. As with Hell's Elevator, taxis in the Underworld usually kept you waiting. Car after car would pass you, whether or not they were empty, probably due to the orders of some demon dispatcher. Yet the options for traveling horizontally in Hell, that is, across the surface of an individual Circle, were limited. I hated the buses, because they were driven by ill-tempered demons. Walking was always a possibility, but since I didn't know where I was going, a guide, even if he or she was a blind cabbie (all of Hell's taxi drivers are blind), seemed like a good idea.

"Sixty-nine Lovers' Lane," I told the gruff old fellow, after consulting the scrap of paper Lilith had given me earlier in the day. "Do you know where that is?"

"Yeah. Get in."

I still don't know how a blind taxi driver could navigate city streets. Certainly they made their share of mistakes, like inadvertently running over one of their fellow damned souls, or slamming into a curb, running a red light ... that sort of thing. At a macro level, though, the cab drivers seemed to have a pretty good handle on the general layout of whatever town they served.

We pulled away from the office tower, merging with only minor mishaps into the herky-jerky flow of traffic along Main Street. Horns honked with regularity, not that anyone could see a possible collision coming. I think the honking was just to add a little extra irritation to the ambient sounds of the city. It worked pretty well for all the blind cabbies, though, for they seemed to use them as sonar blips, and in that fashion could avoid most collisions.

The driver went about ten blocks, past the hotels, motels, bordellos, sex shops and adult video stores that dominated the street frontage in Lustland, then turned left onto a numbered avenue. We passed under a highway overpass, and the scene abruptly changed. There were fewer buildings here, mostly factories and warehouses that made or stored the wares of the city. I saw the corporate headquarters of noCumco, makers of erectile dysfunction medicine, that is, medicine that prevented the lustful from being able to achieve sexual arousal or satisfaction. Though its primary purpose was to keep the old schwanzstucker as limp and little as a piece of overcooked macaroni, this was in fact a unisex medicine, very egalitarian. When taken by women, it completely destroyed their libidos, ensuring that they too had a lousy time in the sack. Oh, everyone who in life had committed the cardinal sin of Lust was required to take this medicine on a daily basis.

Not far from the noCumco headquarters, there was a small motion picture studio that specialized in the hideous excuses for porn films that could be had in the video stores along Main Street. When I say hideous, I'm not kidding. The stars of these movies were grotesque parodies of human beings, and watching one of the films was guaranteed to turn your stomach. Or so I'd been told. Fortunately, Lust was not my cardinal sin, so my knowledge of these videos was second-hand.

I had expected Lilith to live in some high-rise flat near her work, but the driver took me to a cozy little suburb a few miles outside the city center. We passed through the entrance to the development, a stone arch supported by two brick pillars. Carved into the arch were the words "Amorous Acres."

The neighborhood was a pleasant one, which meant it was for devils and/or demons, because humans didn't get to live in pleasant neighborhoods. Oh, if one of the damned really hated suburbs, they'd get stuck in one, like Virtual Bob, the virtual reality magnate and frequent client of mine. He was spending his eternity in a cheap 1950's cookie cutter home among a thousand other cheap Fifties cookie cutter homes, receiving eternal damnation through a VR device he himself had invented. Bob's suburb made the Love Canal, that chemically-laced neighborhood in upstate New York that had to be evacuated in the late 1970's because of deadly pollutants, seem like a garden spot.

But if a neighborhood was nice, like this one was, the residents had to be part of the upper echelon of Hell's society. Probably everyone here was a demon, though, since a devil would be more likely to live in a high rent district, with mansions and private country clubs and servants. Still, Amorous Acres beat the crap out of my shabby little sixth floor walkup down on Five.

I thought it odd that Lilith would choose to live in a suburb. As a professional femme fatale, the action of the big city seemed more her style. Yet I also could not deny that there was a sweetness to Lilith, almost a wholesomeness, that seemed compatible with the gentle living of this community. You didn't always see that sweetness, because you were generally overwhelmed by her rampant sexuality. But sometimes, when she didn't think I was looking, her remarkably blue eyes would practically glow with a sort of innocence.

This seems at odds with the whole notion of succubus, I know, but as I've said, the father of all the succubi is an archangel. There has to be some good in Lilith. In her case, it displays most obviously as sweetness and an unexpected

175

kindness, unexpected because kindness is just about the last thing you find in Hell.

My driver turned into a quiet little cul-de-sac. Near the end of the street, he bumped into the curb and stopped the car. "Here ya are, Mac. That'll be seventeen thousand dollars."

Yes, runaway inflation had hit the Netherworld, but I was used to it, and carried a quantity of cash, in large denominations whenever I could, since no one would give one of the damned a credit or even a debit card. I pulled out three ten thousand dollar bills. "Here's thirty. If you'll wait for me, I'll give you thirty more after you drive me back to the city." I wasn't sure I'd be able to get a cab to drive me back to the Escalator, and I didn't want to call BOOH out here if it wasn't necessary.

"Sure thing. You're still my fare, as long as you pay me."

"Great. I'll be out as soon as I can." I handed him the three tens. The exorbitant fare didn't really bother me. I'm on an expense account. Just needed to remember to get a receipt, or the demons in Accounting would bloody every bit of my flesh.

Sixty-nine Lovers' Lane was a modern brick colonial sitting on about a quarter acre of land on the loop of the cul-de-sac. The rich green zoysia of the lawn was perfectly manicured; you could have practiced your putting on it. Artfully pruned shrubs were under the windows. A large and stately oak was the centerpiece of the front yard. I couldn't tell anything about the back, though, because it was obscured by a tall privacy fence.

The sidewalk leading to the front door was flagstone. The door itself was stained a rich cherry. To the left of the door was a white button, which I pressed, rewarding me with a gentle "ding dong."

"I'll be right there!" said a familiar voice. "I'm just taking something out of the oven."

176

The door opened to the accompaniment of my sharp intake of breath. Lilith stood before me in a pale blue and white flowered print dress and a white waist apron. She was holding a baking sheet covered with a dozen chocolate chip cookies. Now, if memory serves, Toll House cookies bake at about 375 degrees, so that sheet of metal they were resting on must have been just about that hot, yet Lilith had nothing between it and her lovely, delicate bare hands. They may have been comely, but they were also impervious to heat, a general requirement for all devils and demons.

Lilith had on very little makeup; her auburn hair was tied back with a bow. Her look was relaxed and completely natural. I'm not sure I had ever seen her more beautiful. She was like a combination of Donna Reed and Samantha Stevens - with a little Jane Mansfield thrown in to account for the difference in cup size.

"Hi, Steve! Would you like a cookie? I just baked them." She held out the sheet.

I took one of the cookies and bit into it. "Delicious!" I said, with my mouth full. It was a little hot - the chocolate chips were almost liquid - but they were great. My diet did not normally consist of delicious cookies, bitter sardines and decrepit oranges being more my standard fare, so I did not mind the heat, grabbing a couple more to nibble on as we talked.

She went to her breakfast table, which was placed in a charming cherry-paneled nook off the kitchen, and set the rest of the cookies down on a trivet to cool. "Would you like an iced tea? We can take our drinks and sit on the patio out back."

I stuffed another cookie into my mouth. "Well," I said, talking with my mouth full, and hoping she wasn't offended, "I don't have a lot of ... "

177

"Nonsense!" she said, going over to a pitcher full of tea. She poured two glasses. "This is the first time you've been to my house. Surely you can spare a minute for a glass of tea."

"I ... I guess so."

"Wonderful!" she beamed, then, carrying the two glasses, wove her way through the modern living room furniture, past the fireplace, and headed toward the two French doors leading to the back yard. Since her hands were full, I hurried ahead of her and opened the doors.

The back patio was a large oval of the same red brick as the house. In the center was a round glass-topped table, on which Lilith placed our drinks, and a chaise lounge, which she claimed, draping herself across the cushion in a most appealing way. I took a chair nearby.

Her backyard had climbing roses against the fence, more manicured bushes, and, in the very back, an arbor. Inside the arbor was what looked like a hot tub.

Though I'm a city boy, I grew up watching shows set in the suburbs, gentle sitcoms like 'The Donna Reed Show,' 'The Dick Van Dyke Show' and 'Bewitched.' I loved the houses of that time period and had always wanted to live in one. This home could have fit the neighborhoods for any of those shows. Well, maybe not the hot tub: I associate that more with the Seventies than the Fifties or Sixties, during which these sitcoms ran. But everything else about Lilith's home had the wholesomeness of those timeless TV neighborhoods. Even Lilith.

That the irresistible Lilith, temptress *par excellence*, would choose to spend her off hours in such quarters was just one more example of the contradictions the succubus embodied. And boy, did she embody them. I noticed that the two top buttons of her dress were open now, and I could see more than a bit of cleavage. A wholesome succubus, but a succubus nonetheless.

And this seemed to explain everything, in a way. A succubus is a sexual chameleon who subconsciously adapts to be optimally attractive to a man. In this case me. And because I had crushes on Donna and Samantha (and Laura Petrie and a few others from back then), Lilith was projecting that vibe too.

To find these paragons of domestic housewifery attractive may seem on the surface to be chauvinistic, contrary to my lifelong support of feminist issues, but the housekeeper role wasn't what turned me on. Donna, Samantha and Laura were just the first really attractive women that penetrated my consciousness during my pubescent years. Well, them and Raquel Welch in "One Million Years BC."

Yowza.

Considering the situation in retrospect, I was dimly aware at the time of the disconnect between the simple, black and white sexual roles projected by the sitcoms that played out in these neighborhoods and the confusing grayness of the feminist revolution that hit its peak just a handful of years later. Think about it: In 1966, at least in TV land, Mary Tyler Moore, for example, was still the stay-at-home mom, dependent on and at least somewhat subservient to her husband. Four years later, she was the quintessential liberated woman.

Belonging to the generation that came of age at that time, floating between two very different social sensibilities, the fact that I found many attractive things about both the old and the new is not really so surprising. After just seeing Asmodeus make a mockery of the feminine mystique, I guess I felt comfort in regressing to the simpler if lopsided values of an earlier age.

"You're awfully quiet, Steve," Lilith said. "What are you thinking about?"

179

Sorry," I said with a wistful smile. "I was just thinking about what a nice house you have, Lilith." I took a sip of my tea, my eyes widening.

"Thank you. Do you like the tea?"

"It's a long island iced tea, isn't it?"

She grinned mischievously. "Of course. I'm wholesome … sometimes … but not so wholesome that I'm gonna drink the regular stuff. Besides, it goes down smoothly, doesn't it?"

"Sure does," I said and drained my glass.

"You know, Steve, if you became a demon, you could have a house like this. Or," she added, shyly, playing with another button on her dress, "you could just move in here with me. There's lots of room."

"Lilith, I … "

"Oh, please, Steve," she panted, leaning toward me. I noticed now that her dress had three buttons open, as if her breasts simply would not be confined by the modest domesticity that was attempting to hold them. She was an eyeful, that's for sure. Samantha never looked that good. Not even Raquel was as stacked as this hot little redhead. "You know how much I care for you."

"And I care for you, Lilith," I said, meaning it. "But this isn't the time to discuss any of this."

"If not now, when?"

"Uh, maybe later," I said, my face reddening, whether from embarrassment or guilt I wasn't sure, since I was feeling a bit of both at the moment. "Now, though, I have to ask you about Flo, that is, Miss Nightingale."

"Humph!" Lilith pouted, blowing an errant lock of red hair from her forehead. "Her again. Okay, Mr. Detective. Ask your questions."

I looked carefully at Lilith. As I've said before, I've never met a demon who could fool me, only the occasional devil, and of those, only the most powerful ones. I nodded. "I'll just ask two. Before I do, though, I want to tell you a couple of things. First, I think you're wonderful."

She looked at me in surprise. "You ... you do?"

"Yes. I also believe you when you say you care for me. And a person who cares for me would never lie to me."

"Really?" This concept seemed novel to Lilith, yet, to her credit, she gave it several seconds of thought before she nodded. "Okay, I guess it stands to reason that you wouldn't lie to people you care for. They would, what's the word, trust you?"

I smiled. "Yes, that's precisely the word. Trust. So, Lilith, did you have any involvement in Miss Nightingale's disappearance?"

My favorite seductress stared me straight in the eyes. "No."

"And do you know of anyone who did?"

"Nope."

"Thanks. And because we care for each other and trust each other, I know you're telling me the truth." *Also, my super sensitive bullshit-o-meter isn't going off. She's on the up and up.*

She smiled warmly then stood, scooping the two empty glasses from the table. "Good. I'm glad that's over. Now, let me get us some more iced tea."

"Well, I really need to be go ... "

"Won't take a second," she said hurrying into the house.

It took about three seconds, not one, but she returned with two full glasses. She had magically changed from her Donna Reed dress to a white terrycloth robe. Stitched over the left breast pocket was the word "His."

Lilith placed the glasses on the table, pulled over the chaise so it was next to me, and sat back down. She took my hand and placed it on 'His." I blushed, and felt a stirring beneath my tool belt. Seems I couldn't spend any time around her without that happening.

I stood and kissed her lips, gently, as I'd done once before. "I've got to go hon, while I still can."

I was halfway to the doors when she called to me. "Steve." I turned. Lilith had untied her robe; she let it drop to the patio bricks. I felt like I was looking at a *Playboy* centerfold, bunny of the year, or the millennium.

I think my jaw was hanging open. That at least explained the fly that was stuck to my tongue.

"Wouldn't you like to spend some time in the hot tub with me?"

With an effort, I spat the fly onto the patio brick. "Ga … ga … gatta run!" Then I bolted.

Behind me Lilith screamed in frustration. "This isn't over, Steve!"

Chapter 17

The cab driver was still parked against the curb. I opened the car door quickly and hopped inside, half-fearful that at any moment an enraged succubus would run out of her house wielding a meat cleaver with my name on it.

"Hell's Escalator, please. And step on it."

"Sure thing, bub." The driver did a U-turn in the cul-de-sac and pulled out of Lovers' Lane. In minutes, we'd left Amorous Acres behind. The density of buildings along the sides of the road increased; we went under the overpass and were back in the city.

The entrance to Hell's Escalator was sandwiched between a porn shop and a brothel and looked more like a subway stop than the primary mode of downward transportation in the Netherworld. I paid the fare, giving the cabbie an extra ten (thousand) as a tip; he'd been a good driver, transporting me in both directions with nary an incident, except for one time when we almost had a head-on collision with a cement mixer. He responded to my yell, though, with a deft weave around the truck. We spent a few seconds on the sidewalk, but no one was hurt, and then we were back down on the street heading for our destination. All in all, a relatively uneventful cab ride.

After paying the driver, I stepped onto one of the treads and began my descent to Five. Since Lustland was on Level Two, there were three levels for me to travel to get back to the office. That gave me an opportunity to think, without the distractions so common to an afterlife in Hell.

Jeez, that was close with Lilith. When she dropped that robe, man! What a body! Another few seconds, and I would have been a goner.

183

All in all, not a bad way to go. Of course, I *was* a goner, being dead already, yet this would have been another sort of no-going-back moment. If I ever had sex with Lilith, there would be no going back to Flo, not because I might not want to, but because I was pretty sure she'd find a boyfriend who'd had sexual congress with a demon to be a bit on the unsavory side.

Yep, major turnoff. No doubt about it.

Still, it was hard to see Lilith in all her glory and not fantasize about what it would be like to, well, shampoo the strawberry wookie. Yep, there now could be no doubt about it, since seeing Lilith unrobed left nothing to the imagination. That was one spectacularly attractive succubus.

Still, I reflected, not any more beautiful than Flo. As I thought about my missing girlfriend, Lilith faded from my consciousness. Was Florence okay? What did I know, really?

Well, for one, no one in Hell can hurt her, not even Satan. Her FloZone protects her from harm. Could she be captured, though? Held against her will? Maybe, though even that isn't certain.

Once again, I assured myself that while Flo might be missing, she was not in mortal, or in her case immortal, danger. That familiar pain in my chest, my worry reflex, which had been progressively building up again, eased a bit. I was still concerned, but I would not allow myself to panic. Not yet. I could always panic later if I wanted to.

A shadow flitted across the sky. I looked up and saw BOOH, sans hat and sunglasses, streaking across the sky. He was probably running an errand for Satan. I waved, and BOOH waved back companionably, which put him in an unplanned barrel roll. He "Skree"d his irritation, but recovered quickly. The whole maneuver looked like he planned it, which was good. In his way, BOOH was very dignified; he *was* after all the original Bat out of Hell, and he had a reputation to maintain. He hated

184

doing anything that looked uncool. He "Skree"d once more, this time in satisfaction, put on a burst of speed and disappeared from my sight.

I went back to my musings. Flo was missing, but Shemp, Asmodeus and Lilith, my three best suspects, didn't seem to be involved. I was hard-pressed to come up with others who might wish her harm. Maybe one of the other Hellions was more miffed at her than Shemp, but I doubted it. Still I was interested to hear what he would have to say, provided of course, that the Stooge was a man of his word and did what he said he would in the first place.

Stepping off the Escalator on Five, I started to turn toward the office then thought better of it. I still had not paid a visit to Flo's apartment. There might be a clue there that would help me, so I zagged instead of zigged and headed toward the Victorian quarter of the Fifth Circle, where Flo had a nice flat on the second floor of a brownstone.

The many chimneys on the crushed-together buildings were working overtime, not to generate heat for the residents of the neighborhood, but to create plume after plume of sooty smoke. As a result, there was an unusual amount of smog in the quarter. Still, it fit the ambiance of the neighborhood. For the moment, I imagined myself in London town on a foggy day, a bit of a stereotype, I know, but that's what it seemed like. Along the cobbled streets were horse-drawn carriages, phaetons and hackneys both, and wagons and carriages ladened with coal, sulfur, rotting vegetables, wilted flowers and offal.

The air was heavy with the odor of raw sewage. no enclosed sewage system in the Victorian quar drooled from the ground floor of each buildin that ran along the sides of the road. H shoveled off the cobblestones and straight

185

some of the damned whose job it was to clean the streets. Between the waste produced by the residents and that from the horses, there was a pungency to the neighborhood that made it hard to draw a breath.

Funny, I reflected, that whenever Flo was around, this odor was nonexistent. Her FloZone must have counteracted bad smells as well as evil intentions.

A wagon drove past me. "Top of the morning to ya," I said in a friendly manner to the driver.

"Fuck off!" he groused. I'd startled him, and his horse, since both of them were blind.

"And to you too," I said cheerily, knowing that would irritate him more than anything. He tried to catch me with his whip, but since he didn't have a real good idea where I was, he missed by a good foot.

I was guessing the fellow's Cardinal Sin was Sullenness, which is not really a Cardinal Sin but sort of a corollary of Sloth, like Apathy and Sadness are. He certainly seemed sullen to me. Most of the damned in Hell try to give each other a little slack. It's bad enough having devils and demons beat you up all the time; we generally don't compound our problems by contributing to the unpleasantness. Of course, his Sin could have been Wrath, but his swing at me was more ill-tempered than angry, so I was betting on Sullenness.

The entrance to Flo's brownstone was never locked, so I let myself in and climbed the stairs, slipping twice on the frayed that loosely covered the steps. Flo's apartment was only the top of the stairway on the second floor. The n and the doorjamb had some of that yellow d in an X across the portal. The consultant ID ied me was still firmly attached to my breast

186

pocket, though, so without hesitation or fear of retribution, I stepped between one of the gaps in the X and into her flat.

The furniture in the living room and library was tossed this way and that, drawers pulled out and contents dumped on the floor. For a moment, my heart began beating rapidly. That's when I happened to spy two eight by ten glossies on the kitchen table. Both were in protective mylar sleeves with the Hell's Police Department decal on them. The one labeled "Apartment of Florence Nightingale, Before" showed a tidy living room. The second, marked "Apartment of Florence Nightingale, After" displayed the same chaotic scene I was looking at now. Yet the two photographs were timestamped only a few minutes apart. I concluded the mess was caused by the demonic cops themselves. Either they were looking for evidence or just an opportunity to cause some mayhem. *Probably the latter,* I concluded with irritation.

Also on the table was a pile of mail, and it made me think of the letter Flo had mailed just before she left the hospital and disappeared. *I wonder who she had written.* The top piece of Flo's mail was the most recent issue of *The New England Journal of Medicine.* I looked with some interest at the cover story, "Advances in Rhinoplasty." Since I have a nose the size of a beagle's, I picked it up, thinking there might be some good before and after photos.

That's when I discovered the note. There was a half-sized piece of paper, slightly crumpled, as if the reader of the note, presumably Flo, had been upset by it. The short message on it, composed with letters cut out of magazines, said,

I'LL GET YOU, MY PRETTY!

My heart began to beat rapidly again. This was the first scrap of concrete evidence I'd found that indicated someone wished Flo ill. Looking around the kitchen, I found a Ziploc bag, the gallon size, and using my needle-nose pliers, picked up the note and dropped it into the bag, sealing it closed. I had no idea how to get fingerprints off the note, but maybe Pinkerton could do it.

Those clowns! They were so interested in trashing Flo's place that they didn't even bother doing a proper search.

I quickly looked over the rest of the apartment, which was in a similar state of disarray, so trying to find any more clues was pretty much impossible. All of this vandalism, in Flo's sanctuary, offended me. Still, I was grateful. That I'd found anything at all in the chaos was an unusual stroke of good fortune.

For a few minutes, I examined the scene in Flo's bedroom. The mattress and linens had been yanked from the bed frame and tossed against the wall. A lamp that normally sat on her small round bedside table had been knocked to the floor, cracking the porcelain. I picked up the lamp and placed it back in its accustomed place. Then I took a moment for myself, for my memories, thinking back to that one magical evening when Flo and I had made love. With a sigh, I turned back to the living room.

A few more minutes convinced me that nothing else was to be found, or if there was something, the bedlam created by the demon cops had obliterated it. I finally had a lead, though, a piece of evidence, maybe a good piece. Carefully, I tucked the Ziploc bag inside my coveralls - my tool belt was cinched tight enough to prevent the bag from falling down a trouser leg, so I was confident it would stay put. I zipped up my work suit, stepped through the X, headed down the stairs and out the building. Then I hoofed my way back to the trailer.

Chapter 18

The office was empty. While waiting for Orson to show, I poured myself a cup of coffee, sat down at my desk. The work orders in my wire inbox, dumped there one after another with a juggernaut persistence by the pneumatic tube system suspended two feet above my desktop, looked to number about two hundred. I pulled them out to make room for any incoming ones, placing them on a far corner of my desk. *On second thought* … I grabbed the pile and dumped them in File Thirteen.

That would be the waste basket, in case you didn't know.

Throwing the work orders away without reviewing them first was taking a bit of a chance, but at most there would only be a couple that needed doing. A one out of a hundred chance that I'd get nailed for ignoring my duties: I'd take those odds, spending the time normally allotted to triaging the work orders to focus on Flo's disappearance.

From inside my coveralls, I extracted the Ziploc bag. With my pliers, I pulled the note out of the bag, laying it on the metal surface of my desk.

At that moment, the door opened, and Orson ambled into the room. Seeing I was drinking coffee, he grabbed his Blimpie's mug and went over to the Mr. Coffee. I'd left him some, but it was the dregs of the pot. That didn't make the coffee any worse, just a bit thicker. Nonetheless, he dumped out the burnt remains of the morning's pot and made a fresh one.

"What took you so long?" I asked, still studying the note.

"What else? That damn Elevator!" he cursed. "I must have waited over an hour for it."

"Did you discover anything at the mine?"

189

"Only that no one could be seen." The Mr. Coffee gurgled one last time then fell silent, as if someone had choked it. Orson poured a cup and sat down on his stool. He cursed again when he burned his tongue on the hot black liquid.

Everyone in Hell drinks their coffee black, no milk or cream, not that we'd have access to them down here anyway. Caffeine condiments would be too much of a treat to allow the damned to have. Hell, after all, has never been described as a land of milk and honey. We *can* get non-dairy creamer, but since it tastes like bauxite, no one uses it. Sugar doesn't exist in Hell, except in the hands of the Underworld's elite, individuals like Lilith, I noted to myself, who could even make a respectable chocolate chip cookie with it. My stomach grumbled as I remembered my little treat, thinking ruefully that if I were a demon, I'd probably get to have as much sugar as I wanted. With a sigh, I went to our crate to grab one of the shriveled, decrepit oranges we kept there. It was a new container, so I used a crowbar to open it. With little enthusiasm, I took one of the oranges from the crate. Usually the fruit had little flavor, but it was something to eat, so I sat back at my desk and began to peel off the rind. I stuck a slice in my mouth, and my lips puckered. This fresh batch was unusually tart. Exceptionally tart or incredibly tasteless: it was hard to decide which was worse.

"It was really eerie, Steve. Well, everything about Hell is pretty eerie, but the mine is usually like a termite mound. It just teems with activity. To see it virtually abandoned was beyond strange."

"Virtually?"

Orson shrugged. "Well, I can't be sure. There was no one at the entrance, and all of the equipment was as still as corpses, which I suppose is appropriate enough. All of the time cards - man, there must have been thousands of them - were in their

190

slots next to the time clock. I pulled out a few to check them; they all showed the workers as off the clock."

My friend blew across the surface of his coffee, cooling it down a little. He took another sip, this time without burning his tongue. "The entrance to the mine was gated closed, with a big chain and padlock connecting the two doors. Still, it's a big gate, and there was enough wiggle room even for me to slip between them."

"I traveled a few hundred yards into the mine. Still nobody: the ground didn't even have footprints, as if the mine had been deserted for years, instead of a few hours, and the dirt and dust had shifted, removing all traces of activity. It was really weird."

"Humph. That *is* strange."

"Yeah. The farther into the mine I went, the darker things got; all the lanterns had been extinguished." He shuddered. "It was kind of unnerving. Anyway, soon I was traveling along the edge of the main corridor, my hand against the rock, going forward by feel alone. Another hundred feet and the corridor split. I decided at that point it was the better part of valor to get out of there before I got lost or fell into a pit. But before I did, I thought I heard something."

"What?"

"There was a furtive scraping sound coming from the left fork of the tunnel. And I thought I heard whispers or people mumbling."

"So the mine is not completely deserted?"

Orson shrugged. "I can't be sure, because I barely heard anything, but I don't think so. Still, I wouldn't want to go in there again without my hard hat and a flashlight."

"Interesting, though I don't know if it's relevant to Flo's disappearance." I ate another slice of sour orange, grimacing at the taste. "I found out some interesting things as well."

"Yeah? Like what?"

There was the moist plopping sound of a couple of work orders coming through the pneumatic tube, but we ignored them. "I talked with both Asmodeus and Lilith. I'm sure Lilith is innocent."

Orson rolled his eyes. "Says the horny maintenance worker."

"Stop it," I said, kicking gently at his stool, which chose that moment to pitch Orson to the floor. The kick didn't destabilize things - the chair often and without warning dumped off my friend all by itself - but my kick was ill-timed, and I sure looked like the culprit. Orson shot me a dirty look as he righted his stool and climbed back aboard. "Sorry. Anyway, I've never met a demon yet who could lie convincingly to me."

"Yeah, I've noticed that you're pretty good at spotting dissimulations."

"You mean bullshit."

"That's what I said," he replied haughtily.

"Whatever. Anyway, I'm sure she's innocent. I'm pretty sure about Asmodeus as well, though it's harder to tell with devils, especially with Hell's royalty."

"Why do you think he's innocent ... at least in this?"

"Like what we told Azazel earlier. Asmosdeus views Flo as a challenge. He wants to seduce her, not force himself on her."

"Yes, that makes sense."

I nodded. "When I got back to Five, I stopped by Flo's apartment. It had been ransacked."

"Now that's interesting too," Orson said, leaning forward on his stool and almost tumbling to the ground again, before he caught himself on my desktop. "Any clues as to who did that?"

I grimaced. "Oh, I know who did that. The Underworld's version of cops. But they were just tearing the place up for the hell of it."

192

"Oh." Orson looked disappointed.

"But because, unlike them, I actually was looking for a lead, I found something that they didn't."

"Yeah? What?"

"A note." I beckoned to him with my index finger. "Come around to my side of the desk. Don't touch it now. The clue, I mean. You can touch the desk if you want to." Orson stared at the ceiling in exasperation, sighed once and looked at the note. "I've been careful not to get any fingerprints on it. I don't know if there will be any, and I haven't a clue how to dust for prints anyway, but maybe Pinkerton could help us check."

Orson read the note aloud. "'I'LL GET YOU MY PRETTY!' An obvious reference to the 'Wizard of Oz.'"

"Yeah. Maybe he likes Judy Garland."

"Or old movies."

"Or both."

"Nineteen thirty-nine. Did you know, Steve, that 1939 is considered by many to be the greatest year in Hollywood history? An amazing number of great films were released then."

"Interesting. Did you have a film out that year?"

My friend shook his head. "'Citizen Kane,' which I think you know was my first movie, came out in 1941. But 1939 saw, in addition to 'The Wizard of Oz,' 'Gone With The Wind,' 'Destry Rides Again," 'Mr. Smith Goes To Washington,' 'Jesse James,' 'The Hunchback of Notre Dame,' 'Goodbye Mr. Chips.' Oh, and 'Ninotchka,' 'Gunga Din' and a raft of others."

"Wow!" I said, impressed. "That's amazing though essentially useless information."

Orson snorted. "Tell me it's useless the next time you play *Trivial Pursuit*."

"Fine. I guess you noticed the letters were cut out from magazines."

193

He snorted again. "Yes, a trite but I suppose time-tested method of disguising one's handwriting. So, what do you think this note tells us?"

Frowning, I slid the paper back into the Ziploc and placed the bag in my top desk drawer for safekeeping. "Mainly, that Flo had been threatened before she disappeared. But why didn't she tell me at coffee this morning?"

"She probably didn't want to worry you. I think the note also implies that she was the victim of foul play."

"I ... I think you're right." My chest bunched up in a knot again. *No one may be able to hurt her down here, I keep telling myself, but maybe Dora was right about imprisonment. Why not? It's not like she's got super powers,* repeating to myself what we told Allan earlier. *Just her FloZone.* "Which puts us right back at the original question. Who would do something like this?"

"Nobody that I know," said a voice from behind us.

We almost jumped out of our skins. Putty Face was standing just inside our office door. He had let himself in, not bothering to knock, and we'd been so engrossed in our conversation that we'd not heard him.

"Shemp! Ah, Mr. Howard," I amended.

"Shemp is fine, or Sam if you prefer. My given name was Samuel. Shemp just stuck because my Lithuanian mother couldn't pronounce Sam. Shemp is what came out."

"Well," I said, standing and offering him my desk chair, which he took, "if you don't mind, then, I'll call you Shemp. That's how I knew you, growing up."

"Growing up? You watched my movies?"

I grinned. "You bet. Every Saturday morning for a decade. I loved the Stooges."

He shrugged. "A lot of people did. They especially liked Curly," he said in a wistful voice.

"What can we do for you?" Orson asked.

"Well, it's what I can do for you. Or can't, rather." He rubbed his chin in thought.

"What do you mean?" I asked, offering him some coffee in another one of our spare mugs, the "Satan rules. Humans drool" cup. He accepted it without comment, then took a sip. "Jeez! This stuff tastes like shit!"

"Is yours any better?" I asked, looking at Orson skeptically.

"Actually, yeah. Not much, but a bit."

This was a staggering revelation. Somewhere in Hell, you could get better coffee than we could brew. Of course, Orson and I might not be able to. That was likely part of our damnation, because we both loved the drip from the old bean. Perhaps Shemp didn't care as much, so he got better coffee than we did.

"Still," he added, in an attempt to be civil, "it's the thought that counts." He took another sip, winced and set the cup to one side. I guess civility only takes one so far.

"You were saying?" Orson prompted.

Shemp shrugged. "I was sayin' exactly nothin', which I suppose is information of a sort."

"Please," I said, sitting on the edge of my desk. "Explain."

He shrugged. "Well, as I told you I would, I put out a call to the Hellions about Nightingale. We have quite a network, you know," Shemp said, his chest swelling with pride. "We have this phone tree, see, where one of us can call ten Hellions, then each of them calls ten Hellions, et cetera, et cetera. It only takes four levels of calls to reach the entire network. We always know where everyone is, since they're more or less chained to their eternal damnation, so connecting is pretty easy. Funny," he said, drawing a smiley face in a bit of spilled coffee on the desktop. "It's one of the few things that works really well in Hell."

"Anyway … " Orson said, trying to restrain his impatience.

"Anyway, no one has seen hide nor hair of Miss Nightingale. We have Hellions in all the big cities, down here on Five, of course, but also in New Rome, Lustland, Gluttons' Gap, Sloth City, Glasgow by the Kraken. We even have contacts in Shit Town, uh, Tae Bayan on Seven, and Badhgag down on Eight. Nothing." He shook his head. "There have been rumors, naturally, that she's disappeared. That kind of news travels fast. And something else," he said with a frown.

I sat on the edge of my desk. "What?"

"Well, apparently there are some other people missing as well. A cabbie here on Five and some farmer up on Four."

"Hmmm." I hadn't heard this. "Got any names?"

He shook his head. "Nope. Sorry. One thing I can share, though, is that to a soul, every Hellion swears they had nothin' to do with this."

"And you believe them?" Orson asked.

Shemp looked up at the big guy. "Yeah, I do. What's more, none of them believe a human is involved in her disappearance."

"Why's that?" I asked.

"The same reason I told you earlier. Everyone loves Nightingale. I mean, how could you not?" Shemp stood. "That's all I got. Now I've gotta scoot. I have an early shift at Red Square, and the maître d'evil there will pull my nuts off if I'm late."

Since that was a common form of torment down here, one I'd experienced myself a time or two, I knew he wasn't exaggerating. "Well thanks for your help."

196

Shemp paused at the door. He looked appraisingly at me. "Speaking of balls, it took a lot of them for you to stare down ten thousand Hellions like you did that day on the Stairway to Heaven. Did you really stop all of us so that the rest of the damned wouldn't suffer?"

"Yeah." *That, and Satan and Beezy didn't really leave me any choice.* "Sorry you fell down all those stairs."

"Eh, no big deal. Kind of reminded me of the old routines in our movies." He opened the door.

"Oh, Shemp?" I called after him.

"Yeah?"

"Just curious. What was your Cardinal Sin? Anger? Sullenness?" He had always seemed so angry to me that I figured it must be one of the two.

He blushed. "No. Envy. I was jealous that Curly got all the attention. Everyone seems to have forgotten that I was the original third Stooge. I actually spent more years with the team than he did."

That explained so much to me. Shemp had spent the last twenty-five years of his life in Curly's shadow, not to mention another hundred or so down here. No wonder he looked sullen. *Time for a little truth telling.* "Well, Curly was a comic genius, no doubt, but he was so over the top that sometimes I thought it was more like watching Curly and the Two Stooges. For what it's worth, I think the group as a comic ensemble always worked better with you in the third slot. Everything was more balanced, and you three worked off each other better. That's my opinion anyway."

Shemp looked at me in surprise. Then the most amazing thing happened. His face unfolded from the perpetual frown that he seemed to always carry around the Underworld, the frown that made me think he was so ugly, the frown that got me calling him Putty Face to begin with. And he smiled.

He had the most beautiful smile. It transformed his face, and there was Shemp Howard, the nice, gentle guy I'd read about, admired in the movies.

Shemp reached out his hand and I shook it. "You know, Minion, I mean, Steve, you're alright."

"Thanks Shemp. So are you."

When the smoke cleared, Orson was holding out a rag for each of us. I guess he saw this coming.

"Got creamed," Shemp mumbled, wiping the light brown pudding from his face.

"Me too. Hey, what's your poison?"

"Butterscotch," he said, as Orson helped him to his feet. "You?"

"Coconut."

Shemp reached down for my hand and pulled me up from the floor. "Oh. Those welts look like they hurt."

"They do. I'm allergic, but they'll be gone in a few seconds, so no biggie."

He nodded. "That's good. See you around Steve, Orson."

"Bye," we both said, and then the Stooge was gone.

Chapter 19

"Well, that was interesting," Orson said, as he closed the door behind Shemp. "Nothing conclusive, but in a couple of hours his Hellion network covered more of the Underworld than we could have in a year."

"You said it. I think, without evidence to the contrary, we should assume that ... "

"Wait a second. What have we here?"

"What? What did you find?"

Orson reached in my trash can and pulled out the pile of work orders I'd discarded. "Steve, Steve," he said, in a tsk, tsk sort of tone.

I flushed. "Well, I was in a hurry."

"But that's not how we do things around here." Orson wiped Shemp's coffee spill off my desktop with a corner of butterscotch-soaked rag then plopped the work orders on the surface. "You, of all people should know that."

"Give me a break, Orson. That's my girlfriend that's gone missing."

My friend blew at his mustache whiskers until they floated parallel to the floor, a trick he often performed when showing his disapproval. Since I wasn't much good at growing facial hair, I always found this impressive. "Maybe so, but if we don't at least make a token effort at performing our duties, Beezy will pull off *our* nuts."

"Fine, fine. Triage away."

Satisfied, Orson settled his capacious personage in my chair and began to sort. "No," he said after examining the first order, placing it to one side. "No, no," and two more went on top of the first. He straightened his small discard pile then returned his attention to the big stack of unsorted orders. Orson held up a fourth work order, read it twice. "Ah ... no," he said.

Trying to contain my impatience, I stared at the ceiling, though I knew no help would come from that direction.

"No, maybe ... on second thought, no." The discard pile was growing, and the time clock on the wall ticked away the seconds with a deliberate click ... click ... click

"Jeez, Orson! Would you hurry it up?" I finally blurted out.

"It would go faster if you'd help, I ... "

A gray mote of smoke floated in the air before us. The mote turned to a wisp, the wisp to a plume. Then the smoke curled in upon itself, forming a ring. The ring began to spin and darken, until it was the color of pitch; tongues of flame erupted from its center.

"Minion," a deep voice said from the disc's heart. I was fast becoming familiar with that basso profundo, though I would never grow comfortable with it. If evil and anger could take the form of sound, this would be it. My heart was pounding in my chest like a punching bag being pummeled by a heavyweight.

"A ... Azazel?"

"You will now report to me," the voice continued, "in person." The disc of smoke grew until it stretched from floor to ceiling, then an irresistible force like gravity came from the center of the vortex and pulled me into it.

"STEEEEVVE ... !" Orson screamed behind me, but his voice was soon drowned out by an ear-splitting rat-a-tat-tat. I felt like a BB, spinning and slamming repeatedly against the sides of a tin can. For a moment, I lost all awareness, unusual in Hades, especially for me. After all, I had dropped four times through the Throat of Hell, which would make most anybody pass out, and still managed to keep my wits about me.

200

When I came to my senses, I found that they weren't providing me much information. I couldn't see anything, nor could I move. Well, I thought, I might be able to move if allowed, but something was restraining me.

Without warning, an intense light stabbed at my eyes. Screaming from the pain, I looked away, downward, and tried to will away the bright colored circles of the afterimage from the glare. Still blind, I closed my eyes for a moment to give my shocked pupils a chance to recover. On finally opening my peepers, I saw why I couldn't move. I was shackled to a stiff wooden chair.

That was about all I could see. The space I was in was undefinable, with walls that were either black or so far in the distance that they might as well not have existed. I couldn't even see the floor on which the chair sat. There was only me, the chair, my restraints and that intense, white light above me.

"Minion." It was the same evil voice I'd heard coming from the disc of smoke.

Slowly I looked up at the light. It was still searingly bright, but I forced my eyes to adjust to it as best they could. Behind the glow, against the black background, I could detect a presence, little more than a silhouette, but enough to know someone stood very near me.

"Why am I chained to a chair?" I gasped.

A creepy laugh came from the shadows. "I find I get more information from humans this way."

With an effort, I took a few calming breaths. My mouth was dry, and I had to force out my words. "Azazel," I said slowly. "This isn't necessary."

"Just tell me what you know."

I swallowed hard. "Yes, of course I'll tell you. You don't need to treat me like a criminal."

Azazel's whip lashed out from the darkness, slicing diagonally across the full of my face. I howled in pain and instinctively tried to pull away from him, yet my bonds held me fast.

"Do not dare to question my methods! Now, tell me, what have you learned of Nightingale's disappearance? Do not make me ask again."

I nodded wearily. He couldn't really hurt me, since I was already dead, but the survival instinct in a human is strong, and an aversion to pain stays with you, even down here. "We investigated our primary suspects, Asmodeus, Lilith, the Hellions. None of them seems to have a motive, and I don't believe any were involved."

"Belief? What kind of evidence is that?"

"It's … it's all I've got right now, but I've always been able to read demons. None of them has ever been able to lie to me."

Azazel laughed again. "That you know."

"Yes," I said slowly. He had me there. "I suppose that's true, but I'm pretty sure Lilith wasn't lying."

"Tell me, human, do your magical powers of discernment extend to devils?"

"Some of the lower level ones, yes, I think so."

"But not a prince of Hell, like Asmodeus?"

I shrugged, or I would have, if I hadn't been rendered immobile by my shackles. "No, but in his case, he has a good motive for leaving Flo, Miss Nightingale, alone."

"And what would that be?" he asked with amusement, the kind of amusement a sadist would get from sending a paraplegic down a flight of stairs.

"Like I told you earlier, he wants to get her in the sack of her own free will. He admitted as much to me when I interviewed him a while ago. Also, there were at least forty women up there

202

he'd been screwing all day. They all insisted he had been nowhere but his office."

"And why would you trust what they say in the presence of the very devil who had them in his power?"

I licked at the blood that was now flowing freely into my mouth. "I guess I can't completely, but this was a group of feminists, all very strong personalities. They spent a lifetime fighting against sexist males like Asmodeus. He might have been able to cow some or even most of them, but I can't believe Stanton would lie for him, or Ayn Rand for that matter," I added, remembering the look she gave me before enacting that X-rated scene from Star Trek.

"Humph," Azazel grumbled. "Ayn Rand was not a feminist."

"No, I don't think so either. We studied her in my Twentieth Century literature class in college, and my professor ... "

"Shut up."

I swallowed hard. "Yes sir."

The devil was silent for a moment "Very well," he said at last. "I will accept his alibi, flimsy as it is." He paused. "What about the other princes of Hell?"

I hadn't really checked them out for this case, but I'd gone through this drill only a few days earlier so felt I could answer the question. "None of the others really has a motive, except for Satan himself. He has told me he wasn't involved, and I have to take that at face value, because there's no way I can check up on him. For the rest, Mammon never leaves his Pantheon, Leviathan never leaves his ocean and Belphegor is just too lazy to bother."

"What of Beelzebub?"

"Again, no motive, but I haven't checked him out. I could ask him. He'd probably tell me the truth."

Azazel snorted derisively. "Yes, he probably would. That fat boob. What kind of devil tells the truth?"

"Got me."

"Assuming then, for the moment, that the princes aren't involved directly, that still doesn't rule out their underlings." He mulled what little information I'd provided. "What of the humans?"

"I don't think they could have managed it ... sir."

"And why not?"

I told him what the imp had said about Flo disappearing in a flash of light outside the hospital.

"WHAT?" he roared. "This is new information to me. How do you know this and not I?"

"TNK-el told me," I offered reluctantly. I didn't particularly dislike the runt devil, and I didn't appreciate being forced into the role of snitch either. (Nobody likes a snitch.) Still, the prospect of another taste of the devil's lash was not particularly appetizing. Blood was now dripping in my right eye; it started to water. Stung a bit too.

"And he did not tell me. ARGH!" Azazel sent a jet of flame straight up. I tried to follow it, but the Hellfire seemed to go on forever, like a laser beam shot at the moon or something. "TNK-el shall pay for withholding this information! For that matter, why are you telling me only now? Did you just learn about the flash of light?"

"No, sir. I, well, I forgot about it the last time we talked." I cringed, expecting the whip to fall again.

But instead the devil only did his creepy laugh. "You forgot. Now that I can believe. Moron."

I guess that was deserved. "Sorry. Anyway, I figure a human couldn't make Flo disappear magically like that. Besides, we're all kept on a pretty short leash down here. As I told you, the

Hellions have been checking things out for me, and they haven't found anything that points to the damned being a part of this."

"The *Free* Hellions. What a joke! Still, no human could hide information from me, and certainly not a gang run by the Three Stooges, so you're probably correct. Then, based upon your pitiful investigation, know one knows anything."

For some reason, I thought I detected relief in his voice. *Odd.* "Not that I can tell, no. Flo just disappeared without a trace." A spark of rebellion in me stirred, and I decided to withhold information about the one piece of concrete evidence I had, the note from her apartment.

The lash flashed out at me again, striking my face from a different angle. Wincing, I imagined myself branded with a bloody red X. "Why should I believe you?"

My lips were wet. Reflexively I licked them again. Tasting the hot saltiness of my blood: that was good. It distracted me from my fear, allowing me to think again.

I'm dead. He can't do anything to me, not really. Yet, I'm frightened. No, terrified. Why does this guy scare me so much?

I tried to clamp down on my thoughts, suddenly remembering that earlier in the day Azazel seemed to demonstrate the ability to read my mind. I had always found Satan's mind-reading powers just about the scariest thing about him. It allowed him to peel me like an onion, expose me completely. I might have been one of the damned, but I always prided myself on the power of my mind. That Satan could violate my brain so effortlessly was what kept me in perpetual fear of him. I thought this guy could do the same, yet now, curiously, he was quiet. Perhaps he was just a good guesser.

Azazel remained silent, which was just what I needed at the moment, for it gave me time to get mad. "Why should you believe me? Call it a hunch, bub," I said at last.

The devil's sharp claws raked across my chest, but I bore it. *It's only pain. I'm used to pain.*

"Insolence!"

"Listen, you asshole, I'm not afraid of you!"

"You lie!" said the voice.

I exhaled heavily, but it was in exasperation, not fear. "Maybe I *am* afraid of you, but I'm not scared enough to put up with this shit. You may be a big-ass devil, but I don't work for you. My boss is Beelzebub, and my boss's boss is Satan himself. They're they only ones who can push me around like this."

Azazel hissed like a snake. "Satan! The trivial dictator of this trivial domain. Ha! By rights I should have his job." The devil paused. "If things had gone differently, *I* would have been the Antagonist, not that pretty boy, Lucifer."

A hand reached around the light and turn it upward, illuminating the devil's cruel face. "It was I who was the serpent in the Garden of Eden, I who tempted Adam and Eve, I who made them fall." The voice continued. "It was Azazel who was the Scapegoat for all the sins of the Jews. I am Evil Incarnate. Not Satan! Azazel! Bwahahahahahaha!"

That settles it. This guy is a definite nut case. Sheesh.

As Azazel talked, I watched his face glide from anger to rage to madness. His eyes turned from red to onyx then back to red again; spittle ran out of his mouth. After a while, it was hard to look at his hideous visage, and I averted my eyes.

That's when I saw that I was not in a huge empty space; there was in fact a black wall behind him. And, curiouser and curiouser, on the wall hung a gallery of black and white photos, like individual mug shots in a police station. Abruptly I realized that that was probably exactly where I was, in some interrogation room of the HPD, in view of Azazel's position in Hell. With a gasp, I recognized each face. Flo, Nikola Tesla, Louis

206

Braille, Pinkerton. Even Orson. All friends of mine. Across the pictures of Flo, Nicky and Louie, someone had drawn X's with a thick black marker, like a Sharpie.

"What are those photos doing on the wall?"

In an instant, Azazel's face shifted from insanity to paranoia. I was sure of it. He looked like a kid, a big evil kid with horns on his head, but a kid nonetheless, who had just been caught stealing hubcaps or something. Quickly he swung the light back in my eyes, blinding me again, making me turn my head back to the floor.

"Bah!" he said in disgust. "You and your assistant are useless to me." I felt a tingling in my breast pocket. "I have rescinded your consulting status and taken back the badges I gave you."

"Badges?" I said, licking more blood from my lips. "Heh, heh. We don't need no stinking badges."

"You and your old movies! Get out of my sight."

Everything went black again.

For a time, I was suspended in the darkness. I could no longer feel my shackles, nor the hard surface of the chair beneath me. There were no sounds, no smells, no sights.

For some reason, this frightened me more profoundly than anything I had ever experienced. Even when I'd died, I hadn't had a moment like this, of consciousness between states of being. I tried to cry out, to make a sound, to proclaim in some fashion that I existed, even if it was an afterlife existence, but nothing came from my lips. Then I realized I couldn't feel my lips at all, not even the wounds on my face. I could no longer feel my restraints because I couldn't feel anything at all.

All that seemed left to me was my mind, and yet, as I pondered my own consciousness, my thoughts became confused, fewer. Even my mind - my pitiful human brain of which I'd always been so proud - seemed to be deserting me. It

207

was growing smaller and smaller by the moment, capable of less.

With great effort, a thought came to me. A horrifying thought. Was this true death? Was my soul being destroyed? Did Azazel have such power that he could destroy the seemingly immortal me? Could he do this to anyone, even Flo?

My mind was going black, and with dreadful surety I knew that if my mind failed, so would I. Forever. Somehow, I had to fight this inexorable force trying to shut down my brain. I had to keep thinking, to survive, if only to help my Flo, my friends.

Think, I willed. *Think! Think!*

The clanging started up. I was aware of my body again as it spun in an inky vortex, and then I was spat from the mouth of the smoke disc. I landed on top of my desk, belly first. "Oomph!"

My friend was with me in an instant. "Steve!" Orson shouted in concern. "Are you okay?"

For a moment, I could not speak. The memory of that awful time-away-from-time in the black void was haunting me, would probably haunt me forever.

But I had to keep moving. Movement was existence. Thought was existence. Speech was existence. "Okay enough," I said finally, as he helped me off the desk. I wiped off the remaining blood on my face with my sleeve. Staring at the bright crimson brought me back to myself.

Thought was existence. Speech was existence. And, at least for me, so was sarcasm. "Azazel just *loved* my report."

"Really?"

"No," I said. "I think we're off the case."

Orson, nodded. "My badge disappeared just before you popped out of that vortex of smoke. Looks like yours is gone, too."

208

I laughed. It must have sounded pretty grisly, because Orson flinched. With an effort, I smiled my best, normal smile and watched my friend relax. "Like I told that lunatic back there, we don't need no stinking badges."

Despite himself, Orson chuckled. "Good one. But what about Flo?"

I thought about the black X through her photo, as well as those through the faces of others on that wall. I thought about the nothingness from which I'd emerged and hoped that my friends had not endured that. Then I looked at Orson. No X for him, not yet, but his picture was on that wall too. "No problem," I said to my assistant, patting his arm. "We'll go freelance."

Chapter 20

Orson took a damp cloth to my face, cleaning off some blood that had clotted around the cuts. They were taking longer than usual to heal.

"Man, Azazel really let you have it."

"You said it." I winced as he got a little too near one of the slices during his ministrations. "I tell you, Orson, that guy is completely crackers! He summons me to report, then immediately treats me as if I were a POW or a murderer or something."

My friend sat down heavily on his stool. That, of course, is what he usually did, i.e., sit down heavily. Unavoidable, really, for him, considering he weighed in at over 28 stone.

Those English. Still hanging onto a stone as a unit of measurement after all these centuries. Still, in Orson's case, it seemed to fit. But I digress.

"So, do you think he's more crazy than evil?"

I shrugged. "Who knows? I mean, devils are pretty much evil by definition, but I've never seen one that makes Dr. Moreau look like Ned Flanders."

Orson looked puzzled. "I get the Moreau reference, but who's Ned Flanders?"

"Skip it. About five years after your time. My point is, he's the craziest devil I've ever seen."

"That might make him the most dangerous devil in Hell."

"You said it. Satan is evil, but he is master of his domain."

"Of course he is!" Orson said, puzzled again. "He's the Earl of Hell. Why would you think otherwise?"

"Sorry. Again, a cultural reference from after you died."

"Well, cut it out and stick to plain English. We don't have time for you to keep translating for me."

"You're right, we don't." I looked with paranoia around the office, half-afraid that Azazel was hiding in the corner, ready to come after me again. With a reasonable assurance that we were alone, I told my story. "Orson, he had me chained to a chair, while he gave me the third degree, blinding spotlight and everything. He was ranting at the universe, claiming he should have been the ruler of Hell, not Satan."

"Where were you?"

"I was right there, of course. Oh," I said, when Orson's eyes narrowed in irritation. I rubbed my jaw. "That's hard to say. I think maybe the police station, perhaps an interrogation room, though I can't be sure. Everything was dark, except for that damned light in my face. Yet, at the end, Azazel directed the light at his own face briefly, allowing me to see the wall behind him."

"And ... ?"

"Orson, there were black and white photographs, eight by ten glossies, like mug shots or posters you might see in a police station for wanted criminals. Except the people in the photos weren't criminals at all."

"What do you mean?"

"They were ... they were my friends. I saw pictures of Flo, Nicky, Allan, Louis, even ... even you," I said, hesitantly.

Orson reared back on his stool, nearly losing his balance and falling to the floor. "What ... what else?"

My head was beginning to hurt, not from the whip lashes, or even the lingering memory of that dark place, but from the possible meaning behind the photos. "The pictures of Flo, Nicky and Louis had big X's drawn through them."

"Was there a picture of BOOH?"

I smiled grimly. "I'd like to see someone try messing with BOOH. Devil, demon or human, BOOH could probably take most of them, and anyone he couldn't, Satan would demolish. Nobody puts baby in a corner."

"Huh? Steve, did you just do it again? Never mind. Of course you did. I get it though. Satan is very protective of his pet bat. But what about me and Allan?"

"There isn't an X through either of your pictures." *Yet.*

"Well, that's something I suppose. But what does it all mean?"

I reached a conclusion, double-checked it mentally and nodded. "I think I know. Someone is targeting my friends."

"Who? And Why?"

I stood up from my chair. From my desk, I retrieved the Ziploc bag and put it inside my coverall top again. "I don't know, and I don't know, but it's time to find out. Look, all we've really got is that Flo is missing and that she had been threatened. I think we need to check on Nicky, Louis and Allan. I have a bad feeling about the first two, but I want to go to Nicky's farm and the cabbie dispatch center just to be sure. With Allan, at least we can warn him, if it's not too late, and maybe he can help us figure out something from the note Flo received."

Orson got off his chair. "Sounds like a plan. Or at least, something to do. I'm tired of sitting here. Oh, by the way, you were right. None of those work orders were worth doing. Well," Orson amended, going over to the most recent of the tall piles of ignored work orders in the corner of our trailer. He rifled through the top dozen and pulled out one. "This one we can handle, since we need to go there anyway, and it will show Beezy we're still doing our jobs." He showed the order to me.

It had been filled out by a demon so was a little hard to read, but after I puzzled out the scribbly cursive, I nodded. "Right. As

212

long as it's an easy fix. We've got a lot of ground to cover. Still, we might as well start there. It's close."

He nodded, and we exited the office.

We left the industrialized section of Level Five, where our trailer was located, and headed into the citified portions some ten blocks away. Here there were office buildings, tenements, fast food restaurants, the inevitable Starbucks on every corner. Not to mention the grid of city streets, choked with traffic, all but halted by traffic lights on every corner. Car exhaust commingled with the already noxious scent of burning brimstone, making Orson and me cough like a couple of three-pack-a-dayers.

There were thousands of pedestrians on the busy sidewalks, crossing the streets. Very few of them were getting run over today, which was unusual, but that's probably because the traffic was so snarled in the city center that most vehicles couldn't move fast enough to catch a walker who was paying attention. Oh, occasionally one would get clipped, but that was just an artistic touch by Hell's management.

If you really wanted to get creamed, you needed to get out a little ways, on one of Hell's tollroads (there are no freeways here) or its broader avenues, like the Highway to Hell, where a vehicle could work up some speed.

Anyway.

Our destination was a large rectangular box of a building with garage bay doors on the ground level and automobile-wide ramps coming down from its second story. We stepped inside the structure; dozens of yellow cabs were parked on the large garage floor. Swarming over the taxis were their drivers.

"Blam!"

"Shit! I told you to stop pumping. Now you've gone and blown the tire."

"Sorry, Ray. I'll get another one," said an old man, who grabbed a cane lying on the concrete and tapped his way over to a rack of spare tires. He ran his fingers across the tops of a few, found a likely one at the end and pulled it out of the rack, knocking off a few extra in the process. These proceeded to bounce on the floor a couple of times and then roll with unerring accuracy toward three other cab drivers who were bent over their vehicles. Predictably, the tires flattened all three of them, eliciting a whole bunch of completely justified cursing.

Hell's cabbies must not only navigate the streets of the Underworld without benefit of sight. They are also responsible for doing their own car maintenance. It must be a bitch changing a headlight by feel alone.

"Aagh!"

One of the cabbies was in the middle of a lube job; he had just gotten a face full of oil. "I can't see! I can't see!"

His colleagues were unsympathetic.

The dispatch office was a glass-enclosed station on the second floor in the center of the building. From there, the demon who sent out the cabs had an excellent view of the garage floor. We climbed the stairs and knocked on his door.

It flew open. "What the fuck do you want?" growled the demon dispatcher. "Oh, Minion, Welles. It's you. Have you come to fix the intercom?" He stepped back and let us into his office.

"Among other things. What's the problem?" I asked. Orson was scanning the floor of the garage, looking at every cabbie. He caught my eye and shook his head no. I nodded.

"The thing keeps fading in and out. Look, I'll show you." The demon picked up his microphone. "AFFLECK! Affleck! Get out of that stupid daredevil costume and head to Twelfth and Main."

"What came out of the intercom was "A ... FLACK, a ... flack, cough, whisper, whisper."

"Hmmm. Why don't you show us the guts of the system?"

"Okay." The demon walked over to a closet in the corner, unlocked the door and opened it.

Well, what do you know? Gilbert Gottfried. They let him in Hell after all. I'd always thought that the comic's voice was so irritating, Satan would never allow him in the Underworld. There he was though, curled up on the floor of the tiny closet, a big set of headphones over his ears, his mouth pressed to a grate that opened out to the garage. Gottfried's hand was on his throat and he was swallowing hard.

"So, let me get this straight," I said to the demon. "You speak into the microphone, and Gilbert here yells what you say through the grate for all the cabbies to hear. Now whose damnation exactly is this supposed to be, the cabbies or his?"

The demon shrugged. "Both, actually. Part of theirs. All of his."

I looked to my assistant. "Got any ideas?"

"Well, one." He reached in his pocket and pulled out an orange.

"Honestly, do you ever stop eating?"

"Hey!" he said, offended. "I mostly just eat oranges and sardines. And drink coffee. Just like you."

"Yeah, but you do it all the time. And I don't carry food around in my pockets like you do."

"Well, it's a good thing I do," he said, slightly miffed. He tossed me the orange. "It's not a lemon, but as tart as this new batch is, I think it might help."

"Good idea," I admitted, peeled the orange and handed Gottfried a slice. "Here, Gilbert. Chew this up a little and then just suck on the juice. It should help your laryngitis."

Gottfried nodded wearily, as he popped the orange slice into his mouth. He did his mastication thing, spat out a few seeds, then let juice combine with his own saliva for a few seconds before swallowing. I gave him another slice, which he popped in his mouth, then the rest of the orange.

"Any better?" Orson asked.

He nodded gratefully. "Tha … anks."

We winced. Boy, his voice could have etched glass. I turned to the dispatcher. "Try it now."

The demon nodded and grabbed his mike. "Testing. One, two. One, two."

"TES … TING, ONE, TWO! ONE, TWO!" I noticed that all the cabbies on the floor visibly cringed. Well, visibly to me. Not to them.

"Seems to work okay now." The demon said.

I pulled a pad and pencil out of my coveralls pocket, scrawled something on it, tore off the sheet and handed it to the demon. He turned it upside down, and for a moment I thought he might be illiterate, like Digger. "Boy, Minion, your handwriting sucks."

"You're handwriting wouldn't win any prizes either, so bite me."

"Don't tempt me," he said absently as he read the note. "Prescription for Gilbert Gottfried. Take one orange, or if you can get it, a lemon, as needed for laryngitis." He looked at me in disgust. "Do I have to? I mean, I'm supposed to be punishing him here."

"Just do it when he runs completely out of voice," I said, trying to placate the jerk. "His throat will hurt plenty, don't worry."

"Okay. Where do I sign?"

I handed him the work order and indicated the signature box. He scrawled his sigil, which looked vaguely like a taxi meter.

"Thanks," I said, pocketing the work order. "Say, do you know where Louis Braille is?"

At the mention of Braille's name, the demon turned red. "No. He didn't show up for his shift this morning. His cab is missing too. I'm getting ready to report him AWOL."

"You might want to hold off on that," Orson said. "We believe he's been abducted."

The demon look skeptical. "Who would bother to abduct one of the damned, unless they intended to torture him?" The dispatcher brightened. "Well, that's okay then. I guess I'll see him when I see him."

"That's okay for you, but we're in the middle of investigating the disappearance of several damned souls."

"Yeah? Oh whose authority? Show me some authorization, badges or something."

"Badges?" I said, chuckling. "We don't need no stinking badges."

"Steve," Orson said, putting his hand on my arm, "stop flogging the horse. It's past dead."

"Oh. Sorry." I turned back to the demon. "Well, let me just say that it's *not* Azazel? Get it?" I said winking conspiratorially at the dispatcher. "We definitely do *not* have badges from Azazel."

"Azazel!" the demon looked at me shocked. "Is he still around? Shit. I don't want to get in trouble with him. What do you need?"

"I'd like to talk to the cabbies. Could you gather them together?"

"No problem." The demon picked up his microphone. "All cabbies meet in front of the dispatcher office, stat!"

"ALL CABBIES MEET IN FRONT OF THE DISPATCHER OFFICE, STAT!"

Orson and I reflexively cringed. If I had to listen to that voice all day, I'd go nuts.

The cab drivers were moving quickly toward the base of the stairs, some navigating by cane, others feeling their way along the walls, car tops, etc.

When they were all gathered, I spoke my piece. "I'm looking for Louis Braille. Has anybody seen him?"

Catcalls.

"Okay. Sorry. SORRY! It's just a figure of speech, okay?" *A bad choice of words though.* I continued. "Anyway, Louis a good friend of mine. Does anyone know where he is?"

"I had a pint with him last night, at Grshnsh's Pub, down the street," said Turlough O'Carolan, the Irish Harper. At least I assumed that's who it was, since he was lugging around a folk harp. I suppose it could have been Rory dall Ó Catháin, another Blind Irish Harper - funny that there were two of them - but I seemed to recall that he was stationed in Lustland. "He left shortly before me. Don't know where he went after that."

"Thanks. Anybody else?"

They all shook their heads.

"Well, if he turns up, let us know, okay?" Orson said.

"Sure ... great guy, Louis ... hope he's okay."

"Missing, just like we feared," I said, as the two of us headed to the exit.

Behind us, we heard the demon - via Gottfried's voice - through the intercom. "HELEN KELLER, GO TO THE WILKIN'S BUILDING AND IGNORE SALMON P. CHASE, WHO'S TRYING TO FLAG A CAB THERE ... . OH, RIGHT, YOU CAN'T HEAR EITHER. CHARLES! SPELL IT OUT FOR HER!"

Chapter 21

"I don't like it, Orson." I said, as we stepped onto the sidewalk. "That's two for two."

He nodded, a serious look on his face. "It looks like someone is targeting your closest friends. You said Tesla's photo was also X'ed over. Do you want to go there next?"

"Yeah, I do. If Nicky is also missing, then I think that seals it."

"The Elevator is only a few blocks away. Let's hurry over there."

I shook my head. "The time for stealth is over. I'm calling BOOH. Let's just hope he doesn't get in trouble."

A whistle and a shout was all it took. Two seconds later, the Bat out of Hell was hovering above us, his thirty foot wingspan stretching from the taxi depot to a building across the street.

I'd like to see someone try and kidnap BOOH. Good luck with that.

BOOH had discarded his hat and sunglasses. I guess he thought the time for sneaking around was past too. "Skree?"

"Could you take me and Orson up to the farm on Level Four where Nikola Tesla works?"

"Skree!"

In the space of a few heartbeats, the three of us were flying above a flat, arid stretch of dark dirt. The afternoon was windy, and spirals of black dust spun in the air. This is what I imagined a farm in the Dust Bowl must have looked like in the Thirties, when severe drought combined with bad land husbandry to suck the nutrients from the soil and create bone-dry fields in which little or nothing would grow.

There were a few humans out in the fields, breaking up the earth with hand-pushed plows. Since nothing would grow here, they harvested dirt, dirt farmers in the truest sense. After those working the plows loosened the soil, some of their colleagues followed behind with wheelbarrows and shovels. They scooped up the rock and earth, dumped it in their carts and carted it off to a silo near a dilapidated barn some distance away. The barn door was open, but there was no sign of any livestock; the animals had either bolted or never been there to begin with. Probably the latter.

I pointed at the farmhouse, and BOOH set us down there. Sitting on the steps, using a pocket knife to whittle a small pitchfork out of a branch, was an old demon attired in denim overalls and a blue work shirt. He was also wearing a John Deere gimme cap.

"Scuse me, sir."

The demon gave me a long look and spat something dark on the ground in front of him. The noxious black loogie could have been chewing tobacco; it could as easily have been just the demon's spit, since it began to boil and eat its way into the dirt. Either way, the tar-colored mucous smelled horrible. The demon went back to whittling.

"I said, EXCUSE ME, SIR!"

"Busy," was all I got out of him. That and a toothless grin.

Orson gave it a whirl. "Are you the overseer of this farm?"

"Who wants to know?"

"He's Steve Minion, Hell's Super, and I'm Orson Welles, his Assistant."

"Be still my heart." The line was out of character, but at least it showed clearly that the demon didn't give a shit about us.

"Hey!" Orson snapped. "You work for Lord Beelzebub, I presume?"

The old demon nodded. "I manage this land, and the humans who work it, but yeah, Beelzebub is my boss. What's it to ya?"

He had the country farmer bit down pretty well, including the cantankerous quality, as long as he kept his focus. But "cantankerous" was wearing a bit thin; now I wanted some answers.

"Well, he's our boss, too," I said, glaring at him. "So how about a little cooperation here?"

He threw his knife at me, but I was anticipating something like that, so I snagged it in midair with some duct tape. The demon stared at me agape. "Pretty good trick fer a human. Now gimme back my knife."

I tossed the blade to Orson, who caught it deftly, spun it in his hand then threw it at the step beneath the demon. It pierced the brittle wood and stuck. The knife quivered slightly from the impact.

"That was a pretty good trick too."

Orson shrugged, and I tried not to look impressed. Of course, I knew he could do that. Orson had learned all sorts of things during his lifetime, including rope tricks from Will Rogers (or so he said) and knife throwing from some circus performer. That's why I'd given him the blade. I hoped it would impress the demon enough to get him to tell us about Nicky.

It helped. A little. The demon laid the unfinished pitchfork to one side, then pulled the knife from the step, folded it and put it in his pocket. "What do ya'll want?"

"We're looking for Nikola Tesla. Have you seen him?"

He looked at us and frowned. "Not sure I should tell ya."

There was a shuffling in the dirt next to me. It was BOOH, and he was frowning. Generally, my friend was an even-tempered sort, but he must not have liked this demon's attitude either. "SKREE!" He blew the guy's hat off.

The demon jumped up straight in the air and caught himself on the side of the farmhouse with his claws. He hung there. "Okay, okay! Just call off BOOH, okay?"

I patted my batty friend on a wing. "Thanks," I whispered, then said more loudly, "Tell me about Tesla."

The overseer climbed down from his perch, keeping a close eye on BOOH. "I ... I haven't seen hide nor hair of him all day. Getting' ready to report him for, what's the word, oh yeah, dereliction. Dereliction of duty."

Orson and I looked at each other. This didn't look good.

"Dereliction of duty may be the least of Nicky's problems right now," I said, handing the demon my card. "If he shows up, call me, will you?"

He frowned. "Mebbee I will, n mebbe I won't."

"SKREE!"

"I mean, a'course I will. Anything for a friend of BOOH's." The old demon trembled.

"Well, thanks for your help, I guess. Come on, Orson. Let's get out of here." We turned to go.

The demon stood on the steps and stared at the sky. "Looks like a twister."

Sure enough, there was a monstrous tornado heading in the direction of the silo. I whistled for BOOH. "Get us out of here, will you?"

"Skree?"

"Take us down to see Allan on Seven!"

The twister hit the silo, reducing it to splinters. The storm scooped up the dirt from the silo, and we had a black blizzard, hundreds of feet high, heading toward us. Even BOOH was impressed, so he hightailed it into the Throat of Hell just before the dark funnel sucked us into it.

The ride down to Pinkerton's Circle of Hell was not long, but it gave me a few seconds to think. Flo, Louie and Nicky: all of them had X'es through their pictures, and all of them were missing. I glanced at Orson, worrying. His and Allan's were the only other pictures I'd seen. *Will they be next?* At least Orson knew about the danger, not that he was likely to be able to do anything about it, if a devil or demon was involved. He seemed to be taking the danger in stride, though when you're dead and damned, being kidnapped would be a minor inconvenience, I guess. Still, I'd feel better after I checked on Allan and at least let him know what might happen.

BOOH must have picked up a little of the tornado's momentum, or maybe it just gave him the idea, but he spiraled rapidly down to the surface of Seven, next to Allan Pinkerton's workshop, and set us on the pavement. My head felt like it was spinning as we touched the ground. Orson looked a little green around the gills.

BOOH landed on the ground beside us. Last time we were here, Allan had plied the bat with Scotch, and BOOH looked to be anticipating another round or two. "BOOH, we don't have time for a proper visit with Allan."

The giant bat hung his head in disappointment.

"Sorry, big guy. This will only take a few minutes, so if you could just hang tight, we'll be right out." He nodded then flew to the top of the workshop to wait for us.

We stepped into the dim interior of Pinkerton's workshop. As usual, Allan was wrestling with an ill-made keg in the center of the space. It was ill-made by him; he was a terrible cooper, which is a barrel maker in case you aren't current in the professional jargon of the cask-making profession. (It's a barrel maker even if you are.) Allan, who was usually engrossed in his work, making it frequently possible to sneak up on him and go

223

boo, must have been at a stopping point, for he heard the door open immediately. He looked up at me and Orson with his intense, dark eyes.

I sighed in relief. He, at least, had not been taken.

"Hello, my friends," he said, slipping off his leather gloves and apron. "Any word of Flo?"

"Not, directly," I said walking up to him, Orson in tow. "But I have a clue I'd like you to take a look at."

"Very good. Would you two like a drink while we work?"

Orson looked at me with wide eyes. I'd told him about Allan's famously bad Scotch, and my assistant looked to have no interest in sampling it. "Thanks, Allan," I said hurriedly, "but another time."

Orson sighed quietly in relief.

"Ah, suit yourself," Pinkerton said, clearing a jug and some glasses off the rickety table he had in the back of the workroom. "What do you have for me?"

"A note. It was in Flo's apartment. The cops missed it."

Allan snorted. "That's because they're not real police officers. They're just devils in blue uniforms. No doubt they were more interested in ransacking Florence's flat than in finding any useful evidence."

"That's what I thought too." Reaching inside my coveralls, I retrieved the Ziploc bag and laid it on top of the table. "I was careful not to get any prints on it."

Pinkerton smiled approvingly. "That's best practice, though of course we don't exactly have access to a fingerprint database down here. Still, we might be able to learn something."

"So, do you think you can get prints off this?" Orson asked.

"Of course," Allan said. "I'm a professional. Do either of you have a pencil?"

Orson pulled one from behind his ear, where he often kept it.

"Excellent!" Pinkerton set the pencil on the table at the back of his shop. 'Steve, hand me that adze over there, will you?"

"I thought you weren't allowed to use ... "

"And be careful, it's ... "

"Ow!"

"Sharp," he said, sighing. He took the adze from me, and as I sucked the blood from my wound, he placed the tool parallel to the pencil then, with a single blow, bisected it. The pencil, not the adze.

"I'm not allowed to use any of the cooper's tools to make a barrel, but for this purpose, there isn't a problem." He handed the adze back to me. With respect, I put it back in place on the wall. Allan took his Swiss army knife and from the middle of the pencil scraped out the graphite, then ground it into a fine powder using the flat of his blade.

With a pair of pliers provided by Orson, Allan drew the note out of the Ziploc bag. He set the pliers to the side, then studied the note.

"The paper is a very fine grade, as if it had been made by hand for something like origami. As to the letters: *Playboy*, *Car and Driver*, *Hell's Bells*. I recognize all of these fonts."

"Impressive," Orson said, doing his mustache-blowing trick in a feeble attempt to compete.

"As I said, I'm a professional. This doesn't tell me much, though, except that the person who did this is likely a devil or demon, since humans aren't allowed to have magazine subscriptions, oh, except those who hate door-to-door salesmen."

"Interesting that you could deduce that out of something so minor," Orson opined, admiringly.

Pinkerton shrugged, then, like a child eating green peas, he scooped up the pulverized graphite on the blade of his knife.

"We can offer something too," Orson continued, trying to show we weren't complete simpletons.

"Oh?" Allan said, carefully shaking the charcoal powder from his knife across the back of the entire note.

"Wait," I interrupted. "Why are you dusting the back and not the front?"

Pinkerton raised an eyebrow and shot me a quick glance. "How do you hold something you are reading? Do you turn the page away from you?"

"Oh, right," I said sheepishly. "My fingers would support it from the back."

"Just so. I will dust the front now, though, because that's where the thumbs usually go. Besides, we may see some prints where the perpetrator touched the page while gluing on the magazine letters."

"Makes sense."

"Now, what were you going to tell me?"

"Note the text of the message," Orson said.

"'I'll get you, my pretty?' Florence is certainly quite pretty, but you seem to ascribe more meaning to the words than I would."

"It's a line from the movie, 'The Wizard of Oz.'"

"Interesting. Moving pictures were after my time, except for some early demonstrations." Allan turned the note on its side and tapped it against the table top. Most of the graphite fell off the paper. He examined the note by the light of the lantern that hung above the table. "Aha!"

"Aha what?" I asked, coming to stare over his shoulder.

I saw some clear fingerprints, broken in spots by sharp angles. In and of themselves, they told me nothing, but the fingers that made them were long, tapered. There was an elegance to them.

"I would wager these are Florence's prints. At the very least, the hand is that of a woman's."

Orson crowded in next to him. "What are these upside down V marks breaking up the print?"

"Devil claws," Allan said without hesitation. "Florence held this note after a devil touched it." With his palms, Allan supported the note by its edges and deftly flipped it over so we could see the front. It was covered by the V patterns, though I could see what I guessed were Flo's thumbprints at the bottom.

My assistant, who was seldom impressed by anybody, was clearly struck by Allan's conclusions. "How do you know all this? How do you know they are devil claws instead of a demon's, and how do you know that the devil touched it first, before Flo did?"

"Simple reasoning. First, devils have claws, but demons don't."

Orson and I stared at each other. "Of course they do," I said. "I've been raked by demon claws more times than I can count."

"Me too," Orson added.

Allan shook his head. "Demons are would-be devils, as we all know. While some parts of their anatomy do in fact become like devils, their 'claws' are mere affectation. They grow their nails, which are much like what you and I have, extra long and carefully trim them to emulate the claws of devils. Surely you've noticed the demon manicure shops all over Hell."

I thought about the ManiMaim shop not far from my apartment. ManiMaim was a franchise, like McDonalds or, perhaps more aptly, Great Clips or Supercuts, and they were all over Levels Two through Eight. I'd not paid ManiMaim much attention before, but I realized now that I'd never seen anyone but a demon go in or out of one of those establishments.

"So this mark here," I said, indicating one of the V's on the paper, 'is a devil claw."

"Yes. A demon's faux claw is not as rigid as the real one of a devil, and it would not have imprinted itself so precisely on the page."

"Okay, Sherlock," Orson said, "how ... "

"Sherlock. There's that name again." He looked at me sharply. "You called me that once before."

I shrugged. "A fictional detective. His first adventure was published a few years after you died, I think. Anyway, Orson means it as a compliment."

"Oh, well then ... "

"How do you know the devil touched the page first?"

"Now *that* is a very interesting question. Take a look at the paper closely. Do you see anything unusual about the places touched by a devil claw?"

The paper seemed blistered wherever we saw one of the V's. "A burn?" I suggested.

Pinkerton nodded. "After a fashion, yes. Devil claws are hot, like pokers that have been left in the fire until they are white from the heat. We've all, I wager, been scratched by a devil, more than once most likely. Tell me, did you never feel the heat coming from the touch?"

"Well," Orson said, "generally I've been too focused on the slashing part, but now that you mention it, yeah. Their claws burn as well as slice."

I nodded. They were right.

"This is how I read the clues," Allan said. "A devil put together this note. Not a demon. A devil. He then touched it with his claws which, being white hot, fused the pores of the paper together. When Florence picked up the note to read it, the oils from her skin couldn't penetrate the page where the claw marks were. That's why we only have partial prints."

"Hmm. Ingenious," Orson said admiringly.

"You said it, Orson. Thanks, Allan. Now we at least know it was a devil who threatened her." Taking Orson's pliers, I gingerly lifted the note and put it back in the Ziploc, which I sealed shut and returned to the inside of my coveralls for safekeeping.

Allan brushed the extra graphite, along with the remains of Orson's decimated pencil, off the table and onto the floor of his workshop. Absently, he rubbed his foot over the debris until it blended into the dirt. "Is there anything else, fellows?"

"One thing," I said with some reluctance. "I ... I recently had a conversation with Azazel, in his office, and happened to spy a handful of mugshots on the wall. Three of them, including one of Flo, were X'd through. And Orson and I have just checked. The other two, Louis Braille and Nikola Tesla, are also missing."

Orson finished for me. "Steve thinks his best friends are being targeted. My picture was up there too. And ... and so was yours."

Allan's eyes narrowed. "Did our photos have X'es through them?"

"No," I said. "Not yet, anyway."

"Well," Pinkerton said, in his best stiff-upper-lip fashion, which, him being a product of the Victorian Age, was pretty good. "Forewarned is forearmed."

"Not sure what you'd be able to do if a devil came after you, but I, well, I wanted you to know."

Allan smiled ruefully. "Thank you. It's the thocht that counts, aye, laddie?"

"Aye," I said, returning his smile.

Yet the exchange gave me no comfort. I felt that both of them were at risk, but there was nothing I could do about it. "Well," I said slowly, "guess it's time to go. Thanks for your help."

"You're welcome, my friends," Allan said, shaking first my hand and then Orson's. "Take care."

"You too." We watched Allan slip his apron and gloves back on and return to his barrel. Then I followed Orson to the exit.

Chapter 22

Orson and I sat on the rickety steps outside our trailer. BOOH had dropped us off a few minutes earlier then high-tailed it out of there, as if he'd been summoned by the Big Guy to run an errand. I hoped my furry friend wasn't in trouble for having helped us and resolved, if possible, not to pull him into my current mess again.

The sky was tinged with yellow. (It's often that way in the late afternoon, or what we call afternoon down here. That's when Hell's management does one of its periodic infusions of sulfur into the atmosphere.) The jaundiced air smelled bad and looked worse, as if all the Underworld was beginning to rot. The almost overwhelming stench made me cough.

"So." Orson sounded weary. "What do we know?" he asked, repeating my question from earlier in the day.

I sighed. "Someone is making my closest friends disappear, and that someone is, if Allan's reading of the clues is correct, a devil."

My friend nodded. "I'd also wager that said devil left that note in Flo's apartment, after she read it, just so you could find it."

"Really? Why?"

"'The Wizard of Oz' reference. Anyone who knows you is aware you're an old movie buff."

"Well, so are you."

"Yeah, but I don't go around quoting them all the time, like you do. I swear, if you'd said 'we don't need no stinking badges' one more time today, I was going to pop you."

"Sorry about that," I said sheepishly. *But he's right, which means …*

231

"Steve, I think *you* are the target of all this, not Flo or Louie or Nicky."

"But why? What's the point? Just to torture me a little more? Shit, isn't it bad enough I have to do this crappy job for all eternity?" In frustration, I slammed my hand against the side of the trailer. That must have dislodged a shingle, for it fell off the roof and smacked me on the head. *And now I'll have to fix that.*

"You okay?"

"Guess so," I grumbled.

Orson patted me on the back. "I don't know what the point of all this is. I also don't know what to do next."

I stood. "Well, I do. We don't know when or where Nicky or Louie disappeared, but we *do* know where Flo did. I think we should go back to the hospital. You know, we never actually examined the spot where she disappeared."

"You mean where TNK-el said she disappeared. He could be lying. That's what devils do, you know. Hey, do you think he was the one who sent the note to Flo?"

"Naw. His claws are too tiny. Besides, you saw that lovesick, moony-eyed expression on his face whenever he talked about her. I believe he really is distressed by her disappearance."

Orson struggled to get off the stairs, so I gave him a hand.

"Very funny," he said, finally rising. "That's a joke that just never gets old for you, does it?"

I snickered. "Well, it *is* a classic down here. Besides, you trying to scramble up off that step looked like quite a feat, and I felt it deserved a round of applause."

"Some friend you are," he grumbled.

That wiped the grin off my face. "I *am* your friend, you know. And you're mine, probably my best friend ever. Listen, Orson, you need to be careful until this is all over."

He nodded. "I've already thought of that. There's not much I can do if a devil wants to grab me, but so far, at least, no one has been kidnapped in front of you."

"Meaning?"

He smiled ruefully. "Meaning I'm sticking with you like glue until this is all over. If someone *does* nab me in your presence, you'll at least be able to see who did it."

"Fair enough. Let's get our magnifying glasses. We might need them." I headed up the stairs and found a note stuck to the office door. "Yuck," I said pulling it off.

"What's wrong?"

"Somebody stuck this flyer to our door with devil double bubble."

"Oh, crap. That stuff is a bitch to get off."

"Don't I know it." I retrieved a putty knife from my tool belt and scraped at the pink gum. I managed to get it off the door, along with a fair bit of paint, but then the gum was firmly stuck to my putty knife. Shrugging, I threw my knife into the dumpster a few feet away. As I opened the door, I unfolded the flyer. "Oh, this again."

"What?" Orson asked, reading over my shoulder.

FAME! FORTUNE! ADVENTURE! THE LUSH LIFE. MORE BABES
THAN YOU COULD POSSIBLE IMAGINE!
JOIN THE DEMON CORPS!
APPLY TODAY AND RECEIVE LIMITED TELEPORTATION
POWERS!*
*(Offer void where prohibited by law.)

"Wow," Orson enthused. "Teleportation! I thought only major devils could do that, not demons!" He looked at me expectantly.

233

"I'm *not* going to become a demon!" I wadded up the flyer and tossed it into my trashcan. "If you think it's such a great offer, why don't you apply?'

"Demonship - or demonism or demonosity or whatever the Hell it's called - is by invitation only. I've never been asked. Besides, I don't think I meet the physical requirements."

"What do you mean?" I asked.

"Have you ever seen a fat demon?"

I thought back to all the demons I'd ever known, Uphir, Karnaj, Whizzer, Digger and a host of others. Some were built like body builders, but most were rail-thin, and none at all were fat, not even the ones who worked in Glutton's Gap. "Oh. Guess not."

Orson went to the supply cabinet to get our magnifying glasses. "I think I'd make a wonderful demon, but I guess no one will ever know. Ah, well," Orson said breezily. "It's their loss."

"Hey, would you grab me a spare putty knife while you're in there?" I always felt naked without a putty knife.

Orson flipped me one - a knife, not a finger, mind you - and I stuffed it, again, the knife, into the vacant spot on my belt.

The walk to the hospital seemed to take forever. The yellow air was thick, like honey that had been left in the jar too long, almost a crystalline thing, dragging against our clothes. I felt like I was swimming against a rip tide rather than just walking along the sidewalk. (These are two very different images, but at least no one can accuse me of mixing my metaphors. These are similes, after all.) Looking at Orson, he seemed to be similarly struggling. Hell was often like this. The place fights against you, both physically and mentally, and the Underworld's undertow was in full force that afternoon. By the time we reached the sidewalk leading to the entrance, we were both drenched in sweat.

234

The entire plaza in front of the hospital was still cordoned off with yellow police tape. The cops were long gone, though. They'd probably just left the tape there to trash up the place. I was pretty confident the D&D squad couldn't care less about my missing paramour.

"Isn't that where TNK-el said Flo disappeared?" I asked my friend, indicating the plaza.

"Yeah, but it's a pretty big area. Maybe we should hunt up TNK-el and have him show us exactly where it happened. That could cut down on our search time."

"Good idea."

Turns out he wasn't very hard to find. TNK-el was hanging around the waiting room, darting out in front of the humans who regularly milled around the area, waiting interminably for their admission papers to be processed. The little guy was tripping any human he could then stabbing his pitchfork into whatever body part was within his reach. It wasn't much as far as torment went, but he was still contributing to the cause, which was all that really mattered.

TNK-el was standing on the butt of an old guy with gout and taking the opportunity to repeatedly plunge the pointy weapon into the soft flesh beneath him, snickering all the while. But when the little devil saw us, he hopped right off and came over to talk. "Any progress?" he asked, worry in his voice.

"Some," I allowed. "Tinkle, I ... "

The little devil began hopping up and down. I think this was how the expression "hopping mad" came about, as a way to describe the pique of imps. "TNK-el! It's TNK-el!"

"Sorry, TNK-el! We think it would be a good idea to thoroughly examine the place were Flo disappeared. The plaza is pretty big, though, so I thought you might be able to narrow down our search."

235

"Sure. Come on." The small fry took a few steps then abruptly spun on his heels and ran back to give the old man's butt another stab. Satisfied, he pulled out his pitchfork and returned to our side.

TNK-el led us to a spot about ten feet outside the front doors of the hospital. The plaza before the hospital was an impressive feature, complete with a fountain, the centerpiece of which was a thirty-foot statue of Satan in a physician's gown holding aloft a caduceus. The liquid in the fountain was yellow and smelled bad, and it came from an orifice on the statue that I'd rather not mention. In an unusual patch of good luck, TNK-el led us to a spot upwind of the fountain.

The imp took his pitchfork and circumscribed a twenty by twenty foot patch of concrete not far from the main entrance. The scraping of his weapon against the cement set my teeth on edge, but I put up with it, because when he was done, we had a well-demarcated area not much bigger than a living room. "That's the best I can do, but somewhere within the lines was where Florence was standing when the light took her."

"Thanks, TNK-el," Orson said as politely as he could. "We'll take it from here."

"Okay. I was going to get a Slurpee from the cafeteria. I'll come back in a bit and see how you're doing." With that, the imp headed into the hospital.

The ambient light of Hell took that moment to diminish a bit, undoubtedly to make our job harder. We ended up on our hands and knees, on opposite ends of the square, slowly working toward the center, magnifying glasses to the fore.

After twenty minutes of crawling, staring down at the concrete, we collided, heads first. We'd covered the entire space but seen nothing. We stood, working the kinks out of our legs. "Hey, look at that!" Orson said, indicating a mark a few feet away. "I went right by there and didn't see it."

"It's these damn magnifying glasses," I said, pocketing my instrument with disgust. "They had us too focused on the micro level."

We stood above the mark. I noted with interest that it had been made with lipstick, the same shade that Flo sometimes wore when she was dressing up, the same shade she had on that morning for our coffee date. The mark was not accidental, that's for sure. It was too elaborate, and the lines were too straight. It looked something like this:

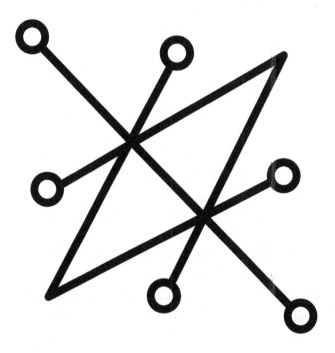

"Any idea what it means?" Orson asked me.

"No, but it was drawn with a woman's lipstick. Flo's shade too."

"Hmm." Orson got back on his knees with his magnifying glass and carefully examined the concrete around the mark. "Look at this," he said.

With my own glass, I looked at the spot he indicated. The concrete was dusty, but most things in Hell were covered in dust or grime, so that wasn't unusual. However, in the dust at the bottom of one of the V's was a delicate fingerprint. I pulled out the Ziploc and placed it next to the print. "What do you think?"

Orson frowned, comparing the print in the dust with those on the back of the message. "I think it's her index finger."

"I agree. It's logical to assume Flo drew this. But why?" Sitting on the lip of a nearby planter, I pulled a notepad and pencil from my pocket and tried to replicate the sign.

"You forgot the circles," said a voice beside me.

I almost jumped out of my skin. "TNK-el! Where did you come from?"

The little imp shrugged. "The cafeteria," he said, indicating the Slurpee he was holding with both hands. "Like I said."

"What were you saying about circles?" I asked, feeling suddenly very tired. I'd been going in circles all day, and it was wearing on me.

"Azazel's sigil. You can't just draw the lines. You need the circles to complete his sigil."

"What?" I scooped up TNK-el unceremoniously and carried him over to the drawing on the concrete. He struggled briefly, but not wanting to drop his Slurpee, he settled down. "This is Azazel's sigil?" I asked, indicating the drawing on the ground.

"Well, yeah. Wonder what it's doing there. Hey, would you put me down, now? It's not dignified, a devil being carried around by a human."

"What? Oh sorry." I placed him on the concrete. "I think Flo drew it with her lipstick."

"Really?"

"Yeah. Do you think she was in trouble and trying to call Azazel for help?"

TNK-el frowned. "Nah. The major devils can't be summoned just by drawing their sigil. They're too powerful."

I stroked my chin. "I think," I said slowly, "that she was trying to leave a clue."

The little guy frowned in confusion. "You believe Azazel had something to do with this?"

Click. It all fit. Her disappearance, his irrational behavior, his relief over my not finding any usable evidence. The photos on the wall. And now this. "Yes. I believe he has everything to do with this."

"But he's the chief of police!"

"Yeah," I said, laughing savagely. "The *devil* police." *And what would the devil police do? Probably the exact opposite of what a normal police force would do, that is, perpetrate crimes, not solve them.*

"Steve!" Orson called from ten feet away. "I've found something else."

This time it was on my side of the concrete. In classic "can't see the forest for the trees" mode, I'd also missed something. I walked over to where Orson stood staring down at a large shadow on the pavement. It was a black scorch mark, shaped like a shovel with toes. "What do you think it is?" I asked.

Orson grinned. "Riddle me this, Batman. What demon has gigantic feet that are shaped like shovels?"

239

The light bulb went on. "Digger!"

"Yes!" my friend enthused. "And do you remember what Belphegor said about all the commotion from the mine today?"

I nodded. "I also remember you said you heard something when you entered what you thought was a deserted mine."

"I did. Which means … " Orson said, pausing to give me the opportunity to say it, a very nice sidekicky thing to do, I must say.

"We may know where Flo is."

"So what are we waiting for?" my friend asked. "Let's go save a damsel in distress!"

Chapter 23

Before heading for the Escalator, Orson and I stopped by the office. We wanted to get our spelunking gear. Well, mainly we wanted our hard hats and head lights. We didn't use them very often, but they came in pretty handy when we had to do something like crawl through Hell's sewers to clear a pipe. A stinky job, and not without its share of unpleasant vermin, like giant alligators, rats as big as sofas, that sort of thing. I don't like big rats and even bigger lizards, but they're much easier to tolerate when you can see them coming.

After grabbing our gear, we hurried to the Escalator. I was determined not to call BOOH, nor did I really think it was necessary. The Escalator was only minutes from our office, and the ride down to the mine on Level Six was scarcely a minute more. For once, things were working in our favor, circumstances that would normally make me suspicious. Events seldom work out to your advantage in Hell, especially if you're a damned human. Oh, I was sure that everything would go wrong at some point - that always happened down here - but for now I chose not to question too closely this rare instance of good fortune.

We were silent on the Escalator as we rode it down to Level Six. My palms felt slick against the hard black plastic of the moving handrail, and my heart was pounding. I looked behind me to see Orson, a few steps above, clutching the rail so hard his knuckles were white. His face was grim. "What the Hell are we doing?" Orson said at last.

I maintained my silence, reflecting on the foolishness of our endeavor. Two intrepid handymen were on their way to rescue their friend, and maybe even more than one if Louis and Nicky were in the mine also, from one of the most powerful devils in

Hell, not to mention a demon who was built like a forklift. And those were just the two we knew about. We had no idea how many other devils and demons could have been in cahoots with Azazel and Digger. Hundreds? Perhaps.

I reached to my tool belt, grabbed the top of my hammer, touched my rolls of duct tape. Pretty paltry weapons, though they were familiar and brought some comfort to me. Still, I wish I had brought my staple gun. It might not stop a demon, but those little staples sure could sting. As much as TNK-el's pitchfork, anyway.

We were crazy to attempt this, but who could we have asked to help us? Other than TNK-el and Uphir, I hadn't found a devil or a demon who gave a flip about the disappearance of Miss Florence Nightingale. Well, that wasn't quite true. Asmodeus had some interest in her reappearance, but he could afford to wait. Besides, I doubted he wanted to tangle with Azazel. TNK-el: he was another matter. He seemed to have a real crush on Flo, but I suspected he lacked the firepower to help much. And Uphir, well, he might enjoy having Flo around as the recipient of his abuse, but not enough to risk antagonizing Azazel. The demon seemed to have a genuine - and justified - fear of the big devil.

Satan would be nothing but pleased about Nightingale being indisposed or indefinitely absent. I might have asked Beezy for some help, but as it was, he resented the time I was spending looking for her. Ironically, the only reason he was letting me look at all was because of Azazel, though I guess Beezy didn't get the memo that I was off the case. For some reason, Azazel had some hold on my boss, so help from the office of Beelzebub was unlikely.

Regarding the vast majority of Hell's inmates, the damned, where would they stand? While I hadn't met a human down here who didn't adore Flo, the damned were not the most promising group from which to recruit a rescue party. They were, by definition, a pretty defeated and demoralized lot. There were a few who might risk a fight with a gang of devils and demons. Certainly Pinkerton would, and maybe even Shemp and the other Stooges. Hell, perhaps all the Free Hellions would help, if asked, but they wouldn't stand a chance. From personal experience, I knew that ten thousand Hellions couldn't stand up to a single Beezy, and Azazel seemed to be a devil of comparable firepower.

Orson spoke again. "Do we even have a plan? I sure don't. You?"

I looked mournfully at my friend. "Not really. I think we're about to screw ourselves."

"Yeah, that's how I figure it too."

"Perhaps we could sneak up on them, find Flo, wait until they leave and try to break her out."

Orson looked skeptical. "Maybe, though I'm not really built for stealth, you know."

I held up my hands in defeat, violating the first rule of escalator safety by not holding firmly to the handrail, and almost falling as a result. "I don't know what else to do. We can't just walk away. We have to at least try to help her. Or, at least, I do. I love her, you know."

"Yes, I do know, even though you didn't get creamed just now by a pie. Why is that?" Orson looked thoughtful then just shrugged. Hell was not always consistent. "Anyway, while she may not be my girl, she is a close friend of mine." He sighed. "Of course we have to help her. And who knows? Maybe we'll get lucky."

I smiled ruefully. "This is Hell. Nobody gets lucky down here."

243

Orson grabbed the rail even more tightly. His knuckles were now the color of chalk. "Well, maybe someone will be unluckier than us."

"Maybe."

We stepped off the Escalator. The mine area was still deserted. In fact, it looked as if it had been abandoned centuries ago. The carts used to bring up the sulfur from the depths of the mine were already rusting. Pickaxes and shovels were spread like the casually discarded toys of a child across the landscape. They were covered with a heavy layer of dust. This was a not uncommon phenomenon in the Underworld. Entropy was a powerful force here, and without frequent activity, the place quickly went to hell.

Orson took the lead to the front gates of the mine. He slipped between them, and I followed. We walked beside the rusting main track along which the damned would push handcarts full of the bright yellow crystal so fundamental to the workings of Hell. The track was the best guide we could have for finding our route, at least until the light gave out, which was about a hundred yards in. Then we turned on the lamps mounted to our hard hats.

They didn't work.

Orson grumbled. "Happens every time. Hit me."

I shrugged then made a fist and slammed it hard on top of his helmet. The light blazed on. "Shit!" he yelled. "Did you have to wallop me so hard? I'm seeing stars."

"Sorry. Besides it's your turn. You can get me back."

Despite having recently been brained by me, he pulled his punch at the last moment. My lamp flickered and died. "Go ahead and thwock me like I did you. You know only a good hard whack will do the trick."

244

He nodded, did the deed, and soon I too was seeing constellations. I was also seeing the interior of the mine, thanks to my lamp - and the none-too-gentle ministrations of my friend.

We walked a few hundred yards until we came to the point Orson had described to me earlier, the spot where the main corridor split into three passageways. He went a few yards into each one, listening carefully. When he came out of the one on the far left, he nodded. "Just like I thought. The others are silent as the grave … "

"Well, naturally, I … "

"Don't interrupt," he snapped. Orson's nerves were on edge. I couldn't blame him. "This corridor here, well, I think I hear voices. Check it out and see if I'm right."

I walked about twenty yards into the passageway. There were voices all right, faint, but audible. "You nailed it, buddy. Let's go."

Orson took a calming breath. "Okay, but let's keep our voices down. If we can hear them, they might be able to hear us."

That gave me pause. I nodded, putting my finger to my lips.

The going was slow. The corridor was not as flat as the main passageway but undulated up and down. Large rocks frequently tripped us up. We landed, hands forward, on the ground so many times that our palms were soon scraped and bloodied. Orson reached to his belt and pulled out his leather gloves, waving them at me before putting them on. I nodded and donned my own.

That helped with our falls, but it wasn't helping with the progressive narrowing of the tunnel. By the time we'd traveled perhaps a quarter mile, we were hunched over like Quasimodos. That's when I heard a soft, "hibbidity gibbity, hibbity gibbity" sound behind me. It was Orson, who had stopped walking. His face had a ghostly pallor and he was sweating like a man who had just run a marathon.

"Are you okay?" I whispered.

"N ... no. I'm claustrophobic, remember?" he said, his eyes wide with terror.

I'd forgotten. For me, heights was the problem. For Orson, it was small spaces, and considering how big my friend was, he often had to confront this primal fear of his as we did our work. Orson was having a panic attack.

"Sit down Orson," I said gently, "and close your eyes."

"Steve!" he said as he plopped down in the dirt. There was desperation in his voice. "I ... I can't breathe!"

"Of course you can't. Me neither. We're dead, remember?"

"Steve!" he said, more insistently, clutching at his throat. "I'm suffocating!"

Even in death our phobias can get to us. Now I understood why Orson was so frightened on the Escalator. Hell, it was bad enough that we were undertaking an uncertain but definitely risky venture, where the odds were surely stacked against us. Orson, however, had to deal with his claustrophobia as well.

"Just close your eyes, big guy," I said again. Reluctantly, and with an effort of will, Orson did as I said. I got behind him and gave him a back rub. I hummed softly, hoping it would calm him.

It did. I could feel the tense muscles in his neck and shoulders loosen. Finally he opened one eye and looked at me. "Is that a Bing Crosby song you're humming?"

"Yeah. It was the first thing that popped in my head."

"Really, now," Orson said, sounding like his old self. "'Count Your Blessings Instead of Sheep?'"

I gave him a sickly smile. "Right. I guess not the best choice."

"Whatever," my friend said, getting to his feet. "It did the trick. Thanks."

"Welcome. You ready?"

"Lead on, McDuff."

"Hey! I thought you said that wasn't a real quote."

Orson gave me a companionable shove, which sent me sprawling over a boulder. "Yeah, well ... Anyway, go ahead, Steve. I'm right behind you."

We traveled another hundred yards, and then we came to a sudden narrowing of the passageway. The "hibbidity gibbities" were starting up behind me again. "Orson, have a seat and look the other way. I'll scout on ahead."

He was sweating again, but he nodded then fell heavily to the ground, humming 'Count Your Blessings' in a tenuous, if mellifluous, voice.

I had to get down on my hands and knees to crawl into the narrow opening. Turns out, though, that the skinny stretch was only a few feet long before it opened onto a large cavern. I stood up, splayed my light toward the ceiling, into the distance. The area was as big as an arena.

"Good news," I said, when my head popped out on Orson's side of the narrowing. "This is only a couple of yards long. On the other side, there's a cavern that would put anything at Carlsbad to shame."

"Doesn't matter," Orson said, matter-of-factly. He'd manage to calm himself down again. "I'm too fat. I'd never fit through."

"Sure you would," I said encouragingly. "I'll help you."

"Promise I won't get stuck?"

"Promise. Do you want me to go first?"

"No," he said climbing to his feet. His face was covered in sweat again. "If I *do* get stuck, it will be easier for you to push me through than pull me out." With that, he knelt down and started to crawl.

Orson was right. He *was* too fat and he *did* get stuck, but using a conveniently-placed boulder for leverage, I put a shoulder against his butt and shoved him through. There was an audible "pop," and then he was free and on the other side. Panting from the exertion, I followed.

The cavern was long, with a high vault of sulfur-tinted stone above us. It didn't look like anyone came here very often, for the walkway was free of the littered debris typical of mine workers in Hell, things like cigarette butts, toilet paper rolls, used sheets of toilet paper, condoms and so forth. You would find most of those in other parts of the mine, though many were sprinkled around just for effect. No one, for instance, needed a condom in a place where the very thought of sex with a filthy, sweaty coworker was at the least unpleasant and the most noxious. Such items were completely absent here, not even around for effect, meaning that the damned didn't come here anymore, if they ever did. There was no point wasting effort to decorate a portion of Hell that got no visitors.

Yet we could hear voices, louder now. Someone had come this way recently, or at least found their way here by a different route. And they were nearby. Orson and I made eye contact, and nodded to each other. As quietly as possible, we walked toward the voices, which came from another shaft that intersected the cavern about halfway across. We were just outside the entrance to the passage, when the sounds of footsteps coming in our direction made us scatter for cover. We extinguished our helmet lights.

From out of the shaft, the hulking figure of Azazel emerged. He was trailed by the even larger form of Digger. "We'll leave her there for a while," said the devil. "No one will find her this deep in the mine."

Digger scraped along behind Azazel, creating a wall of dust with his passage. Both Orson and I struggled to keep from coughing. "When we open mine again, master?" he said in his best Igor-inspired voice. "Digger must dig. DIG, DIG, DIG!!"

What a moron.

Azazel looked at him with contempt. "You will open the mine when I say so, after my business is done. Understand, simpleton?"

Digger scratched at his forehead with a huge excuse for a hand. "Understand simple ton. About two thousand pounds. Lots of sulfur to make a simple ton. Lots of digging! Lots!" The demon grinned, and drool fell from his long tongue, which frequently lolled to one side of his mouth as if he were a dog taking a ride in a pickup truck. The slobber was enough to make about a gallon of yellow paste when it mixed with the sulfur on the ground.

The devil closed his eyes and pinched the bridge of his nose. I could relate. Trying to communicate the simplest thing to Digger was like teaching algebra to a basset hound. "Just ... just go take a nap somewhere, okay?"

"Duh, okay!" Digger took two steps off the pathway and collapsed, unconscious, to the ground.

Azazel just sighed then, with a snap of his fingers, he disappeared.

"Well," Orson said. "I guess the coast is clear."

Unless there were a thousand demons waiting for us down the tunnel. I swallowed hard. "Seems so. Let's go."

Chapter 24

We thwacked each other on the head to get our lights going again, then, as silently as possible, crept into the passageway. This portion of the mine was more precisely hewn from the rock than where we had been before. It looked almost like a corridor, with smooth sides and a floor as flat as the concrete of a well-poured garage. The walls had lost their yellow hue and were now a steel gray. The corridor was straight, and very long.

"What *is* this place?" Orson asked. "I feel like we've left the mine and entered Alcatraz."

"Yeah, the walls look more like metal than stone." I ran my hand across the surface. It was utterly smooth. "Orson, I think it *is* metal." As I said it, I noticed that our boots were clanging against the floor. I stopped walking and motioned for my friend to do the same. The echo of our footsteps faded.

"I think we're going to need to tread very softly from now on," I whispered.

"I'll do my best," he replied in an equally soft voice, "but this is where my stealth skills will reach their limits. It's hard to tiptoe when you're as heavy as I am."

I nodded. "Just do your best."

Fifty feet ahead the corridor made a sharp bend to the right. I followed.

"Psst! Steve!"

"What?" I said, looking as far along the passageway as I could for any signs of movement.

"Where the corridor turned. Look!"

I don't know how I'd missed it, but there was a door knob, recessed into the wall. Looking closely, I could see the faint outline of a tightly fitted door. Orson tried the knob, it turned easily, and he opened the door. On the other side was another corridor, much like the one along which we were traveling. "I'm going to check this out," he said. "You go on ahead. I'll catch up with you in a minute."

"Okay, but be careful, and don't let … "

As soon as Orson stepped through the opening, the door slammed shut, making a sound like a thunderclap.

" … the door close behind you." I sighed and reached for the knob. It was stuck. "Great," I mumbled, "just great," and reached for my crowbar.

Before I could shimmy my tool into the tight recess between door and frame, a light began to glow from said recess. It turned white hot then, as abruptly as it appeared, it faded. There was now no evidence that a door had ever existed there. Even the door knob was gone.

"Orson!" I yelled, beating on the wall, where the door had been, only to be answered by a metallic thud, thud, thud. I stopped, realizing that I could be drawing a bunch of unwanted attention to myself. When the echo from my pounding died away, I put my ear to the wall, hoping to hear Orson's voice or some hammering from the other side. Anything. But there was only silence.

I thought back to the pictures on Azazel's wall. Orson's image was among them, and it probably had just received an X through it. One by one, my friends were disappearing. By now, they probably had Pinkerton too.

Sadness overwhelmed me momentarily, but then something else. Anger. I was as mad as I'd ever been, which was good. I'd take anger over sadness any day. I clutched at my ire, nursed it, like a backpacker fanning a campfire flame, until it was a full-burning fury. At that moment, I wouldn't have cared if I was going up against Satan himself. I was ready to take on anyone.

Someone was going to pay for nabbing my friends.

For the moment, there was no way to help Orson, so I continued along the corridor, noticing that I'd pulled my hammer from the tool belt. The thought of bashing someone's skull with it filled me with a savage pleasure.

In another fifty yards, the corridor turned to the left again. What I saw on the other side of the bend made me gasp. There, in a steel cell fronted with a thick pane of glass, was Florence. She was sitting in a chair, her head downcast, her wrists shackled together. There was no one else in sight, so I risked calling out to her.

"Flo!" I yelled loudly.

Florence lifted her head and saw me. Her face lit up. I think she called out my name, but the glass was so thick, I couldn't hear her voice. She was wearing the same dress she'd had on that morning. It was a little disheveled, and I'm sure she would have been horrified if she could have seen herself. Her garment was stained and wrinkled, the top button, which she was always so careful to keep fastened, was unclasped. Her nurse's cap was gone and her hair, which she usually wore up underneath the cap, was beginning to fall in loose chestnut curls around the nape of her neck. Disheveled she was, but still sublimely beautiful.

Flo got out of the chair and walked stiffly toward the glass. That was when I noticed that her shackles were chained to one leg of the chair. The links of her tether pulled taut as she reached the glass. She tried to pound on her enclosure, but all she could manage was to touch the glass before the chain reached its full length. She called my name again, and I heard her voice, very softly, say my name.

It broke my heart to see her treated so. "Stand back!" I hollered. "I'm going to try to break the glass."

Seeing the hammer in my hand, she nodded and stepped a few feet away. I reared back then struck the glass with all my strength. Nothing, not even a chip like what you'd see on a car windshield that had been struck by a rock. Again and again I pounded on the glass, to no effect.

From behind me came the sound manic laughter, followed by enthusiastic applause. "Very good, Minion!"

A dozen feet away, Azazel watched me with a buzzard's glee, as if he'd just found a new piece of carrion. "You finally found Nightingale. Of course, I fed you so many clues, even you had to figure it out eventually."

"Fed me clues? I don't understand."

"You will soon enough. Bwahahahahahaha! And pounding on the glass will do you no good. It's unbreakable. Magic, you know," he said, a savage grin on his face. He wiggled his fingers at me, and bolts of lightning shot at my head. Fortunately I was holding my hammer at the time, and it took the brunt of the electrical charge. Its handle grew hot in my hand, and I dropped it.

In great, bounding leaps, Azazel rushed me. "Boogahboogahboogah!" he cried, and I fell, cowering on the ground beside my hammer.

Madness loomed over me in the form of a grinning, leering Azazel. "You!" I gasped, fighting to contain my terror. I heard a whimper, and glanced quickly at Flo, who was looking on in horror. "This … this was all your doing!"

"Yes!" he hissed. "I kidnapped Nightingale, left the note in her apartment, covered it with my own prints, knowing that Pinkerton would help you determine that a devil had made the note. Ah. AH AH AH!"

That strange, breathy laugh of his: it was creepier than the patented Bwahahahahahaha. A devil who could laugh like that was capable of anything.

"Then there was my sigil, Nightingale's faked fingerprint and Digger's footprint outside the hospital. Ah. AH AH AH! You should have found those first. They had been there all along, from the first moment Nightingale disappeared. Puny human! Too stupid to think to look for them."

"Hey!" I said reflexively. Despite my fear, my smart mouth often worked on its own, and it was doing so now. Yet he was right. I should have examined the plaza first thing. "So ... so you wanted me to figure it out?"

"Of course, clod! I wanted you to find Nightingale, to see how utterly under my power she was."

"And my other friends?" I said, my anger beginning to resurface.

"I have them all. Even Mr. Welles, now! Ah. AH AH AH!" He raised his arms in triumph.

I took that moment to roll away from him, grabbing my hammer as I did. He was so caught up in gloating that, for a wonder, he let me. Never taking my eyes off Azazel, I got to my feet.

"You'd better not hurt him!" I said, clutching my hammer tightly.

"Or what?" he said with a sneer. "You'll hit me with your hammer?" He waved his hands in my direction.

My hand tingled. I looked down and saw a feather in my grasp. I think it was from a mallard, but I've never been very good at my birds. I let it fall to the floor.

"Your friends are in my power, every one of them," he hissed. "And especially Miss Nightingale."

"You can't hurt her!" I yelled, indignant. "She is a saved soul. Not even Satan can hurt her."

"Satan. Ha. You'll find there is very little that I cannot do." Azazel made a fist with one hand and with the other wrapped an invisible line around it.

While we talked, Florence had been watching us, her face full of dread. As Azazel began his winding motion, she was suddenly jerked backward. Her chain was wrapping itself around her chair, and soon she was pulled fast to it.

Azazel snapped his fingers, and Flo's chair transformed into a pyre. My love, chains still around her wrist, was stretched across dry wood, propped up on her forearms. The devil glanced in her direction, and flames began to lick out from the bottom of the pyre.

"You say I cannot hurt her. Let's test that, shall we? First Nightingale will suffer the Fires of Hell. If they do not rend her from existence, I will put her in my special place. The place of darkness. That place you visited. Where souls are destroyed." He looked at me meaningfully.

I gasped. That's why he'd left me there after giving me the third degree. Azazel had almost snuffed out my own soul, just to show me the extent of his power. He seemed perfectly capable of doing what I thought no one could. My chest felt like it would explode from the anxiety I felt for Flo.

In seconds, the small blaze around Flo had become a bonfire. Her eyes were wide with terror. She looked at me and mouthed my name - that much I was sure of, though I could not hear her voice.

Flo was already in agony. Her hair had fallen to her shoulders. Her face was pink and damp from the heat, and her chest heaved, as she tried to catch a breath. The buttons on her nurse's dress pulled open as she strained against her restraints. Despite the awful moment, her beauty took my breath away.

"Stop it! Stop it!" I screamed. "What do you want from her?"

"Bwahahahahahaha! From her, nothing! As you and Welles already figured out, you have always been my target."

"Then, then what do you want from me?"

"Shall I tell him?" Azazel whispered to himself, chuckling. It was really creepy. "Yes, I think I shall." He looked up at me. "I want you to become a demon and work for Satan."

I felt like a three-year old with too much cotton candy in my stomach who had just been spun around by a carnival twirly barf, that is, dizzy and nauseated. "But ... but I thought you hated Satan!"

He leered at me, flashing his sharp canines in the process. Devil smiles always made me shudder. "I hate everyone, human!" He hesitated. "But Satan is my lord and master. I must do as he commands."

The flames were getting higher; Flo looked ready to collapse into the waiting arms of the fire. "Wait a minute, wait a minute!" I said frantically, trying to think through things. "You can't force me to become a demon. I have to choose of my own free will."

"Then choose, Minion," Azazel said briskly. "Understand that I am not torturing you. I am not forcing you to do anything. You are perfectly free to walk away from here, unharmed. Your beloved on the other hand ... ." The devil rubbed his hands together in anticipation.

"Flo!"

"I can't force you, I can't even torture you into signing this contract," Azazel said. He held out his hand and a scroll appeared, along with a Papermate pen. "But there's nothing that says I can't torture the people you love."

"But ... "

"Choose, Minion!" Azazel looked at the blaze and the woman in the midst of it. "Lovely. Reminds me of Joan of Arc. For now, at least. Choose, Minion, and do so quickly, before Miss Nightingale shares Joan's fate."

The flames had almost enveloped her. I did not know if they could destroy her soul, but if they couldn't, the Dark Place would. I turned to the crazed devil. "If I agree, will you release her, and all of my friends, immediately?"

Azazel frowned. "Y ... yes," he said reluctantly. "I would just as soon destroy them, but I must do as Satan commands."

In the end, it was a pretty easy choice. I took the contract and pen from him. "Okay. Where do I sign?"

Azazel indicated a line at the bottom of the contract. "Don't worry about all the fine print. Legalease, pretty standard boilerplate."

And then I knew him for the consummately evil creature that he was. He sounded just like a lawyer.

With a sigh of defeat, I clicked the Papermate and hurriedly tried to scrawl my name where he indicated. The pen was dry.

"You can't sign an infernal contract with ink. Something more binding is required." Azazel took the pen from my hand and jabbed it in my palm.

"Ouch!" I yelled, as blood began to pour from the wound.

"You must sign in your own blood. Ah. AH AH AH! "

Feeling that I was crossing over into a land from which I could never return, I signed, handing him back the contract and pen.

I looked at Azazel. "Okay, I've signed. Now let her go, like you said you would ... and the rest of my friends too."

The devil shrugged and waved his hand. The flames, along with the glass and Flo's shackles, disappeared. I ran to her, helped her to her feet, which she regained with easy poise. "Sorry, Steve."

But the voice was not Flo's. Before my eyes, my love transformed into a sexy, saucy and familiar redhead. "Lilith!"

She shrugged and stepped into the corridor. "Everybody's got a boss. I have to do what I'm told, like everyone else down here."

"Bwahahahahahaha! Minion, you really *are* a chump!"

Before my eyes, Azazel became Satan.

Chapter 25

"This whole thing was a trick?" I covered my face with my hands. "It was all a scam? And I'm a demon now?"

"Righto on all counts!" the Earl of Hell said, a big grin on his face. "Ooo, what fun that was!"

At that moment, Orson came ambling around the corner of the corridor. "Hey, Steve. Sorry, but I got lost for a few minutes." He skidded to a stop when he saw Satan and Lilith. "Uh, what's going on? Where's Flo?"

"A very good question! And I'm just itching to tell you all about it. First, though," Satan said, turning to Lilith, "Well done, Succubus First Class. You may continue with your afternoon off, though I may have an assignment for you later," he said, winking at her.

"Yes, my lord," Lilith said, bowing. She looked at me mournfully, then Satan snapped his fingers, and she was gone.

"Let's go somewhere where I can be more comfortable as I rub your nose in today's happenings." Satan walked over to a door that I had not noticed before, not far from the chamber that had held the faux-Flo. He opened the door and stepped inside, beckoning the two of us to follow.

We were in Satan's office. How we had gotten from the Sixth Circle to the Ninth I do not know, but his domain, his rules, I guess. Satan was in an exceptionally good mood; he even allowed us two modest but comfortable chairs, which he gestured for us to sit in. His own red La-Z-Boy popped out from the floor behind his large, rosewood desk. The Devil hopped into the chair, kicked back to recline the back and raise the footrest then let out a great sigh of contentment.

It had been a good day for the son-of-a-bitch.

"I've invited you both to my office today so that I could gloat. As you once said, Demon Fourth Class Minion, I do so enjoy gloating."

"Er, why am I here, sir?" Orson asked. I don't think he'd ever been in Satan's office before, and he looked more than a little bit intimidated.

Satan lowered his sunglasses to reveal the scarlet version of his eyes. Having those two beady red orbs lock onto you would make anyone shudder. Orson practically convulsed in his chair. "Welles, normally I'd blast you for asking a question out of turn, but I'm in a good mood, so I'll let it pass. Welles, Welles," he said to himself, thoughtfully. "No, that won't do. I'll call you Orson. It's funnier, just like Minion is funnier than Steve, right Demon Fourth Class Minion?"

"You lied to me," I said sullenly. "You tricked me into signing that paper. I thought the rule was I had to agree of my own free will."

Satan grinned. "But you *did* sign of your own free will. A little trickery was involved, yes," he conceded in an offhand fashion, "but nothing of substance."

"Nothing of substance?" I sputtered. "Nothing of substance? You pretended to be Azazel!"

"No I didn't," he replied, grinning. "I *am* Azazel, just like I'm Lucifer and television static. Azazel is simply one of my aspects. Of course not very many know that. Almost no demon or human does. They've just heard vague rumors of a boogyman devil. I don't assume the persona very often, but occasionally I find being Azazel useful, not to mention great fun."

I rubbed my chin in thought. "Do many devils know you're Azazel?"

"Oh, sure. They all do."

"Including TNK-el, I suppose."

"Tink? Of course. He's one of my oldest friends, if I had any friends of course. I've known him forever. Why, he was my roommate in angel school back in the day."

"Angel school?" Orson asked.

"That's where we took courses in adoration and obedience. As you can imagine, I was not the best student."

"Never mind about that," I said heatedly. I was mad. No one likes being made a fool of, especially when the stakes were so high. "So TNK-el was in on this?"

"Why sure! And don't let his small size fool you. He's an excellent devil. Very evil. Very devious."

"That much seems clear." *Grumble.* "But what about my friends? You kidnapped them to use as leverage against me."

"Ah," sighed the Lord of Hell, nestling his head deep into the red cushion of his chair. "That's the beauty of a good plan. You only assumed I kidnapped them. Just like Orson here. He walked down a corridor, got lost for a few minutes and found his way back."

I looked to my friend who shrugged and nodded.

"Braille had a fare that took him three hundred miles out of downtown, and out of radio contact with his dispatcher, I might add. Then his car broke down, and he had to spend hours fixing it. As for Tesla, he is just now returning to the farm from a wild goose chase I sent him on. He has a note from me though, so he won't get in trouble with the overseer. Pinkerton I never even touched. He's still in his workshop making his execrable barrels."

"And Flo," I said with intensity. "What about Flo?"

Satan began to laugh, not his Bwahaha laugh, or even that fakeo Ah. AH AH AH! he affected when he pretended to be Azazel. This was a hearty guffaw; he was genuinely amused.

"Why, she went to a conference on pie charts. Didn't she tell you she was going this morning when you had coffee together?"

Crap. The conference. "She said she was thinking about it, but hadn't decided."

"Oh, I'm sure she would have let you know, like send you a letter or something. In fact, I bet there's one waiting for you when you get back to your office."

That would be the letter she mailed at the nurse's station. Crap.

"She probably did. But where exactly is this conference? No one has seen here anywhere in Hell."

The Prince of Darkness positively glowed. "That's because the conference was in Heaven. One of the Powers there beamed her up as a courtesy."

"The bright light," I whispered.

"Yes. The bright light. Miss Nightingale rushed out of the hospital as quickly as she did so as not to miss her ride, which she only found out about when she read that note at the nurse's station. She could have just taken the Elevator, I suppose, but she hates the demon who runs it." He grinned. "That was just good luck for me, and I capitalized on it, but Nightingale can go upstairs anytime she wants to, you know. That's one of the benefits of being saved."

"Do tell," Orson muttered sourly.

For the first time since our interview began, Satan frowned. "Orson, are you going to demonstrate the same insubordination your predecessor did?"

"No ... no, my lord!" he said hurriedly. "Wait a second, what predecessor are you talking about?"

"Why Minion, of course. He's a demon now, just like Charlemagne after he left the head of Plant Maintenance job, so Steve-o will be moving on to other responsibilities. In the absence of any better, by which I mean worse, candidates I've decided to promote you to Hell's Super."

"Really?" Orson flushed. "But I thought you didn't want me to accomplish anything in the afterlife."

"I don't really. Not to worry. I'll make certain the jobs you undertake are usually beyond your abilities. That shouldn't be hard, since you suck at handyman work even more than Minion here."

"Gee, thanks. I guess." Orson frowned.

"And I think I'll make Edison your assistant."

My friend looked even more shocked. "But, but he loathes me!"

"Yes. Isn't that great? Your experience during the HVAC Affair, working with him, was a bit of a revelation to me and Beelzebub. You two hate each other, and having a mechanical genius work as a flunky to you, a mechanical dimwit, well, it's just too perfect. Besides, it separates him and Ford. I should never have allowed the two to work together. Their buddy-buddy, partners-in-crime crap is nauseating. They'll suffer, you'll suffer, though in a different way than you have over the last sixty or seventy years, and I'll get to watch you for any potential to be a demon."

"Me?" Orson said, shocked. "I'm way too fat."

"Easily remedied!" Satan said. "I've got any number of gastric bypass surgeons down here to take care of that. Or," he said, reconsidering, "Beezy or I could just blast the excess fat from your body. Or maybe both of us could. Yes! That would be perfect, like an archery contest!"

"But that … that would be decades away, right sir?" Orson probably didn't like the prospect of being target practice for the two top dogs in Hell, but he already had the toadying down better than I ever did.

"Yes. You'd have to prove yourself first. Now, get out of here while I finish talking to Minion. I've already sent transfer orders to Digger about sending Edison to your office."

Orson stood quickly, which was good, since his chair had just dematerialized. "Yes sir," he said, saluting. "I won't let you down, sir." With that, Orson left the office.

"I doubt that," Satan muttered.

Something had been bothering me. Well, lots of things were bothering me, but this one in particular. "The Dark Place. The place where souls are destroyed. I didn't know that was possible, but I experienced it myself. It was nothingness. I felt my own brain shutting down."

At this, Satan howled with laughter. "You mean my broom closet?" He pointed to the blackness behind his chair. A spotlight lit up briefly to illuminate an inconspicuous door about forty feet away. "I stuffed you in my closet and suspended you in midair for a while. You know," he said, as if he were giving me a lecture, "your kind's brain is a funny thing. Put humans in complete isolation, deprive their senses of any input, and they can imagine all sorts of things. Usually they come up with some pretty interesting hallucinations. In your case," he chortled, "you thought your soul was being destroyed. Of course, I was pushing that idea on your subconscious while you were in there. Completely understandable mistake on your part."

"I ... I was in your broom closet."

"It's a very big broom closet," he said with a grin.

Closing my eyes, I put my head in my hands. My moan sounded like a tire being deflated.

Satan chuckled. "Yep. I wanted you to think Azazel had the ability to destroy a soul. Upped the stakes, don't you think?"

Sigh.

"Now, Demon Fourth Class Minion, how do you think Orson will do as your replacement?"

Slowly I opened my eyes and looked at the Earl of Hell. "He'll do okay, I guess."

"Tell me, Steve-o, for all these years, why couldn't you have been more respectful, like Orson was just now?"

"I have a smart mouth," I admitted. "It's always gotten me in trouble."

"Well, never mind. It's one of the things about you that first caught my attention. I like humans feisty and independent. They're much more fun to torment when they're like that, especially when they finally cave."

"I never caved, sir," I said with quiet pride.

"No, you never did. I'll give you that. Of course, that's all over now. Beast Barracks will get rid of your last vestiges of independence, now that you no longer have free will."

"I ... what?"

"Oh, didn't I tell you?" he said with mock concern. "Only humans have free will. When you signed on to become a demon, you gave it up."

"But that's ridiculous. I still feel the same."

"Do you? Demon Fourth Class, I'd like you to slam your head into my desktop."

Without a thought I did it.

"Now, poke yourself in the eyes."

I immediately gave myself a Three Stooges special. "Ow!"

"See? No free will. In the old days, you would have argued with me. But now that you're no longer human, that has ended."

The significance of what I'd done finally hit me. Free will. I'd never thought about it before, but the ability to choose between alternatives, especially moral alternatives, was the defining characteristic of humanity. That meant I was now little more than an animal, an animal who could follow orders, but an animal nonetheless. The scope of my loss took the wind from my lungs. "I'm … I'm not human at all?" I finally managed to say.

"Nope. You may still look human, at least for a while, but you're now a demon through and through. But don't worry, being human is vastly overrated. Demonhood is much better, you'll see." He paused. "There will likely be some residual human characteristics, especially for one like you, who has always been of an independent mind, but they'll fade over time, and as I said, Beast Barracks will help you get rid of them."

"Beast Barracks?" I said faintly. I was still in shock.

"Yes. Think of it as demon Boot Camp. That is where you'll learn how to be a demon. We'll tear you down and build you back up into something better. Here," he said, handing me an envelope that he'd summoned from midair. "These are your orders. You have the rest of the day free to get your affairs in order. Tomorrow you report to Level Eight for Beast Barrack."

"And, and tonight?"

"You will bivouac at the demon quarters indicated. It's all in there," he said, with a smile. He had beaten me utterly, and I guess he felt he could afford to be patient with me. "Go on, open the envelope."

With numb fingers, I lifted the seal and pulled out my orders, read through them. I felt sick.

Satan stood, and he motioned for me to do the same, which I did without hesitation. "Welcome to the Devil and Demon Corps, Demon Fourth Class. Now, dismissed!"

Chapter 26

Slowly I walked to the Elevator. Orson was still there, silently fuming over the long time he'd been waiting, but he looked at me with concern when he saw my face. "Are you okay?"

"No. Not really." I pressed the button, and the Elevator door immediately opened.

"Why didn't it open for me?" he grumbled.

"Because you're a human," echoed a voice through the metal of the car, as the doors closed around us. It was the demon who animated the Elevator. "Welcome to the team, Steve."

"Yeah. Thanks," I said woodenly.

"No problem, buddy." Funny, all these years of riding the Elevator, and it had never once talked to me. Now it was a Chatty Cathy. "Where to?"

"I have a few stops, starting with Level Eight, please. I think I should resign in person."

"No problem." The doors closed and the Elevator took off. Almost immediately, there was a ding. I had reached Level Eight.

"This shouldn't take long. See you in a bit, Orson."

My friend gave me a crooked little smile. "Okay."

"Hey, what about me?" said the demon running the Elevator.

I rolled my eyes. "I'll see you soon, too."

The Elevator obligingly set me on the edge of the bazaar, a hundred feet from Beezy's office. With great reluctance, I pushed through the revolving door.

Beelzebub was expecting me. He was sitting at his desk and motioned for me to sit in the guest chair.

For a long moment, I said nothing, and Beezy, surprisingly, didn't push me. In fact, if I thought it was possible for a devil to look sympathetic, that's how I would have described my boss at that moment.

I cleared my throat. "I guess I'm here to resign."

Beezy shook his head. "I guess Satan didn't give you much choice."

"Why, why didn't you tell me Azazel was Satan in disguise?"

The Lord of the Flies snorted. "Come on, Minion. Satan is my boss, whether I always agree with his tactics or not. For what it's worth, I'm sorry it came to this." Beelzebub picked a dead fly from between his teeth. "You've been a good Super, Steve. Orson has big shoes to fill."

"You mean clown shoes, don't you? I've been wandering around like a clown all day."

Beelzebub laughed gently. "You didn't stand a chance. No one does when Satan puts his mind to trickery. He's the Master Manipulator, you know."

"Guess so."

"Buck up, Steve. It won't be so bad. You'll be treated a lot better in the future, I can promise you that."

"Yeah, but I've lost free will."

He shrugged. "Ah, free will. I've always thought that was overrated anyway, not that I've experienced it firsthand, but your precious free will seems to have got humans into more trouble than they would have if they hadn't had it to begin with."

"Not my precious free will," I said standing up. "At least not any more. Now I'm not even human."

"'fraid not. But then, you're not damned either, not anymore than I am."

"Aren't we?"

He shrugged again. "All a matter of perspective, I suppose. See you around, Steve." He reached out his hand, and I shook it.

"Thanks, Lord Beelzebub. You're been a better boss than I would have ever expected down here."

"Oh, drop the formality. You can call me Beezy, at least when other devils and demons aren't around. You've been calling me Beezy behind my back for sixty years, and all my friends call me that anyway, so I don't see why you shouldn't also." He swatted at the fog of insects that surrounded him. "Just don't call me Flyface."

I smiled. Good old Beezy. Somehow he'd managed to make me feel a little better about my new circumstances. We shook hands again and I left.

When the Elevator door opened, Orson was still inside.

"What are you doing here?" I asked.

"I don't know for sure, since the Elevator won't talk to a mere human," Orson grumbled, "but I'm guessing he was waiting for you."

"Now where, Steve?" said the Elevator brightly, ignoring Orson's complaints.

"Five, if you would. I've got some packing to do."

"You betcha. Have you there in two shakes."

When the door opened, automatically I noted, which was unusual on any Level except Nine, we found BOOH waiting for us. He looked miserable. His ears were back against his head, fur matted even more than usual, and his beady red eyes looked a bit misty.

"Hi, BOOH," I said limply. Then I thought of something. "Did you, did you know about this?"

He shook his head no, and I believed him.

"Thanks, pal," I said, patting him on the shoulder. Without my asking he gently lifted the two of us and flew the few blocks to our office. "I guess maybe I'll be seeing a little more of you in the future?"

It seemed to me that he smiled, wistfully, then nodded.

"Well, that's something at least. See you soon big guy."

"Urm," he said, as he stroked my head gently with one of the small hands growing out of his wings. Then he launched into the air and flew off.

I turned the knob on the office door. It opened without protest, and we went inside.

Looking around the office, I realized there was nothing for me to pack. I saw my "I'm not With Stupid. I AM Stupid" mug, but I didn't think I'd be able to take that with me.

"I'll hold onto it for you, in case you ever come by for a visit."

If I come by, I'll likely be here to hurt you, not drink coffee. But what I said was, "Thanks."

I took off my tool belt and draped it across my desk, pulled out my keys, including the all-important Elevator key, and put them in the top drawer. At the last second, I grabbed a roll of duct tape and stuffed it in my pocket. *Maybe they'll let me use it sometimes. I'm good with duct tape.* But then I realized I would need to leave even duct tape behind. I set the roll on top of my tool belt for Orson, hoping he'd practice. Being a good duct tape slinger in Hell was a skill worth having.

"I, I don't know what I'm supposed to wear tomorrow, so I'll keep the coveralls for now. Thank you Orson," I said, shaking his hand for what I feared was the last time. "You have been a great friend."

Was that a tear I saw in his eye? "You too, Steve."

When the smoke cleared, only Orson was on the ground with cream on his face. I had been bypassed, another benefit, I supposed, of being a demon. I helped him to his feet, since no one had told me I couldn't. *Not yet, anyway.*

"I'll swing by my apartment, see if there's anything there I need, then head on to my first assignment." I didn't want to tell him what it was. "Would you … would you tell Flo what happened? I don't think I could face her now. I know how much she hates demons, and, well, now I am one. Bye, Orson."

"I'll tell Flo all about it, including the sacrifice you made. Satan may have tricked you, but what you did was the greatest expression of love I've ever seen." Orson's face could have been the mask of tragedy. He was a very good actor, but I knew his sadness was genuine. He looked at me for a very long time, swallowed hard, then said, "Goodbye, Steve. Good luck."

I gave him a mournful smile. "You too." Then I left.

The walk to my apartment seemed to take forever, and my steps up each flight of the six story climb were weighted with lead. I opened the door. The roaches, who were my constant companions in the small studio apartment, lined the walls, almost like an honor guard. It was creepy, but somehow seemed fitting.

I walked around the apartment. There really wasn't much in there that I cared about. In the end, I took a pillowcase and stuffed it full of my clown suit, my puffy shirt and my mauve hot pants. Heading toward the door, I saw a red velour outfit draped across the sofa. I looked at it with suspicion, but knew instinctively that it was my new uniform. I stripped off my yellow coveralls and dropped them to the floor, where a swarm of cockroaches flowed over them.

I slipped on the tight-fitting outfit and zipped it up. Underneath the garment was a set of demon horns attached to a metal band. I slipped it onto my forehead then examined myself in the mirror attached to the inside of my front door. Apparently, this was supposed to be a demon costume, something to wear until my own horns and tail grew in, but I felt more like a plush Easter bunny. The horns looked like rabbit ears, though the tail, instead of being a giant wad of cotton, was a flaccid spear.

I picked up the pillow case then realized that there would be no more place in my new life for the few garments inside than for the coveralls lying discarded on the floor. I tossed the stuff on the couch.

With a sigh, I opened the door. On a whim, I turned and saluted the roaches, who had reassumed their positions lining the walls of my flat. Remarkably, they saluted me back. Then I closed the doors and headed down the stairs.

Hell's Elevator dinged as soon as I pressed the button. "Where to, Steve?"

I looked down at my orders. There was one person I wanted to see before I started my tour of duty. "I no longer have my elevator key, but can you take me to Gates Level?"

"It's against the rules, but Satan said to indulge you today, so sure."

"Then lets go," I said grimly.

The DMZ of the afterlife was all but deserted when I arrived. St. Peter was leaning on his podium looking bored. For the first time since we'd met, I was unintimidated by the supercilious saint. I stomped over to his desk. "Why?"

"Why what?" Peter asked, then recognized me. "Minion, why are you dressed … oh! You decided to become a demon?"

"Yes," I snarled, "in part because of you."

"Me? Me?" He really seemed nonplussed by the accusation. "What did I have to do with it?"

"Just answer me one question."

"What?"

"Did you know that Azazel is just one of Satan's many aspects?"

272

Peter gave his signature snort, and I almost slugged him it. But he answered the question. "Of course. What of it?"

"When I was here earlier today, you said he was a devil who could not be trusted, a dangerous character."

"And so he is."

"Yeah, but you didn't say he was also Satan. Why not?"

Peter narrowed his eyes as he looked at me. "Because you had just lied to me about BOOH. I don't like being lied to, you know."

I thought back to our encounter. "BOOH had brought me up here without permission from Satan. I was trying to protect him, you jerk!"

Heaven's Concierge looked as if I slapped him. He was preparing a withering response, I'm sure, but then he stopped himself. "I didn't know you were lying to protect him. Do you," he said slowly, "do you mean my not telling you about Azazel played a role in you becoming a demon?"

"Indirectly, yes," I said, fuming. "Satan, as Azazel, tricked me into signing a demon contract, because I thought he would hurt Flo."

"But he couldn't do that. Don't you get it? Flo can't be hurt by Satan. She's saved."

"Yes!" I said, slamming my hand down on his desk. "But I didn't know what Azazel was capable of. He threatened me with the destruction of her soul."

"He can't do that!" Peter said, outraged, then abruptly quieted. "But you, you didn't know that, did you?"

"No, I didn't. But now I want *you* to know something. Because of you, I'm now a demon. I've given up free will, and I've now given up what little hope was left inside me. I'm no longer human, and you played a big part in that, so, well, anks! Thanks heaps." With that, I turned my back on him and headed for the Elevator.

"Minion! Steve! Wait! I ... " The Elevator door closed behind me, silencing his voice.

"Man!" said the demon running the lift. "I've never heard anybody chew out St. Peter like that. Not even a prince of Hell. That was, well it was really cool."

"Yeah, well, fat lot of good it did me." There was no point putting things off any longer. "Take me to Level Two."

"Sure, pal!" There was awe in the demon's voice.

Outside of Hell's Elevator, I hailed a cab. It took me to a cul-de-sac on the outskirts of town. I paid the cabbie, even though, now that I was a demon, it was probably unnecessary. He took off, and I walked reluctantly to the front door of the two-story colonial, which, according to my orders, was tonight's bivouac.

Lilith opened the door before I knocked. She was back in a simple housedress, though on her it looked anything but simple. "Darling!" she said, kissing me warmly. "You're home! Wonderful! I'm just whipping us up some crackhead slammers. Come on in."

I stepped inside, and the door closed behind me.

An extract from the sequel to 'Deal With The Devil'

The Reluctant Demon

(Circles in Hell, Book Four)

Chapter 1

The constant, rapid trudge, trudge, trudge as the platoon trekked across the desert landscape was beginning to get to me – mainly because it was boring. To call our hike a trudge was complimenting the activity. It was more a series of plunges into the sand, as a foot would hit the surface, disappear beneath, then be pulled up by its owner, creating a slurp-pop sound more akin to plunging a clogged toilet. Then the next step would be taken, the second foot would sink in similar fashion and have to be slurp-popped out.

There was no sun in the sky – there is no sun in Hell, even in the arid wasteland of the Eighth Circle – but it sure felt like one was baking down on us, and from above there was a glare, enough to make me squint and point my face back toward my feet.

We were all in full pack, which for a demon meant five hundred pounds of dead weight, and this was a two hundred mile hike, at double time. If I hadn't been so intent on keeping my forward momentum, I might have reflected on the absurdity of it. Twenty recruits in a row, forty legs slipping beneath the sand, being popped back out hurriedly, so we could maintain our forty mile an hour pace, a brisk though not impossible speed that demons could maintain indefinitely. The pop-pop-pop sounded like a bubble wrap popping competition.

Things could be worse, I reflected, trying to keep up my spirits, which had been as low as Death Valley – an apt simile considering the circumstances – since I'd been tricked into becoming a demon. My horns and tail had begun to grow in – the tail was almost full size – which meant I had been allowed to abandon my plush demon costume, with its clip-on horns and fabric tush brush, the latter shaking formlessly as I walked. Now I wore what the other recruits had on, a dark blue tunic and red loose-fitting trousers, though no boots, since the drill sergeants were trying to toughen up our soles – if not our souls, which were pretty threadbare at this point – by exposing them to the blistering hot sand. I also had on a fairly smart looking red cap, with a two-inch visor and a piece of fabric hanging from the back of the hat, presumably to protect my neck from the sun. Since there was no sun, though, it was mere affectation. My new pitchfork was resting on my shoulder, like a rifle might have if I were in the French Foreign Legion instead of the Demon Corps.

I, Steve Minion, formerly Hell's Superintendent of Plant Maintenance, was the Underworld's newest recruit to the Corps. A cohort had started at Beast Barracks a week before I'd become a demon, but Satan, not wanting to delay my training, let me join the group late, forcing me to play catch-up. That said, I was holding my own, and then some, with the other, more experienced cadets. In fact, when the sergeants weren't performing their primary function, which was chewing us out, calling us the most miserable excuses for demons they'd ever seen, they'd privately told me I was the most promising new recruit they'd seen in centuries. I was already as strong as a demon, first class, and my strength was increasingly daily. I was also faster than even the most experienced members of the Corps. This last bit didn't surprise me as much as the strength thing; years of slinging duct tape at preternatural speed had me halfway there already.

Still, my natural aptitude in these areas was a bit of a mystery to me. The staff at Beast Barracks was as perplexed by my talents as I was.

And then there was my ability to teleport. The other recruits looked on me with envy, because I was the only one who had signed up during the "limited time offer" and gotten this special ability – very special, since apparently fewer than two dozen creatures in all of the Underworld possessed it. Of course, I wasn't very accomplished with teleportation yet. For example, I couldn't just do it at will. Yet sometimes, when I ate something that disagreed and belched, or when I got a case of the hiccups, I would transport ten or twenty feet. The end result usually left me slammed against a wall or boulder, tripped by an inconveniently placed cot, that sort of thing, but Sarge, the tall demon with primary responsibility for my training, said I'd get control over the ability soon enough. The power would be limited – it was unlikely I'd be able to instantaneously travel more than a mile at a pop – but that was more than almost any demon and even some devils could manage, so that made me something special.

Yep, I was going to make a great demon, just like Satan always said I would. That might have been a point of pride for me, if the consequence of my joining the Corps hadn't severed every relationship I'd built and cherished with a handful of other damned humans down here.

And one, undamned one. Flo, Florence Nightingale, who was in Hell trying to make the Underworld a little bit better place, would no longer have anything to do with me. Well, I didn't know that for a fact, since I hadn't seen her since agreeing to become a demon and being swept up into Beast Barracks for my basic training. Yet Flo loathed demons, perhaps even more than devils. Devils had had no choice in becoming what they were. They were intended to rebel in Heaven and fall to Hell. Demons, though, were generally former humans who elected to become demons of their own free will. Flo found this particularly despicable, that a human would choose to become a demi-devil - which, by the way, may be where the word "demon" came from in the first place, though some people think the word is shorthand for "devil-man" - a stand-in for Satan and the rest of senior management.

In my own defense, I had good reason for agreeing to be a demon. Well. That's not exactly true. It wasn't a good reason, but a stupid if well-intentioned one. I had been a dupe, a patsy. Satan had tricked me into thinking Flo's eternal soul would at best be tortured for all eternity and at worst be destroyed completely if I didn't volunteer for the Corps. To protect my one true love, I joined, not thinking things through carefully. If I had, I would have known that Satan had no power over Flo. He could bury her in as many slings and arrows as he'd like, and she would emerge unscathed.

I should have known that, but like I said, I was conned. My motives were good, but this was a time when letting my heart overrule my head didn't work out very well. Sourly, I reflected that I probably didn't even have a heart anymore. Now that my body was changing to the anatomy of a demon, there was likely some other organ that pumped the yellow ichor that served as demon blood through my veins.

Probably the spleen handles that.

"Pick up the pace, you goldbricks!" yelled one of the sergeants. The overseers of today's hike were traveling quite comfortably in a jeep. "I want to see you hit eighty miles an hour before we crest the next sand dune." He floored the accelerator and took off.

You want us to go fast? I'll show you fast. I kicked up my pace and practically flew across the sand. Shit, maybe I *was* flying. I could do all sort of things that used to be impossible for me.

Soon I was running faster than the jeep. I sped past them at what must have been a hundred miles an hour. My tail, which had been slapping limply against my butt all day with each step I took, was now stretched out behind me. I imagined it looked like an arrow, traveling at high speed but in reverse.

One of the sergeants looked at me in wide-eyed wonder, and I gave him a saucy little salute before leaving the jeep in my dust. I reached the top of the sand dune fifteen seconds before they did. That's when I saw the rock outcropping fifty feet ahead of me. At that moment, a mote of sand got lodged in a nostril, and I sneezed, teleporting the extra distance and plastering myself against the stone.

"Ooh ... " I felt a little woozy.

"Break's over!" yelled Sarge, my sarge, who was in the passenger seat of the jeep. "Get back in formation!" The vehicle zipped past me, followed in close order by the line of cadets.

"Show off," said the guy on the end, kicking sand in my face.

Well, I deserved that. Painfully I got to my feet and started running again. In a few seconds, I reached the back of the line, matching my pace with the rest of the crew.

The remainder of the day was spent in pitchfork practice. We started with one-on-one sparring, each trying to pierce the skin of his or her opponent first. I was coming along with the demon weapon-of-choice, but I had a long way to go. I quickly defeated my first partner, a buck-toothed fellow who reminded me of Gomer Pyle. He was probably too dim to realize he'd signed up for an eternity of being the guy in the black hat. I think he just liked the pitchfork. My second opponent, though, was a demon named Maximus. He was a natural fencer, not to mention being near to graduation – due to some pressing need for an additional demon in one of Hell's other circles – and he handled his weapon with a skill that I could only admire if not yet emulate. He also had a longer reach than I had, if not my speed. I tried to use my main advantage to get behind him, but as I swung by his right, he snagged the tines of my pitchfork with those of his own. With a deft flick of his wrist, he twisted the weapon out of my grasp. "Tag!" he said, snickering, as he poked me in my now-exposed side.

"Minion, you miserable maggot!" yelled Sarge. "That's the fourth time you've fallen for that maneuver. You're out of the game. Tomorrow morning, O four hundred hours, you'll train with me, and I promise that when I'm done with you, you'll never fall for that sucker ploy again." He grinned evilly at me.

Oh, shit. And that's two hours before reveille.

"Go practice transmutation, while the real fencers continue the game."

Discouraged, I walked over to a low wall and sat down. Then I began the transmutation forms I'd been taught. First, my pitchfork became a sword, then a tommy gun, like what Capone or one of his men might have used. After I'd practiced all the mandatory transformations, I was allowed to use my own imagination to come up with new forms. I turned the fork into an umbrella, a belt, which I thought would be a good way to carry it if I wanted to be incognito. I transformed it into a pink feather boa, draping it around my neck and doing a Carmen Miranda impression before a dirty look from Sarge cold-cocked me. Quickly I transformed my pitchfork into something more threatening, a spear.

"Better, maggot!" he said, walking over to me. "But it's easy to change a pitchfork into something with a similar shape. Try one that's completely different."

I nodded and concentrated. The spear collapsed in on itself, becoming a small, plastic container the size of canned peaches. Except it wasn't a can, it was …

"A jar of Vaseline? Why the hell did you do that?"

I picked up the jar and opened it, smearing some of the petroleum jelly on my lips. "I really hate chapped lips," I said, mildly embarrassed.

"Wha ... ?" Sarge broke out laughing. "You know, maggot, you're all right. For a maggot, that is."

"Thanks, Sarge," I said, blushing slightly, as I returned my jar of Vaseline to its original form.

He wiped a tear from his eye, still chuckling. "Tell me, maggot, do demons always carry their pitchforks?"

"No," I said, thinking back on all the demons I'd ever known, which in over sixty years of being in Hell, had been quite a few. Uphir, the demon physician and chief administrator of Hell's Hospital, for example, never carried his. "Well, some do, I guess, though they look pretty junior. Don't know what the more experienced demon does, but that's why I practiced the belt just now."

He shook his head. "That's not how it's done. Put it someplace else, where no one but you can get at it."

"Where would that be?"

"Figure it out for yourself."

I frowned. I'd seen some demons make their pitchforks appear out of thin air. That seemed to be a clue. I closed my eyes and imagined a little pocket universe that floated around with me, a place I could reach at any time, but that no one else could. Then I took my pitchfork, put it there, and closed up an invisible seam.

There was the sound of applause, and I opened my eyes. "Bravo!" said Sarge. "It takes some demons years to master that little trick."

"Can I put other things in there? Besides my pitchfork?"

"Yeah, a change of clothes, for example. I know one demon who plays the bassoon. He keeps his in his secret place and practices when he's off duty."

A demon bassoonist. Oh boy.

"You're a natural, Minion. I mean, maggot! You're the most talented new demon I've seen in almost two millennia of training you scum."

"Two millennia?" I said, appropriately impressed. "That would make you a pretty early Christian."

"You have no idea," he grumbled. "Oh well, forget about that. What I'm trying to say is, you're talented ... but don't let it go to your head!" he said abruptly, realizing he wasn't doing a sergeant's proper job of treating me like shit. "You still have a lot to learn. Now, get back out there and spar some more with your squad."

My pleasure at being praised for being a good little demon wasn't exactly rational. The last thing I'd ever wanted to become was a devil wannabe, yet, here I was, a new recruit. But Sarge's praise had its intended effect; I did a little better afterward, winning two out of three bouts.

Around eighteen hundred hours – or at least what the drill sergeants called eighteen hundred hours, since time really means nothing in Hell, and any reference to days, weeks or hours and minutes for that matter, were all pretty random – we headed to the mess hall. Standing near the back of the line, I grabbed a metal tray and an oversized spoon. Cookie took a large ladle out of a simmering vat and dumped its contents in one of the compartments of my tray. It spread out on the metal, filling the space and nearly overflowing into the next compartment.

I looked with distaste at the thin yellow gruel, punctuated with slightly more yellow larvae moving sluggishly through the boiled oats. Maggot stew for the maggots. I had long since gotten used to it, though. Besides, the stew was filling and nutritious, a good source of protein. It stuck to the ribs, when it wasn't slithering around in my stomach.

Added to my tray was a biscuit filled with nails that, surprisingly, my demon teeth had no trouble chewing, and a quivering mass of green Jello. In some ways, the gelatinous mass was the least appetizing item on my tray. I'd always hated lime Jello.

The food at Beast Barracks didn't fit the promotional brochures. For that matter, our accommodations in general were a far cry from the sun-drenched sandy beach prominently featured in all the PR. Not exactly Club Med. More like Club Dead, I suppose. About the only thing they got right, I thought ruefully, was the sand. Sarge told me the scene I'd experienced in Satan's office, the one with the beach babes and the umbrella drinks, was just a demo, a demon-stration if you will, although he promised that after Beast Barracks, frolicking by the ocean with someone of the nubile persuasion was entirely possible for a demon.

After having my tray loaded for me by Cookie, I went over to the large drum in the corner. I picked up a tin cup and filled it from the spigot sticking out of the barrel. This was my favorite part of the meal: demon rum. It was dark and rich and slightly sweet. It also packed a wallop. One of the things I was enjoying about being a demon was that I could now drink booze and get a little buzz from it, not enough to impair my job performance, from what I'd been told, but enough to mellow me out a little. The thought of a mellow demon seemed oxymoronic, but there you go.

285

I looked for a place to sit. Most of the tables were full, so I plopped down next to Gomer. In a few seconds, Maximus joined us.

I wasn't the most popular demon at Beast Barracks. My talents had manifested themselves too early, too forcefully also, and most of the others were either envious of or intimidated by me. That suited me fine. I really wasn't looking for friends in the ranks of the demons; I was still mourning the human ones lost upon joining the Corps. That said, I didn't have any particular aversion to my new colleagues. They weren't much different from me, except they'd willingly volunteered, while I'd been tricked into enlisting.

Most people ignored Gomer; as I said earlier, he was a little short on mental wattage, and so not exactly the best conversationalist. He was a simple soul, and my heart, or what would have been my heart, if I'd still had one, went out to him. He smiled at me when I sat down, then went back to consuming his gruel with unusual relish.

Maximus was another matter. Other than me, he was the most talented demon at Beast Barracks, and since he was getting ready to get his orders, he felt himself senior to and at least as good a demon as me. Certainly with a pitchfork, he was better, and that one advantage seemed to be enough for him. We actually got along pretty well.

"Hey, Steve," he said, sitting down next to me. "I loved that little maneuver you did on our hike today, the way you blasted past the jeep."

I smiled wryly. "Thanks, Max. Did you like the part where I slammed into the rock?"

"Yeah!" he said chortling. "That was hysterical."

"Have you gotten your orders yet?" I said, biting a chunk off my hardtack. One of the tacks got stuck between my teeth, and I used one of my carefully cultivated claws to pry it out.

Demons, unlike devils, don't really have claws, but grow their nails out and file them to sharp points to emulate the claws of their superiors.

"Yep. They were waiting for me when we came back from our hike. I'm going up to Four to work for Mammon."

Mammon's domain was a golden reproduction of ancient Rome. It was one of the best assignments in Hell. "Oh, that's fantastic! You'll like it there. Pretty spiffy setup up on Four, and with your pitchfork skills, they'll make you a demon centurion in no time."

He grinned. "Hope so."

I lifted my cup. "A toast to your new assignment. Best of luck with it!"

"Thanks. Hey, Gomer, you want to get in on this?" Apparently my nickname for the goofy little demon had stuck. Still, asking him to join in the toast was a magnanimous gesture on Max's part that was not lost on me.

The other demon looked up from his plate, startled, then seeing what was going on, he raised his drink as well. The three tin cups clanked together, then we all drank down the rest of our rum. Gomer made himself useful and took the empty containers back to the drum and refilled them. Max and I thanked him, and we all settled down to finish our meals in companionable silence.

The movie that evening was 'Sahara,' starring the incomparable Humphrey Bogart and the comparable Lloyd Bridges. I'd seen it many times, and it had never been one of my favorite Bogie films anyway, so I excused myself and headed for my bunk.

I wasn't really tired – it's hard to tire out a demon – but I wanted to be alone. I stretched out on the cot, which was surprisingly comfortable for a piece of canvas supported by a few slats of wood, much more comfortable than the old Murphy bed in my former apartment. Yes, even in the worst demon circumstances, which everyone assured me was Beast Barracks, my afterlife as a demon was much more pleasant than what I'd experienced as a damned human. I could even sleep, if I wanted to, not that demons needed sleep, but I could do it if I was of a mind. Humans never really slept in Hell, but tossed and turned in insomniac misery the whole night through.

Right now, though, I wasn't in the mood for sleeping. I was thinking of all the friends I'd lost by becoming a demon, of Louis Braille, Nikola Tesla and Allan Pinkerton, even of Shemp Howard, Thomas Edison and Henry Ford. The last two were not friends by any means, but they had played a part in my damned afterlife, and I missed them. Of course, Orson was frequently on my mind. I wondered how he was doing as the new Hell's Super, and if that role was a better or worse damnation for him. Flo popped into my head constantly, but I tried not to think about her. It simply hurt too much.

And of course I thought about Lilith. She may have been a succubus, but she was also my friend. Since a succubus was a demon, she was really one of the few people in Hell I could continue to have a relationship with.

A relationship. Yes, our friendship had become a little more intimate of late. As I thought about Lilith, my mind went back to my first night as a demon, before I'd checked into Beast Barracks.

leather
centipera
yards Bill
Like Blue

Made in the USA
Las Vegas, NV
06 January 2023